# The Chosen

The Heart of Seras: Book Five

Joe Evener

Published by Rogue Phoenix Press, LLP


ISBN: 978-1-62420-898-0

Editor: Amanda Armstromg
Cover Art: Designs by Ms G

# Prologue

Everyone says high school goes by fast, but no one believes it until it's over. For Julie Ayers, those four years felt like a blink of an eye. She met the school's new English teacher, Marcus Campbell, as a freshman. From the moment she and her best friends, Claire Bennett and Jimmy Warner, witnessed Mr. Campbell breaking up a fight between two senior football players, Julie knew there was something different about him. It turned out to be more accurate than she could have imagined.

Marcus Campbell was a warrior from another dimension, Seras. He had been sent from Seras to find Seras' prophesied savior, not knowing it was Julie. Once he discovered she was the one, Marcus reluctantly took the young girl to Seras to prepare her for the fight to come. To help in her training, Marcus introduced her to Callista, the warrioress of the Hemoor tribe, and her two companions, Otta and Seren.

Julie Renee Ayers's birth resulted from the Elder Tolth's need to protect the world of Seras. He brought four of the five Elders together to create the Gifts. Tolth took it upon himself to visit Earth and plant seeds in two parts of the world, knowing they would combine to produce a champion, the Heart, who would be powerful enough to stop the Elderess Eryx from ruling all of Seras and beyond.

While it was an inconvenience to juggle life traveling between Earth and Seras by way of the strange design drawn in Mr. Campbell's basement, Julie learned the powers of the Gifts of the Elders from the immortal Redderick Bobo: the Bones of Azahleah, three rocks which allowed the travel from one dimension to another; the Breath of Ostram, using this potion would give a person the ability to influence people's minds; the Blood of Vestus, an oil which, when set free and warmed by fire, could slow time; the Body of Eryx, personified in secret by the Elders in the form of the Solia Custor, Marcus; and the Heart of Tolth, which Julie discovered to be herself.

Her adventure turned deadly during the Battle of Yellow Fields when a giant killed Callista right in front of Julie. Since then, Julie lost many others to fight the evil desires of Queen Pallanex and her right-hand man, William.

Pallanex had been a wandering follower of the Elderess Eryx, displaced by her temple leaders as being dangerous and unholy. Little did they know that was exactly the type of follower Eryx preferred. In her youth, Pallanex was beautiful and flirty. She seduced the aging Canis, King of the Skorei tribe, who was also Marcus's father. Pallanex became his queen...and his downfall. Pallanex convinced Canis and his men to attack a tribe of Corven women devoted to the Elder Tolth. In doing so, Canis, his two sons, Marcus and Darius, and the men who were involved in the attack were cursed, turning them into demons. She murdered Marcus's mother, Raewin, poisoned his father, which eventually led to the old man's death, and tried to assassinate Marcus, Freya, and their brother, Darius. Marcus killed Pallanex, only to have her revived by the Elderess, Eryx. Marcus, William, Darius, and the surviving Skorei ruled Seras through blood and fire. They separated to rule over more land, not knowing William was loyal to Pallanex. Marcus was betrayed by his best friend, who plotted against him and turned his brother, Darius, against him. They fought in the Battle of the Betrayer, where all the remaining Skorei except Marcus, William, Darius, and the brothers Angus and Malcolm were killed.

Once he was back to full strength, he met Callista, who brought him to Allon, a small fortress where the immortal Bhjuda Heilshorn gathered refugees from the wars raged by Queen Pallanex, and even Marcus himself, where he learned his role in the fate of Seras from the immortal Bjhuda Heilshorn.

There, he was to be assisted by the leaders of Allon, most notably his sister, Freya; Commander Argos, his wife, Gwendolyn, and their three sons, Julius, Jakob, and Edwin; Commander Griffus and his wife, Laila; Commander Pertheus; the Hemoor warrioresses, Callista, Otta, and Seren; and Jayna the Tarrack, the last of her kind, who can change into a bear, hawk, and cougar, to find the Heart of Tolth in a place called Earth.

Unbeknownst to Marcus, he was the only person from Seras who could move through the portal. Once on Earth, he assumed the role of a teacher to find the Heart. Much to his chagrin, he discovered it was a young student named Julie Ayers.

Over the course of four years, Julie and Marcus's relationship had been tested in ways beyond comparison. None more so when Julie and Marcus fought against the Skorei brothers, Angus and Malcolm, and she discovered his secret. Marcus was not just a warrior; he was a Skorei demon—the most dangerous and feared demonic warrior in all of Seras. The secret almost destroyed them.

When Marcus ran off to face his former best friend, it was Julie who insisted the warriors of Allon go after him and save Marcus from the clutches of William and possibly himself. Words could not describe the relief she felt when they found him alive, bringing Julie and Marcus closer. Unfortunately, it cost the people of Allon several strong warriors, including Commander Pertheus. William was able to escape, even though Julie learned she had developed powers beyond her comprehension.

Through it all, with unfathomable trust, compassion, and something even deeper than either knew, Julie and Marcus's strained friendship found a way to survive as they continued to grow closer and closer.

# Part One

Into the Abyss

# Chapter One

## Julie—Earth

Julie's professor scribbled excessively on the whiteboard in front of the class. Is it possible that one country has a comparative advantage in producing a good while the other country has an absolute advantage in producing that same good? The room was tiered in ten rows and angled to allow students a complete 180-degree view of Dr. Morris, a short, bald man who reminded Julie of the Muppets' Professor Honeydew. The room was well-lit, with large windows allowing natural light to fill the space during the day. Most of the two hundred students sitting in the lecture hall jotted notes on their laptops, some with pen or pencil, and notebooks, while others left their phones on their desks to record the lesson.

Most of the students, except Julie Ayers.

"The answer is yes!" he shouted. "All it requires is the comparative advantage or..." He paused.

"The opportunity cost," a few front-row students answered in unison.

"Good," he continued. "The opportunity cost of making that good for, let's call it, country A is lower than country B, regardless of absolute figures." He marked across the board again. "So, if country A produces, oh, how about twenty laptops and forty phones, and country B produces ten laptops or thirty phones, then country A clearly has an absolute advantage in making phones, but the opportunity cost for country A in producing a phone is half a laptop while the opportunity cost for country B is only a third laptop< so it has a lower opportunity cost, and we say country B has a comparative advantage."

Julie sat, barely keeping herself awake.

"I'm sorry, Miss Ayers, am I boring you?" Dr. Morris looked

perturbed.

Julie straightened up in her seat. "I'm sorry," she said. "It's just been a really long day." She felt the eyes of her classmates staring at her.

"Miss Ayers, it's eight twenty-seven in the morning."

The students around the lecture hall chuckled.

"Perhaps a long night, but not a long day."

Julie averted her eyes. Little did he know she had already spent the better part of the day working out with Marcus, training for a war that seemed never to come. "I am so sorry." She stood and excused herself from the room. Julie's steps clattered and echoed down the marble floor. She hopped down the stairs and raced to her car. Once inside the purple 'Jellybean,' she started to cry.

College was nothing like high school. At Cedar Creek, she knew most of the students in her class. She had been popular. She was a cheerleader, track star, basketball player, and even infamous for her role in the Trotter case after he attacked her in the coach's office during her sophomore year. At McPherson College, she was just another number, a nobody. She moved aimlessly from class to class, stopping to get an iced coffee when she needed a pick-me-up, and that was it. Claire was gone. Jimmy was gone. On Earth, Julie was alone. Even her roommate, Brooklyn, was rarely there, preferring to spend her nights partying or socializing away from Julie.

Not that Julie minded. It had been four months since saving Marcus from William. Since then, Julie's attitude had changed. She no longer viewed traveling to Seras as a chore or something she didn't want to do. After graduation, her parents took her on vacation. It was supposed to be a relaxing getaway from the craziness the family had been through, especially the past two years. However, Julie spent most of the trip thinking about Seras, Allon, and Marcus. Even after Pertheus died, Julie felt more at home on Seras than on Earth. Was it the power she displayed in defeating William, or was it seeing Marcus in William's prison that moved something inside her? She couldn't explain it.

"You beat William?" Marcus had said to her in the dark dungeon. "You are an amazing young woman."

"I'm just a girl," she had answered him. "Nothing special."

"No, you are much more than that." His words surprised her and made her blush, and then they burned into her heart.

*Stop, Julie!* she pounded on her steering wheel. *You're just a silly girl!*

## Chapter Two

Pallanex—Seras

"What did you do?" Queen Pallanex bellowed as she entered her chambers. She pushed open the large redwood doors. Her black hair, lined with blue streaks, was slicked straight back, wet from leaving her bath. It hung halfway down her long, golden robe, which dragged across the floor.

William sat on the step by her royal blue throne laced with gold thread. "It wasn't me. It was that wretched girl," he stood to greet her. "My Queen." He reached to embrace Pallanex. William looked worn and beaten, a shadow of the man he once was. His face, the face that had drawn her to him and caused her to break the marriage vows she made to Canis was not the same. Where it had once held a striking mix of magnetism and danger, it now looked defeated. His piercing eyes once gleamed like obsidian and possessed a single-mindedness only matched by Pallanex herself, igniting a fire within her that she thought had long been extinguished, a flame that filled her with hope, for she had found her steadfast companion. She and William would conquer Seras then Earth before attacking the very depths of Hell and free her true love. Those eyes, those same damned eyes, now looked sunken and desolate.

So, as he approached her, Pallanex's thoughts shifted abruptly. She walked past him, and a wave of indignation swelled within her. Pallanex took her place on the throne. She turned to him, her voice harsh and cruel. "Do you realize I need that girl to make my plans successful?"

"No, my Queen. I do not understand."

"I need all five of the Elders' gifts: The Blood of Vestus; the Bones of Azahleah; the Breath of Ostram; the Body of Eryx, Marcus; and the Betrothed of Tolth, the Heart, that arrogant girl!"

"I still do not understand. I thought you wanted me to kill them?"

"I do. Together, they are powerful. Separate, I can defeat them. Get the three remaining gifts and fulfill my duty to the Elderess Eryx. You have let me down once more," Pallanex told him. "You fool! How could you be bested by a girl?"

"The Heart is powerful, my Queen. They attacked me, she attacked me! Destroyed my fortress and killed my men!"

"They were my men!" she shouted then paused. "And what of your pet?"

William dropped his head. "Dead, killed by Marcus's own hands. I tried to get him back. Can you imagine what we could do if I had Marcus by my side?" William begged. "If I could have brought him back, back to what he was...he and I could have conquered Seras for you, and you would not need—"

"He is the Solia Custor," Pallanex yelled, interrupting him. "He will not be swayed back to you." Queen Pallanex raised her hands in anger. "Pour me a drink, you fool."

William walked to her cabinet and poured a glass of wine. "I'm sorry, my Queen. The opportunity presented itself, and I took it." He handed her the drink.

"What opportunity presented itself?" She took a long sip.

"Marcus came to me through a prison wagon. He was picked up, nearly dead, should have been dead, but there he was. He came back to me." William pounded his chest. "He was my friend. I loved him!"

"And it cost us everything," Pallanex roared back. "We have nothing, you damned fool!"

"It did not cost us everything. I know what it takes to make an army of Skorei, the likes of which have never been seen."

"What are you talking about?" She stood from her throne.

"I still have the most important parts. I have my notes, and I have my potions. I can make as many demons as you need for your purpose, my Queen. All I need are men, time, and a place to work."

Queen Pallanex glared at him, unsure if she should believe him or not. "I am growing tired of your games, William."

"Not a game. Marcus might have fooled me, and his army may have defeated my men and destroyed my home, but I have everything I need to honor you."

"Then make it so, William. I will give you what you need. Do not fail me again."

William must have taken that as an invitation. He moved to her; his face twisted with a smirk that usually allowed William to get away with anything in regard to Pallanex. Not this time. She dismissed him with a wave of her hand. His eyes scanned her to see if she was serious, then his shoulders dropped, and he turned to leave.

## Chapter Three

Julie—Earth

"You sure you don't want to go out?" Julie's roommate, Brooklyn, asked as she checked herself in the floor-length mirror in the open bathroom door. With her blonde hair, blue eyes, and long legs, Brooklyn was, as Julie would say, the anti-Julie.

Julie's phone rang. It was a FaceTime call from Claire. "No thanks. I have to take this."

Her beautiful roommate shrugged. "Suit yourself. Don't wait up." She closed the door behind her.

Julie picked up the phone. "Hey, you!" She was sitting cross-legged on her dorm room bed. Her small college dorm room was cozy. The walls were painted in beige. Two twin beds were adorned with comfortable bedding and throw pillows. The beds were parallel, and a nightstand was placed between them. Julie kept her phone charger and her latest book, a story about Persephone and Hades, there along with another reading assignment from her mythology class, her favorite class. On the opposite side of the room, there was a mini fridge nestled in a corner. Next to the mini fridge, a TV was placed on a compact entertainment unit. The room was decorated with white Christmas lights and pink curtains.

"Jules! I miss that face," Claire said.

"I miss your face. How's school?"

"Oh man, the life of a college athlete is nutso. I practice, go to class, eat, go to class, go to practice, go to bed, rinse and repeat," Claire told her. "How about you?"

Julie straightened out her legs. "Not as exciting as that. Take out the practices and add a billion hours of homework, and that's it." Julie chuckled. "High school was so much easier."

"Yeah, but I like the freedom of college better. Oh, and you should see the uniforms we wear, Jules. Coach Langston would have a fit." She laughed.

"Speaking of...are you coming back for homecoming?" Julie asked her best friend.

"I can't. I wish I could, but we have a big cross-country meet that weekend. I have to be there. It's for the conference title."

"That's exciting. I wish I could watch you run."

"You could have joined me here instead of McPherson," Claire reminded her. "Coach Locke really wanted you to."

"I know. It just wasn't meant to be. Besides, my parents would have missed me too much. Patrick already graduated and moved to his new job, about two hours away. My mom was so upset."

"I bet. It's just weird not being in school with you."

"I know. Ten years together. I miss you," Julie said.

"I miss you too." Claire changed the subject. "I don't think I've talked to you since Hawaii. How was it?"

"It was so much fun, so pretty."

"I bet," Claire said. "What all did you do?"

"Mostly swam, went snorkeling, saw a shark. Mom and Dad had us take a tour and see a couple of beautiful waterfalls." Julie went over the list of activities without revealing that she had spent more time wondering about Marcus than enjoying her trip of a lifetime. "It was great."

"That sounds amazing."

"It was." Julie paused. "So-o-o-o-o, what's going on?" Something about Claire's tone and facial expressions on the FaceTime call made Julie suspicious.

Claire paused, not answering right away, and Julie heard her voice catch in her throat. "That's kinda why I called."

"Okay, what happened?"

"Jimmy and I broke up."

"What, why?"

"We decided it was too hard to do the whole long-distance thing. We're still friends. I still love him." Julie saw the tears forming in her eyes. "He said he still loves me." She started breathing more deeply and shallowly.

"Claire, I'm so sorry."

"It's hard." Claire could no longer fight back the crying. "I miss him. I miss you."

"I miss you too! And, hey, I am always here for you. I might be seven hours away, but you can call me anytime, day or night." A tear rolled down Julie's cheek.

"I appreciate you." Claire wiped her face and blew her nose. "I'm sure it was for the best. Heck, we're literally a thousand miles apart."

Julie rubbed her sleeve on her nose. "Yeah, and who's to say you don't get back together after college? Just enjoy this time and see what happens," she told her, trying to stay positive.

"That's why I love you," Claire said. "I gotta go. We'll talk soon, okay?"

"Any time. Miss you!"

"Miss you too!" Claire exclaimed.

With that, Julie's best friend was gone. Julie took a deep breath. Claire and Jimmy had been together since ninth grade. She couldn't imagine them not being a couple. If they can't make it, who can? she thought. Julie fell back on her bed and let her thoughts drift. I wonder what Marcus is doing?

## Chapter Four

Marcus—Seras

Marcus sat with the council; Freya, Griffus, Jayna, Otta, Roderick Bobo, Lord Marek of the Hawkmir, and his two companions, Lord Avery and Lord Atrow. Commander Argos was noticeably absent. They sat at a long, wooden table. Maps were spread out in front of them. Three-pronged candles burned at both ends of the table and in the middle, to illuminate the dark room, which had no windows.

"We can't attack now," Freya told him. "People have not recovered from the loss after the battle against William."

"But that is why we should. He is reeling from the defeat. We have them on the run. William just ran to Pallanex with his tail between his legs like a wounded dog. If we march on them now, there will be no time for them to recover," Marcus argued.

"I wish I could agree with you, Marcus," Griffus said, "but Freya is right. We can't just march from one battle to the next. It's different now. We need time to recover; the people need time to recover."

"We are missing a golden opportunity," Marcus said.

"Think about the men, Marcus," Freya said. "They just lost Pertheus. They need time to mourn for their losses. A new leader must be named. The time is not right."

"What do you think?" Marcus turned to Redderick Bobo. "You know more than you let on. You both do." He looked at Freya. "What do you think the Elders would want us to do?"

Neither Bobo nor Freya said a word.

"Just as I thought. Can we take it to a vote?" Marcus asked, looking each of them eye to eye.

"That is your right," Redderick answered.

"Well, then?" Marcus stood up. "I believe it is in our best interest to attack now. Who agrees with me?" He looked at Jayna. "You have been watching Pallanex for months. What do you think?"

"It's not that I don't agree with you," Jayna said. "I just think they are right." She used her head to point toward the others at the table. "We aren't ready to mount up and go against Pallanex and William so soon."

Marcus looked at his sister. She nodded no, as did Griffus, Otta, and the rest.

"I'm sorry, Marcus," Griffus said.

"Fine," Marcus said. "I can't force any of you to change your mind. I think we are making a mistake."

"It's not that I don't want to," Griffus told him. "We lost a lot of good men against William," the large leader of the ballateers said. It will take a while to get these youngsters ready."

"I know. I am sorry about that," Marcus relented.

"That's not what I meant," Griffus said.

"I know what I did. I put myself ahead of what's important." He slammed his hand on the table. "Because of me, Pertheus and many other good men are dead."

"Pertheus was a friend, a good friend. He was also a soldier. He died fighting. He died a good death."

Marcus stared at him. "Don't use that against me."

"It's true. I know what it sounds like, but Pertheus would not have wanted it any other way."

"I agree."

"Now, Argos on the other hand. We need him," Griffus said.

"How do you tell a father to give up finding his son's killer?"

"I don't know, but we can't attack Pallanex without him," Griffus said. "Of that, I'm certain."

"And I agree with you," Marcus said. "When did you check on him last?"

"Two days ago. I worry about him."

"I will go check on him." Marcus stood. "Maybe...maybe I can help him in some way." He shrugged. "I will see you soon."

"See you soon."

Marcus left the meeting room and mounted his horse. He rode through town in a slow trot to Argos and Gwendolyn's cabin. Gwendolyn was busying herself in the small garden on the side of their home. Marcus dismounted.

"Marcus," Gwendolyn said with a weary smile. "Good to see you."

"Gwendolyn." Marcus bowed his head. "Is Argos here?"

"Yes, go on in. I'm sure he will be happy to see you." There was a sadness in her voice.

Marcus knocked once on the door before entering. Argos was at the table in a large sitting area. At the table were five chairs in front of a fireplace with cooking utensils hanging down from a mantel. Behind Argos was a set of steps that led to a loft for the married couple's bed chamber in the back of the room. Their home was bigger than Marcus's.

"Marcus, how are you?" His eyes were sunken, and it was apparent he had lost a lot of weight. He looked frail and tired.

"Argos, my friend."

"Don't say it. I know how I look." He ran his hand through his graying hair then across his beard.

"What can I do to help?"

"Nothing. I've done everything. I've questioned everyone. I've retraced his last steps. I talked to Leyta. She's as shaken as I am. There are no answers."

"There will be. We will find out who or what did this to Edwin. I promise."

"Don't make promises you can't keep." Argos stood. It was then that Marcus saw the full extent of Argos's deterioration. The once formidable leader of Heilshorn's army could barely stand straight. He looked like a shell of his former self. "Can I get you a drink?"

"No, I'm good. I wanted to check on you. I haven't seen you much the last few months."

Argos snorted through his nose and waved him off. "You have a duty, a purpose, and you must protect the Heart and get her ready to face Pallanex. I have nothing."

"That is not true," Marcus roared through a hushed voice. "You have a wife and two other children. I will not stand here and tell you what happened to Edwin wasn't a tragedy. It was. But you are wasting away to nothing. You are going to lose everything if you continue to feel sorry for yourself. Your family needs you. Your army needs you. Your friends need you."

Argos faced him with bloodshot eyes. "Get out."

"Argos," Marcus pleaded.

The angry father repeated himself through gritted teeth. "Get out of my home...now!"

Marcus shook his head and headed for the door. Gwendolyn opened it as he reached out for the handle. He took a deep breath. "I am sorry. This is not what I meant to do."

Gwendolyn, Allon's matriarch, burst into tears. "I know," she started. "I'm sorry, Marcus."

"No, I'm the one who is sorry. I wish there was something I could do."

Gwendolyn wiped her face. "I'm afraid there isn't anything anyone can do."

With that, Marcus hopped on his horse and rode away.

# Chapter Five

Julie—Seras

"So, college really sucks," Julie grumbled to Marcus as the two of them practiced swords late in the afternoon. "I thought it would be easy. Claire loves it, Jimmy loves it, everyone I talk to loves it." She flailed her free hand in frustration. "My roommate re-e-e-ally loves it."

"It's only been, what, six weeks? It's going to get better. Be patient." He blocked her lunge with a clash of their wooden swords.

Julie scrunched her face. "That doesn't help." She advanced toward him with a flurry of movements learned in her training with Marcus over the years.

Marcus retreated away from her attack. "I'm serious. I was miserable on Earth for two years and see how that turned out."

She stopped abruptly. "Um, I don't think you can compare us. You were on a different...planet, you didn't speak the language, and you..." she leaned in to whisper, "aren't even human." Julie shrugged.

Marcus started to argue back but stopped and shook his head.

"Wow, I left you speechless," Julie exclaimed with a laugh that echoed through the trees during their afternoon sparing. She bobbed her head back and forth, reveling in her little victory.

"Nooo," he dragged out the word. "I'm not speechless. I don't have a good comeback," Marcus said, acknowledging his momentary defeat with a hint of amusement.

"Duh! That's called being speechless."

"I need a drink." Marcus walked to the small mound where they had left their pouches of water, sat down, and took a long drink.

Julie sat beside him. "Man, I don't understand. If I heal so fast, why do my muscles hurt?" She rubbed the area between her neck and shoulder.

"We aren't immune to being sore or getting tired. We just heal quicker from it."

"I'm sorry. I'm just grumpy. I wish college was more like high school."

"You'll be fine. Have you even tried to make friends?"

"Yes...no. But it's not my fault. I'm here whenever I don't have classes." She leaned back against the mound. "I have no chance at a social life."

"Then why don't you take some time off?"

Julie sat back up. "I thought you wanted me here?"

"You know I want you here, but you're right; when you aren't training with me, you're working with Redderick and your powers." Marcus wiggled his fingers in a spooky fashion.

Julie nudged him with her shoulder. "Stop!" She laughed. "I didn't know I could do all of that. Besides, that's not how I do it."

"I haven't seen any of it yet," he said. Marcus stood. "Let me see some of your voodoo."

Julie popped up, shook her shoulders, and hopped back and forth. "I can do this." She moved away from him and took aim at a bush ten feet away. Julie held out her hands. Power emanated from her palms, and the bush uprooted, flying twenty feet back.

"Okay...I'm impressed," Marcus said.

"Watch this." Julie smiled. She directed her attention to a medium-sized boulder, about a third of it was below the surface. Julie mentally pushed the rock out, leaving a hole big enough to swallow up her dad's lounge chair, and tossed it near the bushes.

"That's impressive," Marcus said. "Have you tried it on people yet?"

"No?" Julie thought for a moment. "Only William, I guess."

"Why not?"

"I don't want to hurt anyone," Julie said.

"Then try it on me," Marcus said with a slight shrug.

"What, are you sure?"

Marcus rolled his neck. "Sure. Give me your best shot, little girl." He smiled.

Julie scrunched her nose and curled her lips. "Oh, I'm going to enjoy this now." She lowered her hips and pushed her hands toward Marcus. The force of power flowed from her hands, knocking Marcus to the ground.

He picked himself up off the ground and dusted his backside. "Let's try that again."

"Are you sure?" Julie laughed. "That was kinda fun."

"Can you do it again?"

"I think so. With Bobo, I have moved branches, rocks, and bushes for over an hour," Julie said, hopping up and down, barely controlling her excitement.

Marcus backed up a little further away and braced for another attack.

"Okay, here we go." Julie moved her hands toward Marcus, sending him flying. "Oh my God, are you alright?" She ran to him.

Marcus let out a deep breath then began coughing. "Well. I can see why William ran away," he choked out between gasps of air.

"Are you okay?"

"Yeah, yeah, I'm good." He took another big breath and got back to his feet. "Give me a sec."

"Can we be done now?" Julie asked.

"Not yet. I wanna go one more time."

"You are insane," Julie exclaimed. "I almost killed you."

"No, you didn't. I'm good. You caught me off guard," Marcus said.

Julie drew back. "You told me to do it."

"I know. I didn't know how powerful it would be." He shook his arms. "Ready to go again?"

"Are you insane?"

"It's just like sword practice. You have to get used to using it against people."

"I don't want to hurt you," Julie said.

"Oh, you won't surprise me again."

"Marcus, please," she begged.

"It's okay. I promise."

"Suit yourself." She readied for another attack. Power once again shot from her hands.

Marcus moved to the left of her blast.

Julie sent another wave in his direction.

He moved away from her.

She set her eyes on him and tried again.

Marcus dodged.

Julie used her left and then her right, directing wave after wave of power at Marcus, blasting rock, bushes, and trees until she dropped her hands to her knees. "I give. I can't do it." A tear rolled down her nose.

"Yes, you can," Marcus exclaimed. "That was amazing!"

"You beat me." She straightened up, her eyes blazing red from hurt.

"No, I outran you. That can be fixed, harnessed. You need more practice with him, but not just on stationary objects." He paused. "And I'm here to help you."

# Chapter Six

William—Seras

William strolled into his new home, located in the old arena and training facility, where he spent the better part of his youth preparing to be a soldier of Cauleta. His hair was pulled back into a ponytail, and he was shirtless from a day of training in the heat. He dipped a spoon into the bucket beside the well and took a drink. Then he took the bucket and poured it over his face and body to wash away the dirt and sweat.

He found the arena was the perfect place to do his experiments. The large indoor bunks and training room made it ideal. It had plenty of space and was far from Pallanex, so he could do whatever he wanted without interruption. It was the place where he had met Marcus and the boys who became his closest friends, allies, and family. How many victories did he have in the arena? He remembered those times fondly. It might have been the happiest of his life. Training, sparring, fighting, the Scindo, the plot to reinstate Marcus to the Skorei, all the blood and sweat poured out on the floors of the arena. That was until Queen Pallanex seduced him and brought him into her plans to overthrow Canis, making him the commander of her new army. How could he have resisted? Her beauty, charm, and temptation were more than any boy could dream.

Everything changed the day Pallanex found him peeking at her as she bathed under guarded protection. Later, Pallanex brought him into her chamber. Through intimate conversations in her bed, bath, and other hidden places in between, he felt like a king in the making. She loved it when their passion turned him into the demon. Canis's queen seduced the boy, and after that moment, he would kill or die for her. And he did plenty of killings, the worst of which was killing his best friend's mother.

Pallanex's plan had sounded so simple. She promised to take control of the non-demon Skorei and order them to kill the demon cursed. Pallanex would poison Canis, and William would rid Pallanex of Raewin. He hated the idea but found it easy to do. Pallanex had sent him into the dark of night to butcher Raewin. The old woman who had been nice to him throughout his youth was no match for him. It was an easy kill. He returned to Pallanex's chamber, but she was not there. The revolt against Canis had begun without him. He was shocked to see the chaos. As William moved through the halls, intent on finding Pallanex, he saw Marcus, Darius, and Freya trapped in a stairwell surrounded by some of the non-demon Skorei's best. The three were helplessly outnumbered and would eventually fall if William hadn't entered and taken several of them by surprise, allowing Marcus and Darius to regroup—a mistake, according to Pallanex, as he learned afterward. She wanted them dead, along with Canis. William would be her general.

Then Marcus hunted Pallanex down and killed her. He stayed silent in his role as his friend buried his mother and father. Then, Pallanex returned to him, surviving by ancient magic. She whispered to William in the dark and prodded him to lead Marcus away from Cauleta, abandon him, steal Darius from his side, and return to her. None of his men—Darius, Kralen, or the others had any idea he was taking orders from Pallanex in his dreams. She then sent him back to the north to retrieve something from the Priest of Ostram in the Madena fortress, wanting him to reconnect with Marcus. Later, he found she wanted him to kill both the priest and Marcus. He failed on both accounts. William did not let that stop him. He aimed to impress Pallanex and give her the army she desired to take over Seras and beyond.

"Well, well, well," he said aloud. "What have we here?" He walked over to a row of men strapped to cots. One of the men began to move. William had fed him and the others doses of the potion he formed from years of extracting the blood from Thomen. He had to start over after losing the men when the Heart rescued Marcus. These men, Pallanex brought from across the ocean, were his newest victims.

He leaned into the man, who was struggling against the straps that held him in place. "Come on, you can do it."

"Help me," the man spat out. His eyes were bloodshot, and his veins protruded from his skin.

"I will help you, but you have to survive," William growled in his ear.

"Water," the man begged. "Water."

"Show me what you are!"

"Please." He clicked his tongue to show the dryness of his blistered mouth.

"Show me what you are!"

"Please, no, it hurts." The man coughed repeatedly.

William restrained himself from strangling the man. "You can do it. Show me what I have done!"

The man yelled in pain. "No, no, no-o-o-o-o!" His eyes glowed red.

"Yes, yes, show me!"

His hands clenched as his body convulsed.

"You can do it."

A ridge began to form across his nose.

"Let it go. Let the beast come out." William grinned and grabbed his shoulders. "Show me the demon."

His nose expanded, and his teeth grew.

"That's it! You have done it. You are there. Feel the power coursing through your veins."

The man convulsed, shaking and screaming uncontrollably. His skin began to shred as the beast inside of him fought to get out. He let out a final scream as blood covered him through the lacerations, then he succumbed to the pain and died.

"No, you had it. You were there." Disappointed by his latest setback, William looked across the rest of the room where more than fifty men were tied down, waiting to wake and make the change from man to demon.

# Chapter Seven

Julie—Seras

Julie entered the village as Marcus requested. Candles, torches, and a giant bonfire lit up Allon's evening sky. A group of musicians, accompanied by crude drums, horns, and something that resembled a violin, played upbeat music. It was the time of the Tempora. The grand harvest celebration was when the people of Allon and most of Seras celebrated their birthdays, as far as Julie could gather. It was a strange tradition in her eyes. The fact that they didn't know their exact date of birth always confused her.

The center of town was adorned with garlands, flowers, flowing ribbons, and a variety of colors of cloth. Tables and chairs were arranged in a semi-circle around a white platform featuring an intricate tapestry and additional ribbons. Behind the platform were additional tables filled with food and drinks. Gwendolyn, Argos's wife, busied herself helping to organize the food gathering. The aroma of roasted pig, chicken, and lamb filled the air. There were several bowls of lettuce, berries, nuts, and other assorted fruits and vegetables, and another table with any pie a person could imagine. Still, more tables were set aside for pitchers of water, wine, and a beer-like drink made from fermented honey, much like mead, from what Julie once looked up, after trying it the first time. The memory of crinkling her nose from the bitter taste returned to her. Julie walked to one of the tables where Griffus, his wife Laila, and two children, the twins Beahel and Tuco, were sitting.

"Julie," the burly man said, standing to greet her. "Welcome to the Tempora."

"Hi, Griffus, Laila, thanks." Julie looked around. "Have you seen Marcus?"

Griffus turned to the left and right. "No, but he's probably training somewhere."

"Doesn't he come to this thing?"

"Not really. I think he used to celebrate when he was younger but after the..." Griffus looked around to make sure no one who wasn't supposed to know about him being a demon, namely Lord Marek, Lord Avery, and Lord Atrow of the Hawkmir tribe, weren't nearby, "curse, I don't think they did."

"That's a horrible way to grow up," she said.

Griffus chuckled. "I don't think you know the half of it."

Julie started to tell him she did, but she refrained. It would be too long of a story. "Thank you." She excused herself and found the Hemoor women, Otto and Seren, sitting with Julius, Jakob, and Leyta. "Is it okay if I sit with you guys?"

"Of course, my Heart," Julius said. He and the group stood in her presence.

"Stop, sit down. I'm just Julie." She sighed.

"Forgive us, Heart...Julie," Jakob said.

Julie sat beside Otta. "No worries. I just want to be treated like a normal person."

"But you know you aren't normal," Otta told her.

"I know. But I still want to be treated like one."

"We will do our best," Julius said.

"Thank you." A woman came to offer them drinks. "I'll have a wine, please."

"Yes, my Heart," the woman said.

The other five tried to suppress their smiles and laughed at her words.

"See what I mean?" Julie snorted.

"We can't help it," Seren said. "We learned about you from an early age. You are a goddess to us."

"Trust me, I'm no goddess. Heck, I don't know if I can pass chemistry." The group looked at her. "Never mind." She decided to change the subject. "So, what happens at these things?"

Otto leaned in. "You're about to find out." The Hemoor warrior smiled.

Freya walked onto the staged area and faced the gathering crowd. "Please take your seats." She looked at the parchment in her hand. "Let the Tempora begin."

The audience clapped.

"We will start the Speaking of Names with the family of Barth."

A skinny man stood and walked to the platform. His wife and children joined him. Once onstage, he introduced himself. "I am Barth. This is my fifty-seventh Tempora. My wife, Rella, this is her fifty-fifth Tempora. My daughter, Blythe, this is her thirty-fourth Tempora. My son, Ronald, his thirty-second Tempora. My third child, Jamis, this would have been his twenty-ninth Tempora. He was lost during the Battle of Yellow Fields. He will be missed."

The people of Allon exploded with applause for the family. Barth stood proud and wrapped his arms around his family.

The presentation went on throughout the entire village. Each head of the family introduced the living and non-living members to appreciative clapping. Even the single members of the group without families, like Seren, Otta, and Jayna, stood on the stage and presented themselves.

Julie looked for Marcus, who was still noticeably absent. Even his brother and sister, Darius and Freya, came forward.

The last family to take their place on the platform was Argos's family. Argos looked to Julie as though he had lost fifty pounds. Gwendolyn, Julius, and Jakob joined him. He weakly said their names then choked out, "My youngest son, Edwin, this would have been his twenty-third Tempora." He took a breath. "But he was killed for no good reason," his voice grew louder. "And I swear by the blood of the Elders I will find who did this and—" Julius and Jakob grabbed him to stop his outburst as tears streamed down Gwendolyn's face. Argos collapsed.

The audience clapped pensively at first, but then the applause swelled to show its support for the broken man.

The two sons escorted their parents off the stage.

Freya came back. She looked at Julie and nodded.

Julie felt her eyes grow large. She put her hand on her chest.

Freya held out her hand.

Julie stood. The people of Allon went wild. Julie felt her face grow warm. When she got to Freya, Marcus's sister smiled and stepped back. "I-I-I'm Julie Ayers," she said timidly. Every eye was on her, and she thought her heart would burst out of her chest. Then, she caught a glimpse of Marcus standing in the shadows of the moonlight and torches. She straightened her posture and tried again. "I am Julie Ayers, and while this is my first Tempora, I have celebrated nineteen such events."

The roar she got was deafening.

Julie left the stage and made her way back to her seat, hoping Marcus would join them. But he didn't.

The food was served as the festival continued. Julie hated to admit it, but the lamb was her favorite. She felt a little guilty since they were also the cutest. After the meal, the band resumed playing once more. The celebration became a rousing dance. Julie joined Otta and Seren as they danced with Julius, Jakob, and other warriors from their ranks. The whole time Julie spun around the floor, she watched Marcus, who was busy talking to Freya, Darius, Griffus, and Jayna. No doubt talking about me, she thought. Redderick entered the party with his harem. He delighted in watching them dance around him seductively as he filled his mouth with a large chicken leg. The scene made Julie's stomach turn. "I need to take a break," she told the others who protested at her leaving, but Julie went to find Marcus. When she did, he straightened up as if he was surprised to see her. Freya, Darius, and Griffus were no longer with him; only Jayna remained. The Tarrack woman was practically sitting in his lap, playing with his hair. Julie seethed at the sight but was adamant in interrupting their conversation. "Hey."

"Julie, how are you?" Jayna moved slightly away from him.

"Good. Missed you at the Tempora thingy," she said.

"Yeah, I don't participate in the Speaking of Names."

"That's what Griffus told me. So, you don't know how old you are?"

"I'm not sure. After I left Cauleta, I never kept track."

Julie snorted.

"Why?"

"No reason," she said, "I just wanted to know."

"I'm sorry."

"Fine," Julie started, but before she could continue, Otta and Seren rushed to her and dragged her back to the dancing. Julie played along with the Hemoor women but didn't take her eyes off Marcus. As the evening drew to a close, Redderick Bobo and Freya combined their talents to surprise the villagers with a dazzling display of fireworks.

Everyone gathered around a dock by the river a little more than a mile from the fortress.

Julie sat with Otta and Seren to watch the bright colors explode in the sky.

"Do you have anything like this where you come from?" Seren asked.

"I do. We call it the Fourth of July," Julie said.

"Is it like our Tempora?" Otta asked.

"No, it's a lot different, but I really like your Tempora. I don't think you have anything like our Fourth of July. It's when my country got its freedom from another country." Both girls looked at her with a confused expression. "It's not important." Julie smiled. She turned back to watch the fireworks, loving the way the lights reflected on the water. Over her shoulder, she peeked at Marcus but decided to ignore him.

## Chapter Eight

Julie—Earth

"When do you go back?" Julie asked her best friend, Claire. They were sitting at the newest coffee shop, which was making its home on Sunset Square. Snow covered the ground, ice sparkled in the trees, and the frigid air blew in every time a customer opened the door. The two girls were catching up during both of their schools' winter breaks.

"Thursday." Claire took a sip of her iced coffee. "Indoor track, ya know."

"That's just too soon. I can't believe you're going to be a million miles away again," Julie protested. They talked over the melodic Christmas tunes of Vincent Guaraldi.

"It's not a million, just seems like it."

"It might as well be." Julie stuck out her lip in a pout.

"And you could have joined me," Claire said, mirroring her friend's expression. "With the season you had last year, they would have signed you in a heartbeat."

Julie grimaced. "No, like I said in June, my track days are over." She took a drink. "It was fun, though. I had a great time. It made the last two years of high school amazing."

"I'm glad you finally listened to me and Coach Langston," Claire smiled. A creamy mocha mustache outlined her upper lip.

"Me too." Julie laughed. "Have you talked to Jimmy since you've been home?"

"Not really. I followed his games. I know he wasn't happy with his lack of playing time. But he knows he's just a freshman."

"It makes me sad," Julie said.

"Stop. We're still friends. It's just hard to be in a relationship when we're both so busy," Claire said. She leaned back in her seat. "And how about you? Anyone new?"

"Nah, I'm concentrating on my classes. After that, who knows what will happen." She couldn't tell her best friend that her days were spent training with Marcus in another dimension and that he wasn't a criminal like everyone in Sunset thought...or at least not like the papers and the news reported when the story broke over a year ago when it was discovered the English teacher was not a real, certified teacher, didn't pay taxes, and never existed before five years ago. Her phone pinged. She looked at the message. "Speaking of, I gotta head out. My mom and dad want to know when I'm going to get home."

"No worries. Lunch tomorrow?" Claire stood up. With her college training program, it seemed she had packed on twenty pounds of muscle.

"Sounds good." Julie hugged her friend. "See you tomorrow."

She left the coffee shop in the purple Jellybean and headed for home. She drove around the brick road on the square and passed the now silent fountain. Sunset was decked out for the upcoming holiday season. Brightly adorned wreaths hung from lamp posts, but the manger, where adults and children would reenact the birth of Jesus was empty and quiet. The gazebo had Santa and his reindeer perched on its roof, and the world seemed at peace, at least to Julie. Unlike the feelings she had when in Seras. I wonder if I will ever feel this way about Seras? She drowned out her thoughts with a Bing Crosby song to keep her in the mood.

When she pulled into the driveway, Julie was surprised to see her brother Patrick's car. What's he doing home? Over the past year, Patrick had been spending more time in his apartment closer to McPherson College. Julie had secretly looked forward to going to the same school as her older brother and spending more time with him. That didn't happen; he graduated early in the semester, and she saw him even less than before. Julie got out of her car and bounded up her front porch steps. She was greeted by Shakespeare, who had taken a spot on the front porch swing. "Well, hello there, handsome boy."

The cat stood and stretched. Julie picked him up. When Marcus left Earth, seemingly for good, he gave Julie two gifts: his faithful white cat and the other, a secret he refused to tell her but promised he would when the time was right. His attempt at secrecy was both cute and frustrating but endearing at the same time. Julie opened the door. Her mother's Christmas decorations were nearing completion, even though Thanksgiving was still a week away.

"In here, honey," Michelle Ayers called out.

Julie walked through the living room toward the kitchen. The Christmas tree was up, the stockings hung, and the picture frames were wrapped like presents. Her mom, dad, and brother were gathered around the dining room table. She could tell by their faces something was up. "Hi," she said, dragging out the "i" as long as she could and slowing her pace. "What's going on?"

"Hi, have a seat," her dad, Phil, said.

"Let me get you something to eat." Michelle stood.

"That's okay. I just had a bite to eat at The Square with Claire." Julie plopped down at the table. She looked back and forth to her parents.

Julie's mind raced immediately to, "Don't tell me you're getting divorced!" She stood and began to leave the room.

"No," her dad said. "No, no, no. Nothing like that, honey."

Julie stopped and sat back down.

"Where did that come from?" Michelle asked.

"Looking at your faces," Julie shot back.

"Your mom and I love each other very much." Phil pushed his glasses back into place.

"In fact, that's part of the reason we are doing what we are doing." Michelle told her.

"What?" Julie raised an eyebrow. "I'm confused."

"You're in college now and growing up so fast." Michelle reached out and patted her hand. "Patrick is out of school and living on his own. In a few years, you will be too."

"Okay?" Julie smirked. "What are you trying to say? Just say it already."

"Your mom and I have decided we are going to..." her dad started.

Julie looked around the dining room at the big, beautiful house she had lived in her entire life.

"To take your Grandma Franklin on a cruise around the world," her mom finished.

"You're what?" Julie's voice shrieked. "When?"

"Not right away," Michelle started. "We're going to wait until summer. But we will be gone for almost a year."

"A year?" Julie looked at Patrick. "Are you going to say anything?"

Patrick responded, "Not really. They're right. I already moved away. You'll be gone in a few years. They can do what they've always wanted to do. It's their life, let them enjoy it."

"It's going to be six months," her mother started. "We will fly to Fort Lauderdale, then go to Mexico, the Panama Canal, LA, Hawaii, Japan, South Korea, Singapore, Capetown, Casablanca, Athens, Rome, Alexandria, Barcelona, Cadiz, Lisbon, Normandy, Paris, London, Edinburgh, Dublin, Reykjavik, Newfoundland, Nova Scotia, New Brunswick, Boston, New York, DC, and back to Florida."

"Are you kidding?" Julie stood. "Fine, whatever. Do what you want. I'm so happy for you." She stormed upstairs and slammed her bedroom door.

## Chapter Nine

Marcus—Seras

"Can you believe that?" Julie spit out as she swung wildly at Marcus. Snow kicked up as he backed away. She was dressed in layer after layer of deer and bear fur from head to toe. After her parents told her about their big news, Julie left in a huff and made her way to the little cabin she had built to travel to Seras when Marcus's basement was no longer an option. When she arrived in Allon, she quickly dressed and went searching for Marcus. She found him training alone in the wooded area north of the fortress.

He blocked and ducked away from her attacks so she wouldn't hurt herself or him.

"They want to go on a world cruise!" Her sword struck Marcus's as she chopped it from overhead. "They've already started making payments!" Julie delivered another blow to his sword.

"Why are you so upset?" Marcus retreated a safe distance to try to calm her.

"What do you mean, 'Why am I so upset?'" She threw her sword to the ground. "I don't know. I don't know."

"Isn't it a great experience? You should be happy for them."

Julie blew out a puff of air; it looked like dragon smoke in the cool winter air. "I don't like that they're going to be gone. Like I don't even matter to them!"

"Of course, you matter to them." Marcus walked to the tree where they kept their water pouches. "But aren't you...how do I say, aren't they right? You are grown up; you will be leaving soon. Shouldn't they start doing what they want?"

Julie joined him and sat in the thick snow. "I'm so mad." Tears streamed down her face.

Marcus sat beside her and gently placed his arm around her shoulder. “I hate to ask, but why are you so mad?”

Julie used her arm to wipe her nose. “I don’t know.”

“When are they leaving?”

She shrugged. “This summer. I guess I’m just not ready for the idea of them going their own way, Patrick going his own way, me...me going my own way.” Julie took a drink then handed the pouch to Marcus.

He took a drink. The cold water felt good as Marcus processed what Julie had told him. “You will be okay.”

“How can you be sure?” Julie shook her head. “I’m going to be by myself.”

“You won’t be by yourself.”

“I will be alone.” Julie fell back into the snowbank. “I’m going to be an orphan!”

“Julie, you’re not going to be an orphan. That’s a bit much,” Marcus said.

“Plus,” Julie leaned into him, “what about my cabin? If they decide to move and sell the house, how am I going to get back and forth?”

“I didn’t think about that.”

“I know. I have to do all the thinking.”

“I think you’re getting ahead of yourself. That could be a long way off. Don’t you think you’re overreacting a little?”

“You’re no help.” She threw a clump of snow on Marcus and scrambled to her feet.

“You little brat.” Marcus hopped up after her.

Julie squealed. “No, no, no!”

“It’s too late for you.” Marcus tackled her in a deep drift. Snow flew, engulfing both of the warriors.

Julie broke into laughter. “I’m sorry, I’m sorry. Please don’t,” she begged.

Marcus towered over her with a giant snowball raised above his head. “It’s good to hear you laugh again.”

“Thank you,” Julie said. “I needed that.” She reached out her hand. “Truce.”

Marcus looked into her brown eyes and gave her a warm smile.

"Okay, truce." He dropped the snowball on her before shaking her hand.

The snow covered her face and hair. "That's not a truce!"

Marcus fell over laughing.

Julie rolled on him and started throwing snow in his face.

"Truce, truce, truce," Marcus laughed.

"Now you want a truce?"

"I do, I do." He sat up. They stopped and stared into each other's eyes.

# Chapter Ten

Julie—Earth

"Do you ever think about Mr. Campbell?" Julie asked Claire while talking to her best friend on Facetime. It had been a week since the day in the snow, and Julie had not gotten over the awkwardness of the moment or the feelings that continued to race through her mind.

"Every once in a while. Why?"

"I don't know. I was thinking about him the other day."

"They never caught him, did they?" Claire asked.

Julie was sitting in her dorm room in her green and yellow Cedar Creek tee shirt and shorts. "Nope."

"Man, it's hard to believe he was a con man like they said he was," Claire added. "My dad said the way he disappeared, he must've gotten away with something big."

"Bigger than pretending to be a teacher?" Julie asked, trying to keep her secret.

"Yeah, way bigger than that. He must've robbed banks or something, and that was his cover. Otherwise, why would anyone pretend to be a teacher? It's not like they make a ton of money."

Julie grimaced. "I guess. My dad thinks he might have been in witness protection, and no one told the Sunset police. So, he was discovered when his name turned up on the news for helping me with Trotter."

"Ooh, that's a good one. I never thought of that. That would be why he was able to work as a teacher and got away with not filling out all the government paperwork. He was pretty private and low-key scary. Remember that time he broke up that fight in the cafeteria our freshman year?"

"How could I forget?"

That was when Marcus defended himself from an attacking senior football player with one move: kicking up a chair and using it as a shield. It was the first time she noticed him at school and the first incident that made her curious. Now, she knew he could have easily torn the boys apart in a matter of minutes. "What did you think of him?"

"Mr. Campbell? I thought he was super cool. Plus, he was good-looking. I can admit I had a small crush on him, a small one, not like the crush you had on him."

"Uh, I did not," Julie protested. She felt the heat of embarrassment rise up her chest and neck.

"Come on, Jules. Everyone knew it. Heck, I was a little jealous at times."

"Why? You were with Jimmy."

"Yeah, but you had his attention. The way you looked at him, sometimes the way he looked at you. There was some real chemistry there."

"You're crazy!" Julie forced a laugh.

"Uh-uh. I saw it. You were into him. Heck, you practically stopped dating because of him. Had I not known better, I would have said you were having a fling with him."

"I was not," Julie protested.

"I know. I said if I didn't know better. But you have to admit you two were pretty tight."

Julie relented a little. She knew it was true, and the way she was feeling at the moment was the whole reason she brought up the conversation with her best friend. "We were. But," she interjected, "nothing ever happened. I promise."

"I know. There's no way you could have kept that secret from me."

Julie laughed. "You're right." She breathed a sigh of relief.

"Now," Claire started to change the subject. "Tell me more about your parents wanting to move."

"Oh geesh, don't get me started," Julie said. "They are ridiculous."

"Do you think they'll really move?"

"I kinda do. I think they're serious. I get it in a way. Patrick's gone, and I'll leave the house in a couple of years. They will be free to do what they want for the first time in their marriage."

"I think it's romantic," Claire said. Julie could hear the cooing in her voice. "I mean, think about it. Patrick was young when they got married, and they didn't have time to do much as a newly married couple. Now they can have fun."

"I know," Julie relented. She took a drink from her nearby water bottle. "It will be weird without them."

Claire made a clicking sound with her mouth. "Sure it will, but think about how lucky you are. My parents are divorced. They hate each other. My dad dates girls my age, and my mom is getting married to some guy she met at a singles retreat. I haven't even met him yet. I'm already pretty much on my own."

"Huh, unh, you'll always have me," Julie said.

"I know. Thank you. And you'll always have me," Claire responded. "But, hey, I gotta go. It's the team's weight room time in fifteen minutes. I can't be late."

"Love you", Julie exclaimed.

"Love you!" Claire hung up.

Julie looked around. Whelp. She sighed and looked at the book open with the pages down on the bed. I guess it's just you and me, Mr. Tolkien.

# Chapter Eleven

Julie—Seras

Julie appeared in Marcus's cabin through the Elders' portal. "Hello," she called out. "Hello?" Light shone from gaps in the wood slats. A deer hide partition separated the portal from the rest of the small log home. Marcus built the divider when it became apparent that Julie was now free to come and go from her forest hideout to Seras as she wished, given the state of undress it would leave her in if he happened to be in the room at the time, something Julie was entirely thankful for. He also built her a clothes tree and shelf on the portal side to keep her items when she wasn't there. She lit a couple of the candles in her little corner to dress.

The room was empty. The lack of heat from the fireplace meant that it had either been a warm night or Marcus had been gone for a while. That made Julie a little nervous, after his disappearance a year ago when he decided to go after William by himself. She had to trust he wouldn't do anything stupid like that again. Julie blew out the candles and went out into the town. Where was everyone? The streets and market were quiet and empty. Julie happened into Charlena, Redderick's slave, carrying a load of firewood across the market square.

"Hi, excuse me," Julie said.

Charlena gasped and bowed. "My Heart."

"No, no, please call me Julie." Julie never liked the way Redderick treated Charlena, nor did she understand his control over the strong, able-bodied girl or why he treated her so poorly.

"Yes, my Heart," she said, "lowering her brown eyes."

Julie took her by the hand. "Please, look at me."

Charlena slowly lifted her head.

Julie brushed the girl's sandy hair away from her face. "Thank you.

Where is everyone?" Julie let go of her hand.

"They are at the council house. It's the day of passing grievances."

"Passing grievances? I didn't know that was a thing," Julie said.

"Yes, my Heart. It happens when necessary. If there are conflicts among the people, they present them to the council, and the council will establish what needs to be done to rectify the problem."

"Like a court?" Julie asked.

"I'm sorry, my Heart." Charlena lowered her head again.

"Please, Julie. And thank you." Julie paused. "Hey."

Charlena stopped.

"Can I ask you something?"

The young woman nodded, her expression conveying a hint of humility in contrast to her powerful build.

"Why does Redderick Bobo treat you so badly?"

Charlena slumped. "I do not know, my Heart. It is the way he has always treated me."

"Why do you stay with him?"

"He is my master. I am dedicated to his side."

Julie shook her head. "I don't get it. No one else has slaves. Why don't you go to the council and file a grievance?"

"Oh no, my Heart. Redderick Bobo is better to me than I deserve."

"No, he isn't!" Julie ran her hands through her hair in frustration. "I don't understand. You should be free to do what you want and not work for a guy who is so mean to you."

"I am sorry, my Heart. I really must go." Charlena backed away before turning and hurrying toward Bobo's tent.

*Oh great, Julie. Go ahead and scare a poor girl, why don't ya.* She smacked her hand to her forehead. Julie made her way to the council house, a large wooden building that resembled a barn more than a house.

Julie entered the large room. It was packed wall-to-wall with the people of Allon. Between the heat and the overcrowding, Julie's nose burned, and her eyes watered. Moments like these made her wish someone would invent showers. Rows of pews lined the floor on both sides of the room, leaving an aisle in the middle for access to the front. A platform was raised in what Julie would come to learn was a dais. There, sitting left to right, were Freya, the Corven with her bright colors of orange, purple, and yellow flowing gown; Griffus, who represented the warriors of Bhujuda Heilshorn; Otta the Hemoor; Lord Marek of the Hawkmir people, who looked to Julie like a skinny Santa Claus; and Tanda of the Evandell. They listened to complaints and conflicts between the people of Allon. Marcus stood off to the right side of the raised platform while Redderick, Jayna, and Seren sat in the pew near him.

The room came to a halt when they noticed Julie walking down the aisle. She stopped halfway. "I'm sorry. I didn't mean to interrupt."

Marcus hurried to her.

"Don't be silly, child. The Heart is always welcome," Redderick Bobo said, standing to greet her.

"Julie, what are you doing here?" Marcus asked in a hushed tone, as he took her by the elbow and tried to escort her out of the room.

"Why are you acting so weird?" Julie whispered back.

"I'm not. I didn't think you would want to see things like this."

"Like what? What's going on?"

"We're holding court to settle disputes," Marcus told her.

"I can see that. Why are you trying to keep me out?"

Marcus stopped walking with her and stood up straight. "I'm not."

"Yes, you are. You've never told me about this, and you're trying to make me leave."

"Okay, I didn't want you to see this part of Allon," Marcus admitted.

Julie stared at him with her big brown eyes. "Why?"

"It's not important. If you want to sit in here and listen, you are more than welcome."

She looked at the people of Allon watching her, then glanced at the dais. They were all waiting for Julie to decide what she would do. She turned to Marcus, "I don't want to stay. Maybe some other time. But I do want to know why you hid this from me."

"That's fair." He rubbed the stubble on his chin. "You wanna get out of here?"

"Yes, please."

He nodded to the council and escorted Julie outside.

"What the hell, Marcus?" Julie asked, turning to him as soon as the wooden door closed.

"Let me explain."

"You better believe you will."

"Can we do it someplace else?" he asked.

Julie looked around. No one was walking in the streets. "I guess, but I don't see the point. We're alone right here."

"Okay, but I'd rather do this somewhere else where we can sit down and I can explain."

"Fine, we can go back to your cabin, but I want the truth."

## Chapter Twelve

Marcus—Seras

Marcus and Julie entered his cabin. “Can I get you something to drink?”

“Sure, whatcha got?”

He looked at the pitcher sitting on the table in the corner of the room opposite the dividers that hid the Elder portal. He got the idea for them from seeing a Japanese shoji in Mr. Christian’s home. The old man had traveled there once in college, during a study abroad semester. Marcus built one thick enough. There was no danger of him seeing Julie coming out of the flames if she popped in unexpectedly. “Well, I have water, wine, or something that was supposed to be tea.”

“Is it good?”

“Not really.” He grimaced and shook his head back and forth.

“I’ll take the wine,” Julie said. She sat on the edge of the bed.

Marcus paused.

“Stop. I’m not in high school, I’m not driving, I’m not even on Earth.”

“So, rules like that don’t exist?”

“Hey, you’re the one who mentioned the wine.” She bobbed her head.

Marcus relented and poured her a mug. “Here you go.” He watched as she took a long drink.

“Okay, talk,” Julie said as she sat the mug down.

He sat on the chair beside the table. “I’m not sure what you want me to say?”

“I told you, I want the truth. I want to know why you are hiding the council thingy from me?”

"I didn't hide it from you," Marcus started.

"You never told me about it," she argued back.

"I just didn't want you to see some of the ugliness of the town. Some of the decisions we have to make are very serious. Others are pretty silly."

"Like what?"

"The silly ones? Neighbors fighting over chickens in the yard or barking dogs."

"No, the serious ones. The ones you don't want me to hear about."

Marcus took a deep breath.

"What's wrong? Why don't you want to tell me?"

"It's not that I don't want to tell you." He stalled. "You know how people on Earth are petty and even sometimes cruel?"

"Yeah?"

"We have that here, too. We have stealing, fighting, even murder and rape."

"Oh my God! What the heck?"

"It doesn't happen often, but it has happened. No place is perfect."

"I get that. But why keep it from me?"

"I was afraid," Marcus said.

"Afraid of what?"

"That you wouldn't like it here and would never want to come back."

"Marcus, after everything I've seen and done. I've killed...you're a freakin' demon! You think learning that Allon isn't perfect would chase me away?"

He blew out a breath of air. "When you put it like that." Marcus smiled.

"Is that it?"

"Yep." Marcus hated lying to her, but he had no choice. He could never tell her the whole truth, and he would eventually have to insist that she leave Earth and make Seras her permanent home, as the Heart, and take her place as ruler of the lands. But that conversation would happen much, much later. And for Marcus, the later, the better.

## Chapter Thirteen

Javan—Seras

It had been months of traveling the northwestern coastline of Seras's largest body of land. Captain Javan was the most experienced seaman in what the men who sailed called the Surimira. Surimira was the mainland where Cauleta, the River Linsay, and the northern mountains, including Allon, were located. The very land Queen Pallanex had him traveling the coast of to find a northern passage to sneak behind the fortified home of the Skorei general, Marcus, and the Elder, Tolth's Heart, to stay from Pallanex's reach. Javan was aware of three other major landmasses in his lifetime: Surakora, a smaller body of land south of Surimira where the Crixium Sea separated, and a chain of islands referred to as the Agronicus Islands. He and his crew enjoyed the company of the olive-skinned women with dark hair and dark eyes who entertained them with song, wine, and other activities. Javan had sailed through the isles and around Surakora, something he cannot say about Surimira.

He had also sailed the eastern coasts of Saxaralia, the southern land where the former home of Pallanex, Karros, was located, as well as the northern land of Saxulythia. Javan had not ventured ways around the two massive lands. During their journey, they saw scattered islands along the way. He and his crew made port on an island in the north they named Malitta. They were able to restock their food supplies by trading with the islanders. They also acquired furs to protect against the increasingly cold weather as they traveled further.

"Captain," one of his men interrupted Javan as he labeled the coastal regions they passed. Pallanex wanted it to be a search for a way to get behind enemy lines and destroy them, but Javan saw the opportunity to increase his knowledge and map out areas that had been explored.

“What is it?” He waved the man into the room.

“There is an inlet big enough to sail. Do you think we are far enough north to attempt it?”

“Wait outside,” he told the man. Javan put on his dark red suit, which had a chest plate emblazoned with three circling sharks. He then tied his beard and ponytail with matching red cords.

He met the awaiting man and followed him to the deck—the wooden hull creaked as the ship pitched. Snow covered the ground and treetops. “The water?”

“Flowing inland, does not appear frozen,” the man answered.

Javan walked up the stairs to the helm. There, a man sat on a wooden chair, drawing what he saw. “What do you think, Ranu?”

The man stopped sketching. “Allow the truth to drip from Ranu’s tongue?”

“Yes, of course. I asked, did I not?”

“The days grow colder. If this is not the passage, better to cast yourself into the sea, Master.” He wiped his face with charcoaled fingers.

“That will not happen.” He turned to the man at the helm. “Take us there.”

The pilot nodded and ordered the crew to prepare the sails. He rotated the massive wheel hard to the right as the ship entered the mouth of the river.

# Chapter Fourteen

Julie—Earth

Julie pulled into the driveway of Grandma Franklin's ranch home, nestled in the heart of Sunset. Grandma Franklin was eighty-four years old and was still a force of nature. She met Julie at the door. Her silver hair was pulled back into a tight bun, and her eyes twinkled at the sight of her only granddaughter. "There she is. My favorite granddaughter. Just look at you."

Julie laughed and gave her a hug. "Hi, Grandma. How are you?"

"I'm still kicking. Come on in. Let me get a good look at you." She held the door for Julie. "How are you? How's college? How's life? And more importantly, tell me about the boys?"

"Oh geesh. Well, college is... well, a bit overwhelming. Lots of new things to get used to." Julie followed her grandma to the dining room and kitchen area. She had a pot of tea on the stove and a plate of cookies on the table.

"Sit down, sit down," Grandma Franklin said. "Have you been eating?" You look famished.

"I'm okay."

"Nonsense. Here." She gave her a small plate and placed three homemade cookies on it. "Eat these. I'll make you a cup." She walked to the stove and poured two cups of tea. "Here you go, honey," Grandma Franklin said, placing a cup of hot tea in front of her.

"Thank you."

"Now, you tell me what's on your mind?"

"Huh, what?"

"Come on now. You can't fool this old lady. You're distracted." She sat beside Julie and patted her hand.

"Can't a girl visit her grandma while her parents are out of town?"

*How could she tell her grandmother about her feelings for Marcus? A man fifteen years her senior. A man who is considered a criminal on Earth. A man who is actually part demon from another dimension.*

"Oh, you can, and I love that you do. But I can tell, I can tell," Grandma Franklin smiled and took a bite of her cookie.

"I know. There's nothing to tell. I'm just checking on you," Julie said. She held up her cup with both hands to hide her face.

"Okay, if you won't tell me, I guess we'll have to talk about my love life."

"Grandma!" Julie protested.

"What? An old lady can have a love life, can't she?"

Julie pounded her feet and scrunched her face.

"I met him playing pickle ball," Grandma Franklin continued.

"Can we talk about anything else?" Julie put her hands together in prayer and begged. "Please."

"Listen to this old lady." Grandma Franklin put her hands on top of Julie's. "You are young; the prime of your life is right here. You do whatever you want to do and kick this world's ass."

Julie's eyes lit up.

"I'm serious. Life is too short. Make mistakes, dance, sing, travel, laugh, live. You have so much going for you, young lady. Don't worry about your parents, me, or what anyone in this small town thinks. You be the best you you can be."

"I'm trying, Grandma. But it's everything: school, Mom, Dad, and other things."

"Your mom and dad are going to do what they are going to do. You can only worry about what you have control over. You don't know what they are going to do, and even if they do something crazy like sell their house and move somewhere far away, it's their decision. They might get there and hate it. Who knows?"

"Is that something they're talking about? Moving away?"

"No, no, but being empty nesters, the possibilities are limitless."

"I know you're right. It's all so hard."

Grandma Franklin got up to pour another cup of tea. "You better believe it is. It's hard to lose your parents. It's hard to lose your husband.

It's hard to watch the difficulties of your child having miscarriages. It's hard to watch your granddaughter struggle with things out of your control."

Julie stopped her. "I didn't know my mom had a miscarriage?"

"She had a few of them. After you, of course. That's why she is so protective of you."

Julie wiped her eyes. "I thought it was because I was the first girl. I had no idea."

"Of course you didn't. How would you ever?" She sat back in her chair.

"Your mother loves you like no other." Grandma Franklin smiled. "And all you need to do is love her back."

"I do," Julie said. "I really do."

"I know you do. She knows you do. Just let her see it, even when you don't feel like it."

"Thank you. I guess I'm still trying to find my footing. What am I going to do? Where do I belong?"

"Oh, pish posh! That all comes later. Have a little fun. You need to mix it up, sweetheart."

Julie chuckled. "You sound like my roommate." Julie dipped her cookie into her teacup. "Her name is Brooklyn. She's pretty popular and does nothing but go to parties."

"Well, that's not what I meant."

"I know."

Grandma Franklin stood. "I have an idea. How about we make a pie? That'll give us a chance to take a break from all that studying."

"I love that idea." Julie joined her grandmother at the kitchen counter.

"And I can find out more about this boy of yours." Grandma Franklin winked.

"Oh, Grandma!"

## Chapter Fifteen

Julie—Earth

Julie left Grandma Franklin's house and drove through the quiet town of Sunset. She passed by the neighborhood where Mr. Christian lived. She hadn't stopped in to see him in months. During her last visit, he had seemed better, having recovered from the ordeal Marcus had inflicted upon him by using the Breath of Ostram. The magical potion Marcus used to learn how to speak English, drive a car, and become a teacher was also used on Julie to help her speak the language used in Allon. That was the same visit that Mr. Christian warned Julie about Marcus being in trouble when he decided to seek out William on his own and kill him. *That turned into a disaster.*

As she drove by his house, Julie was surprised to see him outside mowing his lawn. She pulled into the driveway and got out of her car. Mr. Christian stopped his push mower and walked over to greet her.

"Julie, it's so good to see you," he started. "How have you been?" He held out his hand.

"I'm doing great." Julie took him by his hand and patted it. "It looks like you are too."

Mr. Christian smiled. "I must say I am doing quite well. Better than ever, in fact." He shifted to look at his lawn. "I can't remember the last time I got out and did yard work."

"It's been a while."

"I know, and I must thank you and Marcus for taking care of my place while I was incapacitated. I don't know what I would have done if not for the two of you," he said.

Julie refrained from commenting that it was Marcus's fault he ended up like that in the first place. "It was our pleasure, really," she stated instead.

"Would you like a glass of lemonade or iced tea?"

"No, thank you. I'm good. I just saw you out here mowing and wanted to make sure you are doing okay," Julie said. She began to head back to her car. "Can I ask you something?"

"Yes, you may ask me something," he corrected her.

"May I ask you something?"

"Of course." He smiled.

"Are you planning on teaching again?" Julie asked.

"Why, yes, I am. I already contacted the school. As it turns out, they need an English teacher, and I need two more years to get my full retirement. I start in August."

"That's so cool!" She gave the old man a huge hug. "That makes me so happy!"

"Well, um, er," he stuttered.

"I'm sorry. I didn't mean to—" Julie stepped back and regained her composure.

"It's perfectly fine. I wish I would have had you in class," he told her.

"I would have loved that," Julie responded. She walked to her car. "It was great seeing you, and I'm soooo glad you are okay."

"Thank you, Miss Ayers. And if you happen to see Mr. Campbell, please tell him to stop by sometime."

"Will do!" Julie hopped in her car and drove away. The idea of seeing Marcus was etched firmly in her mind.

## Chapter Sixteen

Pallanex—Seras

A raven circled the tower at the heart of Cauleta. Queen Pallanex waited patiently as it landed on the perch of the messenger keeper's crate. The withered old man placed his hand under the raven's claws, and the blackbird climbed on his crooked index finger. He gave it a little morsel as a reward, as he untied the tiny scroll from its leg and gave it to the queen before placing the bird inside the crate with food and water.

Pallanex made her way down a flight of stone steps, carefully unwrapping the scroll and rolling it out. She carried it to her map room and laid it out beside more than a dozen other messages. Three men wearing brown robes stood around the table, which was shaped in the form of a map of the northern shoreline. "Is he getting close?" she asked.

One man, bald and skinny, looked at the message. "I believe he is." He pointed to the area where a second man was adding the miniature drawing that had just arrived to the larger map. "You see. They are turning east into this passage. He would not do so unless he thought he was getting close."

"Or," the second man interrupted, "he is afraid that going further north would lead him nowhere."

"Salius," the third man admonished.

The man named Salius stopped his drawing and looked up to the queen. He was younger than the other two, perhaps having seen forty Temporas in his time. His long, greasy hair was pulled back in a ponytail, and he wore a thick beard and mustache. "I can only tell the truth to my Queen," he said. "We know the depth of cold here. It only worsens as they travel north. Soon, who knows what they may encounter."

"Apologies, my Queen," the third man started. He was thicker around the waist than the other two. His face was wrinkled and worn. “Forgive Salius, he still has much to learn.”

“Nonsense, Barth. I do need to hear the truth.” She nodded her approval to Salius.

“Thank you, my Queen,” Salius answered.

“How much longer?” she asked. Pallanex joined her mapmakers, Barth and Salius, to examine the group’s final member.

“Rondal?”

The bald, skinny man held out a measuring stick to the map. “The land we have traveled goes through here.” He placed the stick marked with notches that represented a day’s journey. “We know this path. Northwest to Fort Madena and Madena to the Lobello Mountains, but we do not know the passage through the mountains as we have never had anyone return from there.” He placed a second stick from the newly added inlet on the map. “I can say that if the angles are matched from here to here,” he overlapped the two sticks and paused for a noticeable effect, “he is close.”

## Chapter Seventeen

William—Seras

William entered the gates of Cauleta. Behind him was a line of fully armored warriors; his most trusted men, behind them, a line of half-dressed captives from their conquest, and a third line of men to keep the prisoners from escaping or slowing the march. His campaign was a success. After his latest batch of experiments had died, it was necessary for him to find more "volunteers." The prisoners and his men were covered in dirt and blood. The dust from the land around Cauleta kicked up around their ankles. The sun was hot against their skin and sweat pooled under their armor.

He spotted Pallanex watching him from the battlement of the wall. Her banners of a dark blue spider on a field of silver cloth were flying wildly in the wind. "She will not be happy," he sighed. William lifted his hand, and the men stopped. He dismounted. "Take the prisoners to their chambers," he ordered. "Make sure they are clean and ready for me."

"Yes, General," one of the men said. He motioned for the procession to continue.

William put on a smile to face her wrath as he headed up the stone stairs. "My Queen." He bowed.

Pallanex turned to him. She was wearing a scarlet leather outfit, cut deliciously down her front, trimmed at the waist, and slit on both sides of her long legs. Her dark hair was braided and pulled tightly under a metallic crown that adorned her head, sitting atop jewelry resembling chain mail, which draped down the sides of her face, around her neck, and down her chest.

"You look lovely, as always."

"William, why do you continue to defy me?" she hissed.

"I see it as getting what I need to fulfill my promise to you, my queen."

"I made promises not to attack the South. They have been supporters since I replaced Canis. You broke that pact."

"Not to worry. They will not be attacking you or anyone ever again."

Queen Pallanex gritted through her teeth. "Get out of my sight."

"You will thank me soon enough," William said and then bowed, turning on his heels.

"Get out!"

William returned to his work. He looked over the new prisoners, cleaned and strapped to their cots. "Thank you." He clapped twice, and his men brought in a barrel. William took a ladle and carefully scooped the contents into small cups. He handed the cups to his men, who then delivered them to the struggling captives.  The men coughed and choked as the vile potion was forced down their throats. One man pinched their nose and held their jaw as a second man poured the liquid into their mouth to make them drink.

"And now, we wait," William said. "Post men outside to make sure none of them escape."

## Chapter Eighteen

Julie—Earth

"How are you holding up?" Claire asked Julie as the two of them were Facetiming during Julie's spring break from college.

"I'm good. Busy, but good. How 'bout you?" She held the phone while sitting on her parents' living room couch. Even though she was less than a half hour away and returned to Sunset whenever she traveled to Seras, it felt like she could relax in the comfort of her home.

"I'm okay. Indoor went well," Claire started.

"I saw that. You were a rock star."

"Thanks." Her friend gave a bashful smile. "Outdoor is going to be even better, I hope."

"Of course it will. I can't wait to see you compete. What else has been going on?"

"Nothing. Track is my life. You know I have no social life," Claire explained.

"That sucks."

"Enough about my life." Claire paused. "Any special guy?"

Julie dropped her back. "You know, no one special, but I have someone in mind."

"No way! Tell me more."

Julie gritted her teeth. "I'm not ready to tell you yet. It's a work in progress."

"Jules, that's not fair. Give me something."

"Okay, he's a...senior...he's athletic."

"What's his name?"

"I can't tell you that. I don't even know if he likes me."

"Give me a hint. Is it somebody I know?"

"Not really. You might have seen him, but you don't really know him," Julie said, trying to be as vague as possible.

"You're killing me, Jules."

The door opened, and Julie's parents walked into the living room. "Hey, kiddo," Phil said. He peeked at her phone. "Is that Claire bear? Hi, Claire!"

"Hey, Mr. Ayers, Mrs. Ayers!"

"Hi, sweetie," Michelle said loud enough for Claire to hear. "How's college?"

"Great, I love it here."

Michelle continued speaking loudly. "When are you coming back? We miss you!"

"Not until after the semester and the season, Mrs. Ayers."

"How's Jimmy?" Phil asked.

"Dad!" "Phil!" Julie and Michelle both yelled simultaneously.

"I'm so sorry, Claire. I forgot."

"It's okay, Mr. Ayers. As far as I know, he is doing great. We're still friends."

Michelle used her head to point out of the room. "Come on, Phil."

"Bye, Claire", Phil said.

"Bye, Claire." Michelle gently pushed her husband into the dining room. "I can't believe you asked that," she said in a hushed voice.

"I'm sorry," Phil whispered back.

Julie continued after her parents left the room, "I'm sorry about them."

"That's alright. At least your parents care," Claire said with a slight sadness.

"Oh shoot, I'm sorry," Julie apologized.

"Don't be. I love your parents."

"Yeah, well, you can have them. They're leaving me for a world cruise in about three months." Julie decided to change the subject. "So, you still talk to Jimmy?"

"Of course," Claire said. "We broke up, but I'm not angry...well, anymore. I get it. Being so far away caused problems."

"That's good. That makes me happy."

"Well, hey, I gotta run...literally," Claire said with a half laugh.

"Okay, I'll talk to you soon. Love you!"

"Love you back!"

Julie's dad peeked around the corner. "So-o-o-o, who's the fella?"

"Huh? Wait, were you listening to my conversation?" Julie shrieked.

"Just a little when I opened the door. So, do we know him?"

"Oh my God, no. He's someone I know at school. I don't even know if he likes me," Julie tried in vain to restrain herself.

"Come on, Jules. I'm just playing." He shook his head. "The joys of being the dad of a teenage girl. But I must admit, you've been pretty easy on the old ticker the last few years." He patted his chest.

"Mom, please make him stop!" Julie threw a pillow at him as he approached her to give her a bear hug.

# Chapter Nineteen

Julie—Seras

Again, Redderick Bobo laughed and clapped his hands. Julie had just lifted a small tree from the ground and threw it twenty feet into a thicket of bushes. "This time, I want you to hold it in midair a little longer."

"Are you serious?" Julie dropped her hands to her knees. "We've been at this for hours." She straightened herself and walked to another tree that was holding her water pouch on a broken limb. "Where's Marcus?" She took a long drink.

"I do not know, my Heart. He said he had something to do and left at first light."

"And you don't know where or why?" Julie took another long drink then poured the water on her hands and rubbed it on her face and through her hair.

"I do not. I told you as such." Redderick sat on a stump.

"But you're the scribe or whatever of Seras. You know everything."

"That I am, but that will be revealed to me when the time is right. I do not pretend to know a person's journeys, future or every detail. Just the finished result." He paused. "Which reminds me, I am falling further behind." He stood up. "We must get busy."

Julie blew out a breath. "Fine." She shook out her arms and rolled her neck. "Tell me what you want me to do."

"That rock there." He pointed to a boulder the size of a motorcycle. "I want you to lift it and hold it until I say otherwise."

"Really?" She had a vague idea about what he was going to do. Julie closed her eyes and gathered her thoughts.

"No, no, no..." Redderick waved his hand. "You are wasting too much time. I want you to react quicker. When you face Pallanex, you will not have time to think about what you must do. You must just do it."

Julie lifted the rock with her mind and crushed it by clenching her fingers together. "There! Happy?" Julie stormed away. "I'm going to find Marcus."

## Chapter Twenty

Marcus—Seras

"There you are!" Marcus heard Julie yell from the courtyard as he entered Allon.

"Julie, what's wrong?"

"Oh, nothing, if you don't consider some fat old man barking orders at you for three hours wrong?"

Marcus rubbed his eyes. "I hate to ask, but did you learn anything?"

"That has nothing to do with it." Julie waved her hands. "Yes," she surrendered. Then, her mood changed. "You should have seen me." Julie giggled and hopped up and down. "I made a tree fly, and I crushed a boulder."

"I guess I better watch out the next time we train," Marcus told her.

"Can we do that now, please?" She clasped her hands and batted her eyes.

"I thought you were tired of training for the day?"

"I never said that. Besides, you're more fun than he is," Julie said, walking backward as she talked.

"I would never consider myself fun."

"Psst. You're tons of fun. I always laugh when I'm with you."

Marcus furrowed his brow.

"Okay, once you get past the grr part," Julie said with a smile. "Come on, silly. We've got training to do."

"Lead the way." Marcus followed her to the northwestern field where they enjoyed practicing the most. "Are you ready?" He held his sword across his shoulders, both arms draped over the blade and hilt.

"More ready than you." She lowered herself and pointed the blade at him.

They began sparing.

"Strike, strike, block," Marcus commanded. "Block, block, block."

Julie began to laugh.

"What?"

"You sound like a chicken." Julie bobbed her head and mocked him like a chicken, "Block, block, block." She laughed again. "I told you you're funny."

"I think we're done for the day," he told her.

Julie wiped the tears of laughter from her eyes. "I'm sorry, I'm sorry."

"But you're still laughing."

"I know, I'm sorry." She bounced toward the bench to get a drink. "Come on, have a seat." She patted the spot next to her.

Marcus sat beside her.

"Can I ask you something?" Julie asked. She turned to him and cocked her head to the side. Her golden-brown eyes sparkled in the sun.

"Always."

"Do you miss being on Earth?"

Marcus chuckled. "Where did that come from?" He paused for a second. "There are certain things I miss about Earth."

"Like what?" He could see her curiosity starting to get the best of her.

"I miss the music. I miss the books."

"Of course you would miss the books," Julie scoffed.

"I miss television, movies..."

"Did you really watch TV or see movies?"

"I don't know. Hmm, maybe it's things I picked up from Mr. Christian? I miss some of my coworkers. I miss Mr. Langston, Mrs. Larson, Schultz, Rupert Doyle, Big Sam, your friends, Claire and Jimmy." Marcus paused again. "I miss teaching a little bit."

"Just a little bit?" Julie questioned, twisting her mouth to the side.

"Well, teaching is not always what it's cracked up to be. There are some students I really, really like; you, Jimmy, Claire, and a bunch of others. Then, some students were quite frankly a pain in the butt."

"Yeah, I always thought I might want to be a teacher, but that's before I paid attention to how many don't do their homework, don't study for tests, and still expect to get good grades and pass. Now, I'm like, forget it, I'll find something else to do."

"That's too bad. I think you would make a wonderful teacher," Marcus told her.

"Anything else you miss?"

"I miss a lot of the food. Yeah, most of the food on Earth is way better. Your mom's food was delicious."

"Really? You should come back sometime to eat," Julie said.

"I can't go back to Earth. I'm a criminal there. Your parents would never let me eat at their table."

"Who needs them?" Julie scoffed. "I can cook just as good as my mom. I can fix you something to eat."

"Julie," Marcus said. His voice cracking.

"I'm serious."

He took a deep breath. "Okay, as long as you think it will be—"

"I do, I do," she said, jumping up and clapping, not letting him finish his sentence.

"Now, can we get back to training?" Marcus stood and picked up his sword.

"Yep!" Julie grabbed her sword. "Let me show you what I can do." She smiled.

# Chapter Twenty-One

Marcus—Seras

Marcus brought his chestnut horse to a stop in front of one of the small cabins once used to fool the army of the giant, Juta, during the Battle of Yellow Fields. Darius was chopping wood at the side of the thatched roof hut. "Darius."

His brother stopped. "Marcus." Sweat dripped from his face from the midday heat as he took a towel to wipe his body. "I wondered when you would come to see me."

Marcus dismounted. "We started something that we need to finish."

"So, are we going to fight?"

"That depends on you," Marcus said.

"I am not sure what else needs to be said. I told you William tricked me. He poisoned my mind against you. He killed Raewin. I was a fool," Darius admitted.

"Not entirely. I know how well he talked. He spent most of our time together lying to me. He was with Pallanex from the beginning. He led us to do her bidding while making me feel like it was his idea or mine."

Darius set the ax down. "Would you like to come in?"

"Sure."

The two brothers headed for the front door. "Has anyone mentioned that you talk funny now?"

"I've heard that once or twice. The result of traveling to Earth and spending time with Julie...the Heart."

Darius moved his hand to a chair, and Marcus took a seat; then Darius poured two cups of ale. "What is that like?"

"I will tell you that after you tell me why I should trust you completely. I mean, I get it. You helped save me, and you saved Julie, but you...we are demons. We killed, you killed people I loved, you killed Arthur."

"How did you get your soul back?" Darius asked.

"You know how. I killed the Priest of Ostram, who I later learned was actually Ostram in disguise. Believe me, it hurt like hell."

"I do not know what that is, but I believe it was painful," Darius said. He opened his shirt and revealed a scar that ran the length of his chest. "Arthur left his mark, and thanks to Freya, I am still here, and her healing power gave me something else, a chance for redemption." He took a drink.

"I know a little of that myself," Marcus said.

"I am sure you do." Darius stood to pour another drink. "So, where does this leave us? Are we friends, enemies, brothers?"

"I don't know," Marcus replied. "But I hope we can be anything except enemies."

"As do I," Darius said. He held up his mug.

Marcus stood and held up his cup. Darius did the same, and the two brothers downed their drinks.

## Chapter Twenty-Two

Julie—Earth

Julie sat at her parents' dining room table with her mother, father, brother, and Grandma Franklin. "So, when are you leaving again?"

The cozy kitchen and dining room gave a warm and cheerful vibe. The kitchen had dark wooden cabinets that matched the floors and featured bright blue and brown accents, just like the living room. A farmhouse sink sat under a window. In the middle of the kitchen was an island with stools around it, perfect for family members to sit and chat while meals were being made. The island had a dark wood finish that matched the cabinets. Next to the kitchen, the dining room had a sturdy wooden table, a gift from Phillip's father, surrounded by matching chairs after he and Michelle were married. A light brown rug protected the floor under the table, and a large, colorful painting hung on the wall. A vintage hutch displayed pretty plates and cups, just like the cabinet in the den.

"We'll leave right after your birthday and be gone most of the summer," Michelle answered. "It's not too late. You can still go with us."

"Mom," Julie sighed, "I can't. I have plans. School starts in August. You won't be back until the first week of September. Speaking of...what are you going to do about the Coffee Festival?"

"Already taken care of," Phil said. "Now, what's this about plans? This is the first time I've heard about plans."

"It's nothing exciting. Claire and I will be getting together. I might go out with a few friends from college," Julie told them, knowing she didn't have any friends from college.

"That's great," her dad said.

"Hmm," Michelle snorted.

"What?" Phil asked.

"Nothing, just wish she would come with us. I thought now that she's out of high school and no more basketball, track, or cheer, we would spend more time together." Michelle teared up. "Patrick is moving away. Julie is busy. I feel so alone."

Grandma Franklin looked at her daughter. "Stop it," she said. "The two of you have raised wonderful children who are doing great in the world. You need to be proud of them, not make them feel guilty. Patrick found a wonderful job. You really don't want him to give that all up just to spend three months with us on a boat. Same with Julie. You said it yourself: she is excelling in school, has amazing friends, and has overcome so much—the incident with that perverted science teacher and Mr. Campbell being some kind of conman who fooled all of us. Only a strong young woman could survive all of that."

"Thank you, Grandma," Julie said.

Michelle blew her nose. "You're right, mom. I'm sorry, you two." She reached across the table and clasped each of their wrists. "I didn't mean to make you feel guilty." She squeezed their wrists and shook them a little. "We are very proud of both of you. I didn't mean to suggest otherwise."

"We know," Julie said.

"Yeah, we know. Grammy is right. You did a great job raising us. Now, it's time to let us live. You guys go and have a great time," Patrick told them.

"It would be a life-changing experience," Michelle said.

"Yes, but you need to have fun, and if we were there, you would spend all of your time wondering if we were having fun," Patrick responded.

"Exactly," Grandma Franklin said with a wink.

# Chapter Twenty-Three

Julie—Seras

Marcus reached down to help Julie back to her feet.

"I'm never going to beat you, am I?" she huffed. They stood at the ready, but Julie was distracted by the rippling definition of his arms.

"Yes, you will. This time, I want you to use both your sword skills and your...um, elder power."

"I call it angel power." She bobbed her head.

Marcus smiled. "Okay, use your angel power at the same time."

"You really want me to?"

"I do. You can't limit yourself. You have this amazing gift; use it. Don't let me hold you back."

"You're not holding me back," she said.

"I am if you are afraid to use it when we are using swords." He moved to attack her.

Julie blocked his advancement with Pale Fire, her sword forged with Evandell magic.

"Good," Marcus yelled. He darted to the right and swung again.

Julie first defended herself with the sword, then a quick blast from her opened left hand sent Marcus sprawling. "Oh my God, are you okay?" She panicked.

Marcus got up laughing. "I'm fine! That's what I wanted."

"You wanted me to kill you?"

"No, I wanted you to use all of your resources at the same time. Use your sword and use your powers. You will be unstoppable," Marcus said. He cracked his neck. "Ready to go again?"

"I guess so."

"What's wrong? You aren't going to hurt me," Marcus said.

"Are you sure?"

"Yes. I'm fine. I promise."

Julie smiled. "Pinky promise?" She held out her little finger.

Marcus chuckled. "Pinky promise." He locked his pinky around hers.

Julie smiled, looking at the size of his hand. Had she really not noticed before? "How big are your hands?"

Marcus gave her a strange look and held out his hand. "This big. I guess." He sneered.

Julie placed her hand on his. "Geesh."

"You're so weird," Marcus said.

Julie smiled. "But ya love me." She bobbed her head back and forth.

Marcus shook his head. "Are you ready to get back to work?"

"Yep. Come on." She hopped up and down, ready to fight.

Marcus took his stance.

Julie did the same.

They sparred, taking turns swinging and blocking with their swords. As they got more comfortable, they increased the speed and the intensity.

Julie freed her right hand from the sword's hilt and aimed at Marcus.

He moved just enough to avoid her blast.

She tried again.

Marcus dropped down to one hand.

Julie missed again.

She took her sword with two hands and gave him a flurry of swings.

He blocked them with little effort.

Then, the two of them locked swords, facing each other in a stalemate.

Julie strained to push the blade closer and closer to him. She could see Marcus struggling to keep her at a distance.

They broke apart, and Julie hit him with a blast from her hand.

Marcus fell back. He rolled through the grass down a slight incline and came to a stop.

Julie waited for him to get up.

He didn't move.

Julie ran to him. "Marcus, Marcus!"

He remained still.

Julie knelt down and shook him.

"Arrgh," he roared.

Julie tumbled to her butt.

Marcus rolled over, laughing.

"You brat! You scared the bejeebies out of me," Julie shouted.

Marcus laughed so hard he began to cough. "I've gotta catch my breath."

Julie slapped at him. "I can't believe you did that to me."

"I'm sorry, I'm sorry. I couldn't help myself." He brought himself up just enough to sit beside her.

"You scared me." She stuck out her lower lip.

"I know. I'm sorry," he apologized again. "But it was funny," he said with a wicked smile. Marcus stood up and offered her a hand.

Julie reluctantly accepted his help. "I'm going to get you for that."

"There's no doubt in my mind." Marcus walked back up the incline. "I need a drink."

Julie blew out a breath and crinkled her nose before following him." I've got a question," she said as they stopped and took turns sipping from a water pouch.

He looked at her. "Okay?"

"I wanted to ask you during the Tempora, but you were distracted."

"That was months ago."

"I know, but I was just curious; how old do you think you are?"

Marcus shrugged. "Like I've told you before, I'm not sure. After I left Cauleta, I never kept track of things like that."

"But what would you think?"

Marcus looked at the clouds as they slowly drifted across the blue sky. "I don't know, somewhere around thirty, I guess."

"Hm."

"What?"

"Nothing. I was just wondering," she said.

"You ready to get back at it?" He dropped the water container on the ground.

"Yep!" As they returned to their spots, her mind wandered a little,

*So, he's only ten or eleven years older than me?*

"You okay?" Marcus asked, breaking her thoughts.

"Yeah, yeah. Let's go!" She hopped up and down. They tapped their swords lightly as a sign to start. They exchanged blows back and forth. Every time Julie thought she had him cornered, Marcus managed to escape. Julie changed her plan. She switched her blade to her left hand and blasted him with her right, knocking him off his feet once more.

"Hey, that's cheating," he said with a hint of sarcasm.

"It's not cheating; it's using my resources. Isn't that what good teachers tell us?"

"Well, yes, but I'm not sure if I like it or not." Marcus laughed.

"Well, well, I know William didn't like it when I used it on him," Julie said.

"So, does Redderick help you find out more and more about your powers?"

"A little, but I think I can do more than he's telling me."

"What makes you say that?"

"Well, it's like that candle I have on Earth. I know it can slow down the passage of time. What else can it do? Or any of the other gifts of the Elders? They might come in handy against a large army. According to you and Bobo, I'm part angel."

"Yeah."

"And you're part demon." A little laugh escaped her lips. "If I'm part angel, can I fly?"

"I think you're watching too many movies," Marcus told her.

"I wish! Between training with you and him and going to college, I don't have time for any fun."

"Oh, come on now."

"Oh, I'm serious. I don't have any free time."

"Well, you need to make some free time. You can't spend all of your time hanging out with me. That's no fun." Marcus got back up on his feet, armed himself, and prepared to fight with her again. "And after this, I want you to go back to Earth, forget about all of this for a while, and find a few friends to go out with. Okay?"

Julie whispered, "What if I don't want to?"

## Chapter Twenty-Four

Julie—Earth

Julie was folding laundry in her parents' living room when she heard a knock on the front door. She answered the knock at the door. "Claire!" Julie hopped up and down, clapping her hands. "Get in here!"

The two hugged. "I need to come home more often," Claire said.

"What are you doing here?"

"I'm on spring break and wanted to surprise you."

"Consider me surprised," Julie said. A buzzing sound came from the kitchen. "I just made myself some cookies and milk. Want some?"

"Yeah," Claire answered with a squeal. "It smells good."

Julie shuffled to the kitchen in her fuzzy socks and returned with a plate of chocolate chip cookies and a glass of milk. They settled onto Julie's living room couch. The scent of vanilla from a candle on the coffee table mixed with the faint smell of fresh laundry on the chair beside them.

"So, what's going on with you?" Claire asked.

"Pretty uneventful. You're looking at my life. Laundry and snacks with the parents out. Wild Friday night." Julie was glad she decided not to go to Seras after class. "What about you?"

"Oh, nothing much. Just checking on my best friend in the whole wide world." She looked around. "Where are your mom and dad?" Claire asked with a slight giggle.

Julie shrugged. "I think they went on a date. I didn't wanna be stuck in my dorm room, so I came here for the weekend." Julie noticed the giant grin on Claire's face. "You seem really happy," Julie said, raising an eyebrow.

"Yep." Claire gritted her teeth and scrunched her nose. "I met a guy."

"What?" Julie crossed her legs and turned to Claire. "Come on, Claire. Spill the beans," Julie insisted, her curiosity piqued.

"What," Claire said, feigning innocence. "It's early. We're just talking."

"Just talking? You wouldn't be this giggly if you were 'just talking'." Julie made air quotes with her fingers. "There's gotta be more to it," Julie said, crossing her arms.

Claire crossed her arms, too. "Seriously, it's nothing."

"Oh, I get it. This is one of those 'don't want to jinx it' situations, huh?" Julie asked, a knowing smile spreading across her face.

"Maybe. I don't know. It's complicated," Claire admitted, looking away.

"Complicated, how?"

Claire shrugged. "How about you?"

"Hey, no changing the subject." Julie popped a cookie in her mouth.

"No, it's not that. It's just...I don't know if I want to get into it," Claire said, biting her lip.

"You know you can trust me, right? I won't push, but I'm always here," Julie said, reaching out to touch Claire's hand.

"I know. Thanks, Jules. It's just...I don't want to get my hopes up. You know how things have been. I haven't dated anyone since Jimmy," Claire said, her voice barely above a whisper.

"Yeah, I get it. Just promise me one thing," Julie said, squeezing Claire's hand.

"What's that?" Claire asked, looking up.

"If he makes you happy, don't let fear hold you back. You deserve to be happy, Claire," Julie said before taking a bite of another cookie and chasing it down with her glass of milk.

"I'll try. Thanks. You're the best," Claire said, smiling. "Now, how about you? You know I want you to be happy, too."

"I am." Julie saw the skepticism on her friend's face. "I promise."

"Have you met any guys in school?"

"Not at school exactly," Julie said.

Claire wiggled closer. "Okay, I'm all ears."

Julie blew out a breath. "It's nothing. I don't even think he knows how I feel."

"Didn't you just tell me not to hold back from being happy? You gotta let him know." Claire stopped. "Do I know him?"

"Nope, he's a guy I see every once in a while, when I'm working out. He's a little older than me, so I doubt he would be interested."

"Julie Marie Ayers, have you seen yourself? You are a babe," Claire said. "And if the guy has half a brain, he's noticed you."

"Well, it's super complicated," she said, using the same line Claire said earlier. "He's a busy guy with a lot of distractions. But he is really good-looking, tall, muscular, intelligent, unconventional, and funny in a way you wouldn't expect from a guy like him. He makes me laugh."

"Sounds like the two of you know each other pretty well," Claire said.

"He's the kind of guy I could see myself with." Julie caught herself, her eyes wide. She ran her hands over her ponytail, not believing what she had just told Claire in so many words.

"I gotta meet this guy," Claire said.

Julie stood up. "Want some more cookies?"

"Sure."

"Okay, why don't you find a movie? We can get off this topic."

"I'm not sure I want to," Claire chuckled. "I think my friend is in love."

Julie went to the kitchen. *Oh my God*, she said to herself.

## Chapter Twenty-Five

Marcus—Seras

Marcus sat on the edge of his bed, putting on his boots, when he noticed the glowing light growing more prominent in the corner of the room behind the partition he placed there for occasions like this. In a few seconds, Julie emerged totally naked. Without the wall to separate the Mark of the Elders, the portal, Julie would have entered his room, and the two of them would awkwardly be scarred for life, especially her.

As predicted, she arrived. "Marcus, Marcus, are you in here?" Julie called out.

"I am."

He heard her make a raspberry noise with her lips.

"Well, don't look back here," she said.

"I wasn't planning on it." He heard her shuffle around, getting dressed. "You've been gone for a while. Everything okay?"

"Yep. Claire was in town for her spring break. We hung out most of the week before she had to go back."

"I hope you had fun."

"We did! It was like old times. We went hiking at Old Man's Cave, went to Kings Island, went to a couple of movies, and it was nice."

"Good."

She emerged from behind the partition in her deer-hide pants and top. "Shoes?"

"Over there." Marcus pointed to a corner by the door.

"What did I miss here?"

"I'm on my way to a council meeting."

"Oh geesh. Another one?"

"Yeah, we have one whenever needed. There have been two

infractions the council needs to rule on." He stood. "I can skip it if you would rather train."

"Nah, we can go. I think it's interesting how this works compared to court on Earth."

The villagers of Allon gathered in the large hall, murmuring amongst themselves as the council sat on the dais at the front of the room. The voices stopped when Julie walked in.

"My Heart, I am glad to see you have come back," Redderick Bobo said. He was among the group sitting in the front row. He patted the seat beside him. "Please, be my guest."

Julie hesitated, looked at Marcus, then sat beside him with an eye roll.

Marcus leaned against the wall near the pew to listen to the charges and verdicts.

Freya spoke first, "Please bring the accused in." She sat between Griffus, Otta, Lord Marek, and Julius.

Two guards stood on either side of a man as they entered the hall.

"This meeting is called to address the issue of Vincent. He was charged with stealing five chickens from Gregory, the merchant, three days ago," Freya said. "How say you?"

"Not guilty," the man said in a quiet tone.

A portly man hopped out of his seat. "Not guilty?" he shouted. "You stole five chickens. I saw you do it."

"That is enough," Freya said. "You will have your say."

The man sat.

"We will hear his side now," Lord Marek said. His two attendants, Lord Avery and Lord Atrow, sat behind the old blind man.

"My Lord," he addressed Lord Marek. "You must believe me. I never stole from him. I found the chickens on my property. I thought it was good fortune."

"You didn't think to ask your neighbor?" Griffus asked, his tone dripped with sarcasm.

"No." The man dropped to his knees. "Please, please. I did not mean to...I got greedy."

"Stop," Freya told him. She looked at the remaining council

members. They leaned into each other before Freya spoke again. "Do you still possess the chickens?"

"I do not," he said. "I ate them."

"You ate all of them?" Julius asked, putting his hands on his head and blowing out a breath.

"I was hungry," the man protested.

"You could go to the market and get anything you want," Freya said. "We sentence you to five days in prison."

"No, please, I am sorry!"

"Five days is more than fair. Guards, take him away." Freya waved her hand, and the guards escorted the man away, protesting.

Griffus stood. "Please bring the next accused."

Two new guards brought in another man.

"This meeting is called to address the issue of Hollan. He is charged—"

Argos barged in, interrupting the council, rushing to the front and pointing at Redderick.

"Tell me who did it."

"Argos, what are you doing?" Freya screamed.

"Who did what?" Redderick asked.

Julie leaned away from Argos. He looked like a man possessed. His face was pale, his eyes sunken, and his hair and beard were unkempt.

"I know you can tell me," Argos insisted. "Tell me now!"

Marcus grabbed Argos by the shoulders.

"Get off me." Argos shook himself free. "I'm sorry, Julie. I don't mean to scare you, but Redderick has the power to tell me who killed my son!"

Julius and Otta hopped off the dais, and Jakob, Seren, and Darius joined to make a wall between the desolate father and the immortal.

"Argos, this isn't the way," Marcus said.

"That's great," Argos shouted, looking at Darius. "The murderous demon gets more respect than I do!"

"Argos, that's not fair," Marcus said. "He has proven himself just as loyal as I am."

"No, no, no, no! You are the Solia Custor. He just happened to survive a fight against another Skorei demon."

"It was more than that." Darius ripped the front of his shirt to reveal a three-inch brownish-white scar that was the length of his torso. "I died. Freya brought me back." He pointed at his sister.

Freya, standing with Griffus still elevated on the dais, said, "It was Tolth's wish."

"Besides, that was long ago," Marcus said.

"It doesn't matter! What matters is that a Skorei is getting better treatment than me! I've been here all along, and my son is dead, and no one cares," Argos shouted at the top of his lungs.

"Did he say Skorei demon?" Lord Marek asked Lord Atrow and Lord Avery.

"Yes, my Lord." Both men drew their swords and jumped down from the dais.

Darius unsheathed his sword.

"Stop, all of you," Freya shouted.

"Kill the demon," Lord Marek ordered. "Kill him now!"

The villagers of Allon started screaming and heading out the doors in panic.

"See what you've done," Freya yelled at Lord Marek.

Lord Marek stood. "I have tolerated the one Skorei, but not two. You have kept this a secret from me."

Lords Atrow and Avery waited, poised to strike, as did Darius.

"Don't do this," Marcus warned.

"I said stop," Freya ordered.

"Kill the demon," Marek screamed. "Kill him for what they did to our people."

Julie stood. "No. Everyone stop!"

Lord Atrow swung his sword. Darius blocked and was ready to retaliate.

"I said stop!" Julie held out her hands, and a wave knocked the remaining Allonians off their feet.

"My Heart," Lord Marek said as he scrambled to the edge of the elevated stage. "The Skorei are evil. They deserve to die."

"No one deserves to die," Julie fired back. "And so help me, if anyone raises a sword against Darius or Marcus, they must deal with me."

"My Heart, please," Lord Marek cried out. "We can't trust them! We can't—" Marek rolled to his back and clutched his chest, his face contorting in pain.

"Lord Marek," Freya screamed, rushing to his side.

Griffus dropped to his knees beside the older man.

"Pound on his chest," Marcus yelled.

Griffus began slamming his large hand on the man's chest repeatedly.

Marcus jumped up on the dais. He began performing CPR. But it was too late. Lord Marek's eyes fluttered shut, and his body went limp. The crowd fell into a stunned silence.

# Chapter Twenty-Six

Marcus—Seras

The body of Lord Marek was lowered into the burial pit. The people of Allon gathered to pay their respects to the once fierce lord of the Hawkmir tribe.

Lord Atrow and Lord Avery stood silent, wearing the armor of the Hawkmir. They held their helmets under their right arms.

"This should never have happened," Avery muttered, loud enough for all to hear. "Lord Marek was betrayed."

Darius snapped his head toward them. His hand clasped the hilt of his sword.

"Silence," Lord Atrow said through gritted teeth. "Do not disparage his memory with your disgust."

Marcus took Darius by the arm. "Let them be."

Freya stiffened at their exchange. She put herself between the two lords and her brothers.

The pyre was lit, and flames roared from the hole where so many of the people of Allon were laid to rest.

Lord Avery proceeded to move toward Marcus and Darius. "You betrayed us. You betrayed him!"

"What are you talking about?" Freya asked, trying her best to keep everyone calm.

"You know who", Avery snapped. "You and your damned brothers. You know what their type did to us, and you hid it from us. You hid it from him, and it cost him his life."

All eyes turned to Marcus and Darius.

"I did not lie to anyone," Darius said. His hand returned to the hilt of his sword. "No one asked me, and I did not say a word."

"You came here with the blood of our people on your hands!" Avery pointed to Darius. "We were forced to accept Marcus as the Solia Custor, but you, you are a heartless monster!"

"Enough," Freya hissed. "This isn't the time."

"No," Darius growled. "Let him speak. Let them all say what they have whispered in the dark."

Marcus placed a hand on Darius's shoulder, but his brother pulled away.

"You're not the one they'll never forgive," Darius said bitterly. "You are the Solia Custor. The hero who gave the world the Heart of Tolth. I am just a monster." He drew his blade.

Lord Atrow and Lord Avery did the same.

Marcus stood with Darius, ready to fight.

"Stop," Freya shouted. "Just stop!"

As they continued to quarrel, another one began. Argos found his way to Redderick Bobo to finish what he started before Lord Marek died. "I want to know who killed Edwin?"

"I know what you want, I cannot tell what you want to know," Redderick answered.

"Can't or won't?" Argos questioned him, using his tall frame to tower over the immortal.

Gwendolyn grabbed her husband by the arm. "Please, not now. There is too much going on."

Argos looked at his wife through bloodshot eyes. "He knows. I know he knows who killed Edwin."

"I promise you I don't," Redderick said.

"Then what good are you?" Argos spat and stormed away.

Gwendolyn apologized to the immortal, and to the villagers watching the fiasco before chasing after her husband.

Marcus and Darius kept their hands at the ready, as did the two Hawkmir lords.

"This is not the time or place," Marcus said. "There was never an intention to deceive you."

"We have to stop," Freya said. She turned to her brothers. "We can settle this in a council meeting."

"The same meetings where you hid the truth," Lord Avery shot back, moving closer to Darius as if to strike him.

Marcus caught his hand. "I don't want to fight you, but I will defend my brother."

"This is not how we do things," Freya protested. "There is too much to lose if we fight amongst ourselves."

"If we fight, Pallanex wins. She is the cause of all of our conflict," Marcus added.

Lord Atrow placed his hand on Avery's shoulder. "Let it go."

"Thank you," Freya responded with a sigh of relief.

Lord Avery huffed, shook his friend's hand off of him, and walked past the group, barreling his shoulder into Darius's as he did.

Darius tensed up and pulled his sword halfway from its sheath.

Freya stopped him. "Let them mourn."

"He is young," Atrow said. "Thank you for your patience."

"We are sorry for your loss," Freya nodded with a sincere smile.

## Chapter Twenty-Seven

Julie—Seras

Outside the gates of Allon, Julie trained with Redderick Bobo. The tension around the fortified town couldn't have been any worse in the days following the burial of Lord Marek. It took the combined efforts of Julie, Freya, Redderick, and the rest of the members of the council, minus Marcus, to convince Lord Atrow and Lord Avery of the advantages of having Darius in their midst. He, being another great fighter and someone who could battle against Pallanex and William, was amongst the group's arguments. Darius, being Marcus and Freya's brother, was another critical talking point to Freya, who had seemed to find an ally in Lord Atrow. In the end, cooler heads prevailed. While it wouldn't be easy, the two lords of Hawkmir agreed to let their hatred of the Skorei brothers be buried with Lord Marek.

That allowed things to get back to relative normal in Allon, and Julie could resume her training with the immortal.

"You are doing fine, my Heart," Redderick said. He wore a brown shirt under his vest.

Julie was relieved that he started covering his bulging belly in her presence. She had just successfully lifted a boulder about the size of a school desk and moved it twenty feet. "Thanks."

"Now, do it again."

"Again?"

"Yes, again. Doing a simple task such as this should become second nature to someone with your abilities."

"This is not simple," Julie argued.

"My dear Heart, this is still just the beginning of what you are capable of."

Julie huffed. "Really?"

"Yes." He gave her a disappointing look. "So much time has been wasted with you not trusting me or liking me."

"The jury's still out on that." She smirked.

"You being mad at Marcus, Marcus disappearing, all of the distractions." Redderick tsked. "You have more. I just don't have time."

"Time for what? What else is there?" Julie argued.

Redderick smiled. "So much. Do you think you are ready?"

"Yes, yes, yes, I'm ready. Tell me what else I can do."

"Julie, you are of angelic birth. It is the sole reason you pose such a threat to Pallanex. But moving objects and knocking people over with flicks of your wrists."

"Show me what you mean!"

Redderick walked to a dirt patch in the field and picked up a stick. He drew the Elders symbol in the dirt. "You know what you have to do next."

Julie pulled her knife from her sheath and ran the blade across her palm, letting the blood trace the emblem, squinting as she tightened and released her grip. "Okay, now what? We don't have the Bones of Azahleah."

"Exactly."

Julie twisted her mouth in confusion.

"Light the portal," he said.

Julie looked around. "I can't."

"You can."

"No, I can't." She patted her clothing. "I don't have matches, a lighter, or flint."

"You can," he repeated.

Julie blew out a breath of air and looked at her hands.

"Point and concentrate."

She did as he said. A small flame emerged and sparked the Elders' symbol. The fire caught and raged. Julie reared back. Her eyes moved back and forth between the fire and Redderick Bobo.

"Now, think about where you want to go, and step through."

"Without the stones?" Julie ran her hand across the top of her head.

"Without the stones. You have to choose a place you are familiar with. A place you have been before."

She took a deep breath. "Okay." Memories of her first time passing through the portal crossed her mind, that day in Mr. Campbell's...Marcus's basement. She remembered how terrified she was that he was going to kill her, and how, now, much she thought about him and cared for him in a completely different way. Julie closed her eyes to think about where she wanted to go. The first place she could think of was wherever he was at the time, but he was hunting with Darius, keeping his brother away from Allon until tensions died off. Plus, if it worked, she did not want to just appear out of nowhere without clothes. The second place she thought of was her little cabin in the woods behind her parents' house. That's better. She walked into the flame. The flames danced around her. Julie felt the coldness as the wind swirled and whipped. Then, she was in her hut made from old barn wood, and decorated like a hideaway to write, just in case someone wandered by. Oh my gosh! It worked.

Julie returned to Marcus's cabin, put on her clothes, and made her way back to Redderick Bobo. "It worked, it worked," she sang as she approached him.

He frowned. "Why didn't you return here?"

"Um, because I wanted to dress first."

"But you went to the places with the Bones of Azahleah," he said. "You can do better."

"What are you talking about? But I'm going to be, you know." Instinctively, Julie's arms went across her chest even though she was fully clothed.

Redderick's mouth clenched, and his nostrils flared. "There will be times when being somewhere is more important than what you are or aren't wearing. You will have to decide when that is."

"Then that will be my choice," Julie snapped back.

"As you wish, my Heart." Redderick seemed to backtrack. "Are you ready to learn what more I can teach you?"

"Such as?"

"Such as, the ability to travel through the two worlds fully dressed," he told her.

"What, I can do that?"

“Yes, my dear, you have been more than capable of that all along. You just never wanted to work with me.”

“Are you kidding me? How?” she practically squealed.

“Let me teach you. Next time you go through a portal, think about the clothing you want to wear,” he said. “It will work. I promise you.

“I can’t believe you kept this from me and Marcus!”

“Marcus cannot do that. You are a goddess, my child. You have more power than anyone in this world or Earth.”

Julie blew out a breath. “You keep saying that, but I don’t believe you.”

“I know, my Heart. But it is true.”

Julie relented. “What else can I do?”

“Very good. Let me show you how to use flames for more than lighting a portal. What if I told you that you can make it more powerful and intense?”

## Chapter Twenty-Eight

Julie—Seras

Julie arrived in Allon through the portal. She was excited to see Marcus for another round of training and show him what she had learned. Redderick Bobo taught her that she could transport to anywhere she wanted when she wanted, and she was wearing the clothes of Seras. It was a relief knowing she could now go back and forth and not be completely naked on the other side. He also showed her how to shoot long streams of flame from her hands. It was all in the wrist and arms, holding her hands close together, opened fingers, and pushing from her arms. He was going to be so surprised. Julie improved every time the two of them got together; now, she had a few more tricks to show him. *I can't wait to see his face when I not only pick up a rock, I blow it up.* She hurriedly put on her clothes and rushed out the cabin door.

Julie had waited a week to return to Allon since Marcus was gone with his brother, but he was due back yesterday. She couldn't hide the smile on her face with the thought of seeing him again.

She looked to the left then to the right, wondering which way to look for Marcus first. She looked at her wrist, where her watch typically was, to check the time. "That was dumb," she said. Momentarily forgetting the portal's drawback of not allowing anything except her and Marcus to pass from one world to the next. Which was a major inconvenience in more ways than one.

As she walked through the village, greeting everyone she passed, she found Seren and Otta. They were bargaining for supplies from one of the vendors in the market shop.

"I will bring you two more wild hens for that sack of vegetables," Otta told the woman behind the table full of produce.

"Otta, you brought me enough. This will do," the woman said. "Take it, please."

"I only want to be fair." The brown-skinned warrior took the bag that was offered.

Seren picked up a loaf of bread. "We will be back in a few days."

"Thank you both. I appreciate what you do for me," the woman patted Seren's hand. Then, the woman bowed. "My Heart."

Otta and Seren looked behind them. "Julie," Otta said. "When did you get here?"

"Just a little bit ago." Julie took the lady's hand, who started to touch her, clasped it between her own, and held it to her chest. "Thank you."

"Thank you, my Heart."

Julie let go of her hand. "Thank you." She turned her attention to the two Hemoor women. "Have you seen Marcus?"

"Yes," Seren said. "He went hunting with his brother."

"He went with Darius, again?" She wasn't doing a very good job hiding her disappointment.

"Yes, an entire hunting party went out at first light," Seren told her.

"I was hoping we could train this morning," Julie told them.

Before the conversation could continue, a massive explosion occurred. All three instinctively drew their swords and rushed toward the commotion.

"Julie, get to the portal," Otta shouted.

"No!"

Seren took Julie by the arm. "You have to go. Marcus would kill us if anything happened to you."

"I know," Julie said, "but I'm not a helpless girl anymore."

Four blondes approached the three female warriors. Otta and Seren moved in front of Julie. Julie could see the chaos around the fortress. Buildings were on fire, and people were screaming.

Otta and Seren advanced to engage the four. They attacked to no avail. The women moved faster than either of them and were more powerful.

Griffus, Julius, and Jakob arrived on horseback with more men.

More women appeared out of thin air. Eight in total. Their

movements were eerily graceful, as though they flowed instead of moved.

Julie watched, frozen, as her friends were being destroyed by the assailants. Griffus was hurled into a small building by one of the strange women. Julie forced herself to shake off the fear and help. She sent a blast from her hands toward two of them, who were simultaneously engaged against the brothers, Julius and Jakob. The two women were sent flying. The strangers reminded Julie of the woman she had seen in the alley the night during her freshman year. “Death Walkers!”

“She’s right,” Griffus yelled, barreling into one of them with all of his might.

“Protect Julie,” Argos said, though weakened by depression, joining in the fray.

While the warriors battled valiantly, they were no match for the Death Walkers.

A Deathwalker approached her. Julie readied her sword. The woman waved her hand, and the hilt burned until Julie was forced to drop it. She started to reach out and blast her, but she heard someone approaching from behind. Julie turned to see another Deathwalker. Before she could motion her hands to attack, one of them touched her on top of the head, and everything went numb. Julie couldn’t move and was barely able to breathe. The second woman placed two fingers on her forehead.

“Sleep, my Heart.” The Death Walkers vanished into the shadows, taking Julie with them.

## Chapter Twenty-Nine

Marcus—Seras

Marcus rode into Allon. He and Darius had a successful hunt. The wagon behind them carried seven deer, two lodear, and five wild boar carcasses. Marcus and his brother had spent most of the morning and early afternoon in the woods. Darius was happy to share what he had learned living in the once-considered haunted forest. He had shown Marcus and the other hunters the best place and time to find the larger animals to feed the village. Marcus was hesitant at first; how often do you willingly go hunting with a man who wanted to kill you for the better part of fifteen years. But the two of them got along better than expected. Between their talk at Darius's new home and the hunting excursion, they found common ground once more.

Marcus told Darius about his time living with the Greagons and what life was like on Earth. Besides showing Marcus his favorite hunting spots, Darius took him to the cave where he made his home. It was tucked away about a mile up a mountain where a waterfall ran. The water was cool and refreshing. The falls fell from high up the hill, which Darius called the upper falls. There was a ridge where a person could walk behind them to get to the other side. There were also the lower falls. Darius gathered most of the fish and occasionally larger prey in the lower falls. Darius' cave entrance was located in a spot where the water rushed through, making it ideal for drinking and bathing. It was almost ten feet from the ground. An average person would find it difficult, if not impossible, to climb. For Darius and Marcus, it was no problem at all. They leaped up to the four-foot hole in the mountain wall. The cave was everything a person could imagine: dark, dank, and smelly. Darius had an area for a fire, a bedding space, and little else.

"I didn't need much," he had said. "I spent most of my time roaming around looking for spies."

"I wish I would have known," Marcus had said.

"You would have tried to kill me. You wouldn't have understood."

"If Freya would have told me."

"It's in the past. It doesn't matter." Darius then led him out of the cave.

When they got to the edge of the faux fortress they had used during the Battle of Yellow Fields, they saw smoke coming from the village. Both he and Darius spurred their horses into a full gallop. When they arrived at the gates, they saw that the men and women had formed a human chain from three of the wells to put out the burning buildings. Redderick was conjuring the wind and dirt to snuff out fires. Freya was organizing those not strong enough to help with the fires to attend to the wounded. He saw, amongst others, those in different states of brokenness, burnt, or scarred: Griffus, Argos, Otta, Seren, and the brothers, Julius and Jakob. They looked defeated.

"What happened?" Marcus yelled from his horse. He looked from Freya to Redderick Bobo, who had stopped what he was doing to follow him.

"Death Walkers," Freya told him. "More than I have ever seen!"

"Julie?"

His sister shook her head. "They took her. I'm sorry."

"Took her?" He hopped down and grabbed Bobo by his cloak. "Where did they take her?"

Redderick tried to catch his breath. "To Speculus. To Azahleah. I'm sure of it."

"Tell me how to get there," he screamed.

"Marcus," Freya placed her hand on his chest. "You can't go there. You aren't dead."

"Neither is Julie."

"She's right, Marcus. Julie could survive. She has the blood of the Elders. You wouldn't."

Marcus seethed. "You are going to help me get there, even if you have to kill me."

"Marcus," Freya gently took one of his hands holding Bobo. "Let him go."

Marcus released him as the immortal clutched his neck.

"We will help you," she said.

"Freya," Redderick said, "we can't. It's too dangerous."

"Is it any more dangerous than letting this fool kill himself to get there?"

The immortal was stunned momentarily. "Well, no," he finally said.

"Good; finish helping with the fires, and we will make the necessary arrangements."

~ * ~

Hours later, once the fires were put out and order had been restored, the sun had started to set. Marcus met Freya and Redderick Bobo outside the village where Allon's dead were buried. There was a funeral pit dug.

"Do I have to die?" Marcus semi-joked.

"In a way," Freya answered without a smile. "We were lucky; no one was killed during the attack."

"As if the Death Walkers had been commanded not to," Bobo said. "It was purely to get Julie."

"Why would Azahleah want her?" Marcus asked.

"Why wouldn't Azahleah want her is the better question?" Redderick asked with a chuckle. "She is the most powerful person in Seras."

Marcus stopped. "What do you mean?"

"My boy," Redderick said, leaning in closely, "you might not believe it, and she doesn't know it yet, but the Heart is more powerful than me, Freya, you, William, Azahleah, or Pallanex. She needs time and practice, and she could rule all of Seras if she wanted."

"I don't understand. I mean, I knew she had some of Tolth's blood in her, but what you're saying is hard to believe."

"I know, I know. But you must trust me. Now, for the problem at hand," Redderick said. He pointed to Freya, who was busy preparing the site.

"Yes, a hand would be appreciated," Freya said, pouring buckets of blood into the pit.

"What is this?" Marcus asked.

"Pigs blood."

"What's it for?"

Freya sneered up at him. "You, you fool. This is how we get you to the Speculus without killing you, though, once Azahleah discovers you in the Abyss, you'll probably be dead anyway."

"You see, Marcus," Redderick patted him on the back, "for as long as we can, we must trick Azahleah and his Death Walkers into believing you are a dead body. Find Julie and find a way out. And be quick about it."

Once the buckets had filled the pit half-full, Redderick said, "Down you go."

Marcus looked at Bobo, then at Freya, and then back at the blood.

Freya nodded. "This is what you wanted."

Marcus lowered himself into the bloody pit. It came up to his waist. "Now, what?"

"This is not going to be anything like the Elders' portal," Freya said. "Time will twist and bend. You will have no idea how long you will be there."

"Great. What's next?" Marcus asked impatiently.

"You have to go all the way under and don't come up for anything. No matter how painful it gets," Redderick said.

"Oh God," Marcus whispered, then held his breath to submerge himself. Through the thickness of the blood filling his ears, he heard Freya and Bobo chanting, though he could not understand what they were saying. The ground around him trembled beneath his feet, then fire from above his head. He cowered lower. The blood grew warmer. He continued to fight for his breath. He felt the need to escape but remembered what Bobo had said, "Don't come up for anything." Then everything went black.

## Chapter Thirty

Julie—Speculus

Though everything appeared to be enclosed, a cold rain began to induce thick fog as the two Death Walkers arrived outside a stone bridge. The women approached a dark tower. The taller Death Walker led, with Julie wrapped against her chest. Julie was in a state of total numbness. She could see everything happening but couldn't move a muscle. The one carrying her did so without any struggle, as if she were a loaf of bread. The thick wooden doors creaked open as they approached.

The women walked through the interior lobby; its tall, pillared arches a dazzling display of art, with speckling flames on the ceiling and walls and a black, reflective surface of obsidian-tiled flooring. Statues of men and monsters lined a Great Hall at an almost alarming rate, like guards standing at attention, and candelabra and torches surrounded every polished table so that the entire room radiated with a soft red glow. The door to another room opened, and a woman, this one a brunette dressed in green, emerged. "Follow me."

The two Death Walkers, obedient to the woman in green, continued their silent march. Julie, still in a state of numbness, caught her reflection in one of the many mirrors throughout the hall. She was wearing a white gown that was too sheer for Julie's liking.

The woman in green waved her hand, and another chamber door opened. "In here," she commanded. "Then leave us."

"Yes, Yarna," the tall one said. Both Death Walkers bowed.

Julie was gently placed on a bed and enveloped by a sheer silk netting surrounding the entire bed frame. The headboard was beautifully carved with intricate details of winged humans, creatures, and monsters, all woven together in medieval delicate designs. *Angels, demons?* Julie thought. She caught the aroma of faint embers with a hint of sweet, erotic spices that filled the air around her. With her senses slowly returning to normal, exhaustion took over her body. She found comfort in the plush pillows, until a man barged in with a grand entrance.

"There she is," he exclaimed.

Julie pulled herself up in the bed. "Who are you?"

"Come, come, my dear. You know exactly who I am." His dark green eyes twinkled with an all-knowing sparkle. His voice was sharp and high-pitched with a hint of childish joy. He stepped out of the shadows, dressed in all white, a stark contrast to the reddish black of the tower's interior. He was thin but toned, with shoulder-length brown hair, and his features were sharp and angular.

"Azahleah," Julie said in a whisper.

"Yes, yes, yes." He hopped up and down excitedly, clapping his hands. Then he took a deep bow. "Azahleah, at your service. Welcome to my spirit realm. Welcome to Speculus." He moved to the silk curtain, threw it apart, and held out his hand. "Come with me, my dear. I want to show you my world."

Julie hesitated.

"Come, come, I don't bite." He winked and flashed a wicked smile.

Julie reached out and took his hand. All at once, the feeling came back to her legs and body. Azahleah led her back through the interior lobby, down a seemingly endless set of stairs, and into a cavernous room of white stone and smoky glass. The room was lit by a soft, ethereal glow, and the air was filled with a faint, sweet scent. He directed her to a dais where two thrones, adorned with intricate carvings and shimmering with a faint magical aura, waited.

"Here we are, dear. Please join me." He danced around her before twirling Julie onto the throne and sitting beside her. "You are home."

Julie hopped up in shock. "What do you mean, home?" Her heart raced as she confronted the enigmatic Elder who wielded power over life and death in Seras.

Azahleah laughed as though he didn't understand the question. "Well, of course. Look at your options, my dear." He stood to face her. "You possess a rare gift, Julie," Azahleah murmured, his voice a low, mesmerizing cadence that echoed off the cavern walls. "The two of us together could reshape the very fabric of existence. Imagine the wonders we could achieve together."

"Excuse me. I think you are mistaken. We are not together. In fact," her voice raised as her memory began to clear. "You took me against my will!"

"Julie, Julie, my dear. We are meant to be together. It was written long ago," Azahleah practically cackled. "You are my betrothed, as I am yours."

The word "betrothed" registered in Julie's mind. You are the "Betrothed," Redderick Bobo had told her. "That's impossible," Julie said.

"No, no, no, think about it. Tolth created you to face the evil of Seras. He is gone, Ostram is gone, Eryx is gone, and Vestus is, well, a cave." Azahleah wrinkled his nose and shook his head playfully. "That only leaves me." He shrugged and did a little jig.

Julie collapsed on the tiny steps leading up to the thrones.

"Come now, Julie. Surely you knew this day was coming," he said. Azahleah looked at Julie with eyes that gleamed like coals in the darkness. He was interrupted by the entrance of the woman in green, Yarna, if Julie remembered correctly.

"I am sorry, my Lord." The lady with raven locks then whispered in Azahleah's ear.

"Handle it." He dismissed her with a wave. "You know what to do."

"Yes, my Lord." She left just as quickly as she entered.

"Excuse the interruption," he said. "I apologize. Now, where was I?" He stroked his chin. "Let me show you something." He offered her his hand.

"I don't want to," Julie said. Then she regained herself and stood, taking a deep breath. She aimed her hands at Azahleah and tried to blast him with her power. Nothing happened. She tried again and again, but nothing.

"I am sorry, my dear. But your power does not work down here. It is one of the powers I have. The halls are enchanted with Enochian Sanskrit."

She looked around at the intricate carvings on the posts and walls, in the tapestry, and markings on the obsidian floor.

"Only I have power in Speculus. It is one of the reasons I have remained safe from Eryx all this time." He reached for her hand again. "Now, if you please. Let me show you how it could be."

Defeated, Julie accepted his offer.

The room shifted into tangled, dark shadows, transforming into a clear, starless night in the middle of a forest glade. Only the waning moon cast its long, dancing shadows across the lake of grass, illuminating the trees. The night was silent, except for the soft, wispy wind that brushed the grass, creating a serene symphony of peace and calm.

Marcus appeared from just beyond the tree line.

Julie ran to him. Thank God. His shirt caressed her cheek as she placed her head on his shoulder. Even with her eyes closed, she could feel his gaze and the peaceful smirk that was always on his lips. He smelled of pine and vanilla. His fingertips moved gently across her back. A quiet sigh escaped her lips. Marcus swept his arms beneath her legs, lifted her, then gently brought her to a blanket. The lush grass formed beneath her body.

Julie slowly opened her eyes, and she met Marcus's soothing gaze. His blue eyes made her forget any problem she may have had. The warm air settled around them. An uncontainable smile spread across her lips as she nuzzled closer into his arms. He kissed her forehead. It took her by surprise. *Did he really just kiss me?* Her confusion melted away with the lingering touch of his lips on hers.

"It could be like this forever if you would like," he whispered.

Julie stiffened. "What did you say?"

"I said, 'It could be like this forever if you would like'," he repeated.

"You," she screamed. "Stop it right now!"

Marcus sat up and transformed back into Azahleah, who crowed with laughter. "If you insist." Suddenly, Julie was back in his throne room.

"No-o-o-o-o-o!" she cried.

## Chapter Thirty-One

Marcus—Somewhere in the Abyss

After sliding through the blood and fire pit, Marcus woke on the dry, hard ground. He checked his body parts. Everything seemed to be in place. He was happy to find himself fully clothed. But where was he? Marcus heard the sound of rushing water. He stood up, brushed the dust and dirt off his clothing, and followed a low whistling sound. Well, here goes nothing. He took three steps before falling endlessly into pitch black.

When he landed, he was deep within a shrouded forest.

"Welcome, Marcus, son of Canis," a woman spoke.

Marcus looked around, ready to fight.

"Do not be afraid."

Marcus chuckled. "You obviously don't know me very well. I'm not afraid, but you should be."

"Marcus, son of Canis. You should not be here." A woman appeared from a mist. She was a tall brunette in a flowing green robe that matched the flora behind her. A black choker was fastened tightly around her neck, with the emblem of a dragon with a ruby eye dangled to her breastbone.

"Good. We both agree. So, just tell me where Julie is, and we'll be on our way," Marcus said.

"I cannot do that," the woman said.

"Then we will have to do this the hard way."

"You are correct, but not in the way you think," she said. "To find the Heart, you must pass my trials."

"What if I just rip your throat out." He started toward the woman. As soon as he reached out to grab her, Marcus and the woman stood behind a wooden door.

"This is your first test," she said, and with a wave of her hand, the door opened to a thunderous roar from a crowd.

A bell tolled before a man's voice announced, "Behold, Marcus, son of Canis!"

The crowd exploded in cheers.

"King Marcus, Solia Custor to the Elders, Defender of Seras, Conqueror of Pallanex, Heir to the Skorei Throne, Protector of Allon and the lands beyond, and Champion of the Heart," the man's voice continued singing his praises.

"What is this?"

The woman placed a thick robe over his shoulders. "They adore you, my king." She guided him to the throne. "This is your rightful place in Seras."

Marcus looked around at the pageantry seemingly directed in his honor. The glow of the day's light filtered through a castle's stained-glass windows. The great hall was decorated with rich crimson and gold tapestries adorning the walls, and banners emblazoned with a crest of his old Skorei ram's head waved from the rafters. The scent of smoked meats filled the air.

Noblemen and women from all over the world stood in the audience, their garments sparkling with jewels. A choir sang a joyous anthem, filling the hall with its voices and praising Marcus's accomplishments and victories.

A herald announced dignitaries one by one, and the most powerful nobles and vassals approached the throne. They knelt before Marcus, each offering a gesture of allegiance. The hall echoed with their vows, their voices reverberating through the chamber as they swore their loyalty and fealty. Then came the moment of gift-giving, a tradition steeped in grandeur. Guests brought forward their offerings: ornate swords with jeweled hilts, intricately embroidered tapestries, and rare artifacts from distant lands. Each gift was presented with reverence and placed before Marcus's throne, creating a spectacle of wealth and generosity. Marcus continued to stare at the woman, wondering what was going on.

She only smiled and nodded her approval at the proceedings. Then she clapped her hands twice, and the grand hall was transformed into a dining spectacle, with long tables laden with roasted meats, pastries, and exotic fruits. The air was thick with the aroma of wine and the sounds of laughter and conversation. Minstrels played lively tunes while jesters performed their entertaining antics. The guests reveled in the merriment.

The feast was followed by a series of tournaments and games. Warriors in the Skorei armor competed in sword-fighting displays. Their skill and valor were met with cheers and applause, adding to the festive air of the evening. Fire-breathing performers and torchlight parades brought an element of drama and spectacle, their fiery displays casting flickering shadows across the hall.

As the night wore on, the king's maids distributed parting gifts, small tokens of appreciation that would forever remind the guests of this magnificent day. As the ceremony drew to a close, the woman directed Marcus to stand.

"What is all of this?"

"Your subjects are expecting a speech," she said.

"I am not giving them a speech," Marcus said. "I have no idea what is going on."

The woman placed her hand on his chest. He suddenly couldn't move. "This could all be yours to rule for the rest of your life; just say the word." Then the woman faced the audience. She addressed the gathered subjects. Her speech started as an apology for King Marcus who was overwhelmed with the pageantry on display. Then she spoke of gratitude and hope, promising continued prosperity and protection under King Marcus's reign. The guests listened, then heaped more love and pledges of loyalty as they left the great hall.

When the last guest left, the woman touched Marcus again.

"What was that?"

"That is the life you could have. Riches beyond the imagination, the love and respect of kingdoms far and wide, and the adoration of your people. Just say the word, and it could all be yours," the woman told him.

"Who are you?" he asked.

"I am whoever you want me to be." She moved closer.

"No, what do they call you?"

"I am called Yarna," she spoke softly, almost wistfully. "The last of my kind." Her voice became more solemn at those words.

"Well, Yarna, you can tell Azahleah you have failed."

"No," the woman shouted. Her eyes glowed red. "I am not finished."

## Chapter Thirty-Two

Julie—Speculus

Julie's heart ached with loss as she reeled from the dream's effect. The overwhelming pain of waking from the possibilities of being in Marcus's arms had been replaced by the unsettling reality of her surroundings—Azahleah and his dark tower of Speculus. Julie trembled, torn between fear and anger. "You are a monster," Julie yelled. "Leave me alone!"

Azahleah's expression darkened, his face contorted with frustration. "You underestimate what I can offer, my dear," he said, his tone tinged with a hint of warning. "But if you choose this path, know there will be consequences." He moved closer to Julie, backing her into a dim, secluded corner. He leaned down into her face. He seemed to have grown two feet in the blink of an eye. His hand gripped her shoulders. When he spoke, his voice came out more like a growl, "You surround yourself with your walls, but do you know what it feels like to play with real flame? I know your secret now, don't I? But you have not allowed yourself to share it with him. Why is that, I wonder? I felt your lust; I heard your heartbeat, the sweat across your skin as you moaned his name under your lips." His mouth twitched into a smirk. He looked pleased to have Julie cower below him. Julie turned flush with a deep crimson hue. "Would you ever dance that chorus with me, Julie?"

"No, never," Julie protested.

"Have it your way." He backed away from her. "Let me show you what is to become." He touched Julie's forehead.

She drifted into an open field, much different from her previous dream. There was nothing but dirt for miles around. There were no trees, no clouds, just the hot sun draining the energy from a large army. Julie moved without walking, floating to the front of the ranks. The murmurs of men preparing for battle rang through the columns. Then the men snapped to attention with a voice carrying over the others.

"Shut up! Form a line now! William's army will be here at any moment, you dogs!" The voice was harsh and commanding, echoing across the field. "The army of Allon will not know what hit them," he chuckled.

"Allon?" Julie looked across the barren field. Nothing was on the horizon. She saw a head officer. His black helmet and shield bore the signet of Pallanex, a red spider. He strode purposefully atop a horse in front of the group of soldiers clad in matching black armor. Despite the heat of the day, some of the soldiers trembled, their fear understandable.

The general dismounted and shook each soldier's armor. He then checked their weapons and ensured they were ready.

Julie could feel the tension in the air, a sense that something terrible was about to happen. She observed a young, shorter soldier nervously trying to stop the bleeding from a cut on his hand from his blade. His hands quivered. The officer's gaze locked onto the boy; his eyes burned red hot. He marched over, his boots kicked up dust from the arid ground. With a swift, brutal motion, he struck the boy across the face with the back of his gauntlet. The boy gasped, clutching his mouth, his eyes wide with fear.

The other soldiers stood rigid and silent. The officer moved on, leaving the boy to his silent suffering. Nearby, another soldier, taller than the one who was struck, spoke to the boy, his voice low and conspiratorial. "It's not just Allon's territory that the Queen wants," the soldier said. "This is just the beginning."

Julie shivered as she listened. "What else did Pallanex want?"

The soldier continued speaking about William. "I saw firsthand what William has created for her. I am sure you have heard the stories about William."

The young soldier shook his head.

"The monsters he is going to unleash are worse. Imagine him without the restraint of human traits."

The boy listened in awe and terror.

As the Captain shouted more orders and the soldiers prepared for battle, the horizon was soon filled with the dark silhouettes of William and his army. Their numbers were too many to count. Julie watched as William's massive, monstrous figure appeared; he had already become the Skorei demon. He wore a black cloak with a purple undercloak and armor with a purple silhouette of a front-facing bull on his chest. His sword, similar to Marcus's, gleamed in the sunlight. Behind him were creatures similar to what she had seen from Marcus, the two Skorei brothers, and William, but different. They were more animal than human. Some walked on two legs, others on all four. They growled and snapped. Slobber dripped from their jaws.

*Oh my God.* Julie clasped her hand over her mouth. William's army moved through the ranks of men, and Pallanex's soldiers shuffled warily away from the monsters. Then, much to her surprise, she heard more commotion. She turned to the front line. Horse hooves galloped toward the assembled army of Pallanex, and William kicked up a cloud of dust.

"There he is," William said, practically foaming at his mouth.

Julie followed his gaze. She saw Marcus, riding atop a brown charger, leading the army of Allon toward them. *Oh no. He has no idea what he is doing.* Julie sprinted toward him as fast as she could, but he, his horse, and a dozen other riders passed through her as if she were nothing more than wind. She turned to run after him once more.

As they closed the gap, William motioned the army to advance.

Julie saw Pallanex lording high above the melee from behind the walls of Cauleta. Her red gown flowed in the wind. She wore a golden crown that fit snugly on her head, with spikes of varying heights sticking out like sun rays. Julie seethed. *I want her to suffer.*

Pallanex's army began stamping their spears on the ground in unison. The sound was deafening. Marcus held his sword out in front of him as he charged forward, as did the brave frontline, consisting of General Argos, his son, Julius, the two Hemoor women, Otta and Seren, and Darius. The men and women in the second line loaded their bows and drew them back, ready to fire, but held as a gust of wind and dust flew from their rear into the faces of the charging army. It blinded them momentarily as the air was filled with fireballs and large spears. Griffus's ballateers wiped out a swath of Pallanex's men.

"Release the arrows!" Freya screamed from the second line. Her magic produced enough distraction to give the Allons an immediate but not long-lasting advantage. She dropped to her knees, exhausted from the power it took to conjure the windstorm.

Arrows flew from both directions. The volley continued as quivers were emptied. Men and women held shields for protection, and many on both sides fell regardless.

"Swords and spears," Marcus ordered. "Advance!" He and the riders charged forward. The arrows and ballateer projectiles ceased as the Allonians took up arms against the strange creatures and Pallanex's army. Marcus rode through the swarm.

William unleashed his monsters. They looked like demon dogs. They ripped and tore at the humans with fierce abandon. Marcus was yanked from his horse. He had no choice but to turn into his Skorei demon self to battle the creatures. He jabbed his spear into one such beast and drove it back into two more. He then hacked off the head of a fourth as it lunged at him.

The soldiers of Allon launched into battle, and their cries of "For Allon!" and "For the Heart!" rang out. Julie ached with the grim realization that they were rushing into a massacre for her. She watched a young warrior sprint headlong into a group of men only to fall at the hands of two Cauleta soldiers who brutally stabbed him repeatedly. His dying scream filled the air.

Griffus caught up with the front group. He severed body parts with each swing of his mighty ax. A demonic warrior ripped the legs of his horse out from under him, making the giant man collapse to the ground. He rose to strike at the Skorei demon, jamming his small blade into its neck. As he reached for his ax, an arrow pierced his back. He arched at the pain. Another arrow caught him in the shoulder. Griffus snapped it off. He hit two more men with his giant blade. A third and fourth arrow struck him in the midsection. It dropped him to his knees. He climbed to his feet a second time and took out an onslaught of warriors at first, but the wounds took their toll. Five of Pallanex's soldiers surrounded him and took turns jabbing and taunting Griffus until the big man succumbed to a multitude of spear and sword wounds. The leader of the Allon ballateers staggered and fell.

As the two armies clashed, blood soaking the dry land, Argos battled his way to a small mound where he could take advantage of the higher ground. At first, he fired off a volley of arrows, trying to keep the enemy at bay, then he noticed Seren as three demon creatures were running toward her, engaged in a struggle against two of Pallanex's men. "Seren!" Argos ran from his position and leaped in front of the pack, blocking their path. Seren cut down both men and joined Argos to fight off the three beasts, but a soldier stabbed him when Argos faced a fourth Skorei monster. Argos clutched his stomach, feeling the blood, and stumbled. As he tried to regain himself, the soldier stabbed him in the back. Argos dropped to the ground.

"No!" Seren screamed. She killed the man who did that to her general and helped Argos to his feet, placing his arm around her neck. He tried to hold his sword in his right hand as she tried to pull him away from the melee. Unfortunately, it was to no avail. The two warriors were overwhelmed and killed in the chaos.

Julie watched the death of two more of her friends; the burden of what she witnessed was too much to bear. She screamed at the top of her lungs for the fighting to stop. It was no use. Then, she saw Otta charging to the body of her dead companion. She sent her spear into one man while ripping through a second soldier with her sword. Otta let out a piercing scream to see Seren and Argos's bodies in a bloody heap, with several dead demon beasts and Pallanex soldiers around them. Otta jammed her sword into the ground and used her bow to send three more soldiers to their deaths. Otta caught an arrow to her chest. The force of it knocked her to the ground. She groaned at the pain but fought to regain her feet. Otta grabbed her sword to steady herself, then used it to block a Cauleta soldier's attack. The Hemoor warrior and the Pallanex soldier squared off. Blood oozed from her wound. Otta held her own with the man until he closed in and used his free hand to push the arrow shaft deeper into Otta's chest. She winced in pain and toppled back. Her sword dropped to the ground, and the man thrust his sword down into her neck and chest.

Julie dropped to her knees, tears streaming down her face. Then she heard a giant roar. She looked up to see Jakob, the leader of Allon's foot soldiers, and Jayna the Tarrack, advancing from a position to Julie's left. They thundered into the fray, catching William and the forces of Cauleta off guard. The battle shifted back to Allon's advantage.

Arrows whirled around just as a rider swung his sword and dropped in a spray of blood. As his brother's troops moved through the battle, Julius faced off against a demon creature. He stabbed the beast in the shoulder. It dove into him, knocking him to the ground. Julius's blade plunged into the demon's chest. He pulled it out, wet with blood. Julius tossed the beast off of him only to get hit with an ax in the back of the head.

Jakob yelled orders to his men. His spear ripped through a group of soldiers. The number of men under Pallanex's command and William's Skorei beasts was overpowering. Jayna flew in as a hawk, then changed to a bear to take out the swarm of men advancing on Jakob. The two fought off as many as they could. Jayna slashed and ripped through men with each mighty swing of her claws. Jakob plunged his spear into one of the soldiers. It snapped off in the man's abdomen, unfortunately leaving him with only the wooden shaft and a short blade at his disposal. Jayna's bear grabbed Jakob, and he mounted her and rode through a gathered group of men. Jakob leaped off her back into the pile with a yell. He slashed through the soldiers until he found himself unarmed and outnumbered. With reckless abandon, he charged with one last breath before falling under their blades.

Seeing Jakob in peril, Jayna changed to a hawk to fly to his aid. She caught an arrow in bird form. She changed back to a bear to protect herself. The wound to her chest slowed her movements. A pack of demons advanced against her. The beasts surrounded the bear. They bit and clawed at her until Jayna, blood seeping down her fur, collapsed as they tore into her dying human form.

Julie watched Tanda and her Evandell warriors trade blows with Pallanex's army alongside Lord Atrow and Lord Avery of the Hawkmir tribe. They, too, fell to crippling wounds.

Darius, who had already turned into his Skorei demon, fought his way back to Freya, who was holding back a small force of soldiers and demons from the wounded she and others were able to pull back from the skirmish. Darius fought and killed several soldiers and a demon to reach his sister. "Come with me!"

"I can't. If I leave, these people will die," Freya responded.

"If we don't stop Pallanex, they will die anyway," he said. He grabbed a horse, mounted it, and pulled her up. "Give me an opening."

Freya closed her eyes and drew her power, sending a white beam of light from her hands. The men in their way were thrown back, leaving a gap for Darius to ride to Cauleta's wall. Darius spurred the horse as Freya held tight to her brother's back. "Stay with me, Freya!" Before getting to the wall, Darius was stabbed in the back with a long spear, knocking him and Freya off the horse.

Marcus saw Darius and Freya. He slashed and stabbed men as he rushed to their aid. Marcus wasn't alone. William saw them, too. He was closer than Marcus was. Darius and William met in the field, both in demon form. Men surrounded William like a wall of flesh, keeping Darius at bay.

"You are a coward," Darius screamed as he fought his way to William.

"But I am alive," William said from behind his men. He picked Freya up by her hair.

Freya kicked and screamed but could not fight back. She was exhausted from her two massive displays of power.

William made sure Darius was looking in his direction as he dragged his sword across her throat.

Freya folded to her knees and then dropped into the dust. Blood seeped into the dirt.

Marcus arrived too late. He and his brother joined, striking down the men as quickly as possible.

Darius started for William. A demon slammed into him, knocking his sword out of his hand. He stabbed the beast with a short knife until it gurgled and died. A soldier swung at him but missed. Darius opened his hand, and the Evandell sword returned to him in time to dismember four soldiers. He finally confronted William as seven demon beasts trapped Marcus.

"I thought you were dead," William hissed. He swung his sword playfully at his side. "But, no, you abandoned me for Marcus."

"You lied to me. You were with her the entire time. You helped her destroy my family. You helped her kill my mother and father. You abandoned us," Darius growled.

The two exchanged blows. They were evenly matched. Unfortunately, Darius had spent a great deal of energy getting this far in the battle while William watched the proceedings from his horse. Darius blocked four of William's strikes. He thrust his Skorei sword toward William's midsection, only to cut his arm.

William slashed at Darius, gashing him on the leg.

Darius faked a jab to the right then clawed William with his left hand. William dropped to a knee. Darius advanced on him, only to have William pull a small knife from his belt as Darius lunged. Darius tackled William, disarming his sword.

William's knife punctured Darius's left shoulder. His left arm hung limp. William moved in for the kill. He called for his sword. It returned to its master. William plunged his sword into the area between Darius's neck and shoulder.

Marcus watched his brother slump to the ground. Blood spurting with the last few beats of his heart. A pile of demons lay at his feet. He exhaled and summoned the last of his strength to face his former friend. He raced toward William.

Julie could see the pure hatred on his face. His demon form seethed and foamed at the mouth. He was covered in dirt and blood. He looked horrendous.

Marcus slammed into a foot soldier who tried to block his charge. He was swiftly eliminated with two slices of his blade.

William stood with a smile. He feinted his attack to the left, then crossed toward Marcus's neck. "What, no clever words?"

Marcus ducked out of the way. "Not for you." He dropped low and took William's feet out from under him, creating a gash at William's calf.

William rolled away from three of Marcus's strikes.

Marcus caught an arrow in the back of his shoulder. It caused him to lower his stance.

William spun behind him, hitting the arrow further into Marcus's body. The point protruded out the front. Then he used his claw to rip across Marcus's back.

Stunned, Marcus turned to counter the blow without the use of his right arm. He switched his blade to his left hand, but William outmaneuvered him, striking Marcus with his sword. It lodged into his side. Marcus dropped his sword.

Julie screamed.

William grabbed Marcus's sword. He held Marcus's head up by his jaw.

Marcus bled from nearly every part of his body. Blood spilled in thick mucus from his mouth.

"You should have listened to me," William cackled, then in one swift motion, he severed Marcus's head from his body with his old friend's sword.

Julie rushed to Marcus's body as William held his head up for those who remained to see. Overcome with unbearable grief, Allon's brave men and women were no longer a match for William's creatures and Pallanex's army. Tears stained Julie's cheeks. "Stop! Stop," she cried, trying in vain to cradle Marcus's body. Just as the nightmare seemed as though it would never end, Julie's vision blurred. The chaos of the battle, the death, and the overwhelming sense of doom became too much for her to bear. She could no longer withstand the pain, and with a final, gasping breath, she fainted, collapsing onto her bed.

# Chapter Thirty-Three

Marcus—Somewhere in the Abyss

The woman named Yarna transported Marcus to a different time and place. She was standing by what looked to him like an ancient oak tree.

"Marcus," she said, her voice seeming to surround him. Yarna had a knowing glint in her eyes. "This Heart must be very important to you. I offered you a kingdom for all eternity, and you refused my gift."

"So just take me to her, and I'll be on my way," Marcus said.

The brunette created a fog. "I am not finished yet."

Before Marcus could respond, Yarna reached out and touched his hand. A blinding light enveloped them. When the light faded, Marcus found himself in a place unlike any he had ever imagined. He was standing at the edge of a bustling village, where towering spires made of gleaming gold and silver rose into the sky. The stone streets were filled with people laughing, drinking, and buying items at the market. Their faces were twisted with a look Marcus did not recognize.

"Why are we here?" Marcus asked.

"Welcome to a place I believe you will love more," Yarna said, her voice echoing.

As they walked through the crowded streets, Marcus noticed the odd behavior of the people. Some were bargaining, others hoarded their goods, and still others stole when no one was looking. Yarna guided Marcus to a grand plaza where a towering statue of a golden Azahleah stood. "Is this how he wants to be seen?"

Yarna grinned. "Something like that."

"So, what now?" Marcus asked.

"We are almost there." She led him down another street away from the vendors. They walked into a dark room. Once inside, the doors and windows were closed shut. In the shadows of the four corners of the room, grotesque men stepped into focus in the torches hanging on the walls. "This is where I leave you. Good luck, demon warrior." She touched the dragon pendant hanging from her neck and disappeared.

The gruesome quartet were armed with swords and maces.

Marcus reached for his sword, but it wasn't there. He cursed under his breath.

They began swinging their maces, gaining momentum.

He dodged one, but a second caught him as he ducked. Flesh tore from his shoulder. Marcus rolled away from a sword, then another mace. He got back to his feet, his arm soaked with blood. Marcus tried to turn into his demon self, but it didn't work. He avoided one more attack from the mace, but a sword got him on the side. The pain ripped through him. Blood oozed down his pants and soaked through his shirt. Marcus dodged another swing; it caught the chain of another mace, and the two weapons clanged to the floor. It gave Marcus a much-needed reprieve. He grabbed one of the men and spun him into the path of the other's sword. As the man dropped to the floor, Marcus picked up his sword and hacked the second man's leg. He went down hard. Marcus grabbed that man's sword in time to move away from another mace attack. He threw one sword into the third man's chest. He collided with the fourth man, and his mace caught in one of the torch holders. Marcus pounced on him with three quick plunges into his chest. He then pulled the mace chain hard enough to pull the torch onto the two men. The flames caught hold of their clothes and engulfed them. Marcus looked around to make sure all four were dead.

The door opened, and Yarna walked back into the room. She looked at the four bodies. An impressed look crossed her face. "Well, you are a hard one to kill."

## Chapter Thirty-Four

Julie—Speculus

"You see, my dear," Azahleah spoke. His voice sounded reptilian. "You should stay here with me to avoid all of that unpleasantness."

"I hate you. Marcus is dead. They're all dead." Her body shook as she wiped her nose across her forearm.

"Ah, but you see. That has not happened yet. That is only what will happen. It's a gift I have. So, you might as well stay here with me," he told her. "You don't want to see your friends die again, do you?"

Julie fell silent, the echoes of the nightmarish dream still vivid in her mind. "If I stay with you, that won't happen?"

"I did not say that," he answered. "Come with me, my dear. I do not think you fully grasp what I can offer." He reached out his hand.

Reluctantly, she took it and climbed out of bed. They walked through the interior lobby once more, down the endless staircase, into the white room with smoky glass. He led her past the thrones to a second set of stairs. They descended lower into the abyss until they emerged from a deep chamber. It was darker than the lobby. Tall archways held cauldrons of flames. There were five massive statues of white marble; three men and two women. Julie recognized one as Azahleah, so she could only consider the other four as the remaining Elders of Seras. They entered a semicircular room with stained glass walls and two doors. Four of Azahleah's Death Walkers lounged on long cushioned benches, while two stood guard at the door to the left, and two more stood guard across from them in front of a door on the right.

"What is this place?"

"This, my dear, if you will forgive the term, is the heart of Speculus. Look." He waved his hand, and the stained glass vanished, revealing glass walls that were almost like a force field.

"You see," Azahleah began, "on this side, you have those who succumbed to wounds on the battlefield. My Walkers brought them to reside here as the blessed of Seras. They are heroes who sacrificed in the name of honor. They live in peace in Taryion." He pointed in the other direction. "These are those who did not die a heroic death. They had succumbed to natural causes or met their ends through non-warrior ways. I call it Hina."

"Why are they here?" Julie asked.

"What do you mean?"

"I mean, shouldn't they be sent somewhere else, like Heaven or Hell?"

"No, it is not like that. They are here at my...what's the word? Disposal, whim? Yes, whim."

"What you are doing is wrong," Julie yelled.

"Why do you care?" Azahleah asked. He sat on his throne.

"Because there are people I care about in there," Julie said. She wiped her nose on her sleeve.

"Ah." Azahleah stood. "That reminds me." He hopped down the steps from his throne and snapped his fingers. The Death Walkers at both doors nodded in unison. They opened the doors and disappeared behind the invisible walls. "Watch this." His smile spread across his face. Less than a minute later, the crowd pressing against the walls parted on the side where those who did not die a warrior's death, Hina, was the ghostly likeness of Argos's son, Edwin.

"No." Julie turned her head away.

"Oh, my dear, it gets much better."

Julie turned to him. Her hands shook, and she could feel her face turn flush. Her worst fear appeared at the other wall. First, Pertheus was shoved into view by one of the Death Walkers. Julie moaned in pain. Then, she wailed as she saw Callista's face.

## Chapter Thirty-Five

Julie—Speculus

"Why did you show them to me?" Julie cried as she flung the door to her bed chamber open. The images of Callista, Pertheus, and Edwin sheared in her mind.

"I want you to understand the power that I have here. The power we could have together," Azahleah told her, following Julie into her room.

"Get out!" She pointed to the door.

"As you wish." Azahleah bowed. "But just think of it. Here, they are not dead. You can visit with them and talk to them any time you want."

"No, that's sick," Julie screamed. "They should be somewhere else. Somewhere better than being stuck here in this, this limbo. It's not right." She stared at him, wishing her powers worked against him. "Get out now!"

Azahleah backed away. "Very well. You know where to find me if you change your mind."

"I won't." Julie followed him to the door and slammed it shut. She walked to the bed and collapsed.

A knock came at her door, and a Death Walker entered with a tray of food and a pitcher. "My Lord has requested you should eat and drink," the woman said.

"Tell your Lord I'm not hungry or thirsty," Julie snapped at her.

She sat the tray on a table beside her canopied bed. "I will tell him." The Death Walker left without another word.

Julie waited until she was sure the woman had left. She picked up a small loaf of bread and sniffed it before devouring it. She hadn't realized how hungry she was. After gorging herself on the bread, fruit, and what tasted like sliced ham, Julie lay in bed and let sleep overtake her.

She awoke a short time later. All but one of the candelabras that lit her room were extinguished. Julie poured a glass of water and took a long drink. She wrapped a blanket around her shoulders and opened the door enough to take a peek. “Coast is clear,” she whispered. Julie grabbed a torch and lit it from the candelabra. She made her way through the dark halls. The pillar’s shadows loomed across the shiny black floors. Each statue made eerie silhouettes as she passed by. Julie went down the stairs and into the throne room, continuing down the second staircase to the abyss. The eternal fires from the cauldrons illuminated the statues of the Elders. They looked as though they were passing judgment on her as she entered the final chamber.

The Death Walkers were gone. *Do they sleep?* Julie tiptoed deeper into the room. The walls were clear enough for Julie to make out the images of people on both sides. She touched the tall door that led to the warriors’ side, Taryion. It opened for her, and Julie stepped in. The first thing Julie noticed was the smell. She didn’t know what she was expecting; blood, sweat, or the smell of a dead animal rotting on the road, but not the sweet scent of lilies. The ceiling above her looked like the sky. Clouds floated overhead, and the sun’s rays shone around the warriors dressed in battle gear. Probably what they were wearing when they died. She approached a group of men sitting at a table.

“You should have seen it,” one man with a husky voice was saying. “When it started to rain, the mud turned a deep red. Men were losing their footing, and it made for easy kills. My sword was covered.”

“Then what happened?” another asked.

“I do not remember,” the first man answered, then bellowed with laughter. “I must have died.” He slapped one of the men on the back. “To the Battle of Broken Bend.”

The group laughed and took a drink.

Julie approached them. “Excuse me.”

One of the men growled. Another said, “You are new here.”

“Ha! Too young to be a warrior,” the most boisterous of the group said.

“I’m looking for Callista of the Hemoors,” Julie said, standing as tall as she could make herself.

“Hemoors? Never heard of them,” another man scoffed. “But I

would not mind plowing you like a fresh field." He stood with a wicked smile.

"You must have forgotten who ran you through with her sword," a voice rang from behind the men.

The threatening warrior quickly sat as Callista approached. "And I do not think you could plow anyone with that." Her eyes drifted to his groin.

The others around him laughed hard. The man removed himself from the group.

"Callista, I am so glad to see you!" Julie ran to hug her.

The Hemoor warrior acted surprised as Julie's body touched hers.

"Is everything okay?" Julie asked.

"Are you dead?"

"No."

"Why are you here?" Callista asked. She towered over her with muscles rippling. Her nose, shoulders, and arms freckled as Julie's did during the summer months.

"Those Death Walkers brought me to Azahleah. He wants me to marry him." Julie shivered.

"That's impossible."

Julie clicked her tongue. "You're telling me. There's no way I'm marrying that guy."

"I mean..." Callista looked at her as though she wanted to say something but held back. "I am glad you are not marrying him." Her smile was every bit as bright as Julie remembered.

"You and me both." Julie hugged her again. "I'm confused. Are you alive here?"

"No, I am not alive. I do not know what this is, but it is not living. I cannot go back to Allon. Not that the Death Walkers would let me. If they struck me down with their swords, I would no longer exist here." Callista moved to a vacant area with a table and bench. "Come, sit."

Julie sat beside her. "You would disappear?"

"Yes, I have seen it. A warrior dared attack them once; when he received a death blow, he was gone."

"So, there is no escape?" Julie asked.

"I do not know about you, but I am afraid there is no escape for me,"

Callista told her.

“How ’bout for me?”

“I do not know.” She looked around. “Where is Marcus?”

“He can’t get down here, can he?” Julie asked.

Callista paused.

“No, no, no, no!”

“He would do that for you,” Callista said. “You know he would.”

“If he dies to come down here to save me, I will kill him.”

## Chapter Thirty-Six

Marcus—Somewhere in the Abyss

"Just take me to Julie, and I promise I won't kill you," Marcus told Yarna as he limped closer to her. Blood soaked both sides of his clothing.

"I am not worried about that, demon." She turned her back to him and walked away. "If you want to see the Heart, follow me."

"No tricks?" Marcus asked. He walked through the door and into a hallway. A gated archway rose, leaving Marcus facing a long corridor.

"Maybe one or two," Yarna said, using her hand to guide him through the gate. "After you, of course."

Marcus gave her a side look as he entered. The floor beneath him turned into a swamp. He immediately went under before regaining his feet. The dark water came up to his chest. The wounds from his shoulder and side stung.

"All you have to do is make it to the other side," Yarna said. "I will wait for you there."

"I will be there soon," Marcus countered. He began to make his way through the murk and mud. He heard splashing coming from both sides of the water.

He heard Yarna's voice echo, "If men cannot kill you, then maybe the animals can."

Marcus hopped as fast as he could to one side, just as an alligator's nose and eyes appeared no more than six feet away from him. He snapped a stick with his left hand and used his right hand to clamp on the alligator's snout, keeping its mouth from opening. The other alligators moved slowly toward him. He jammed the stick up through its soft neck. It twitched and turned to escape, but Marcus held tight until it died.

He removed the stick and positioned the dead animal into the opened mouth of the second alligator. It clamped down on it and moved away from him as the other two got closer. He repeated the strategy of holding the alligator's mouth closed and stabbing it from underneath. The fourth alligator did not take the bait, unlike the others. It continued to move closer to Marcus. Before it could open its jaws. Marcus got a hold of it. The alligator flipped and rolled out of his grasp. He lost the stick used to eliminate the other two. It closed in for another attack. Marcus hopped up and down toward another limb. As he started to reach out, a panther struck his hand, cutting it to shreds. With an alligator on his left and a panther on his right, Marcus had one thought: *I've got to get to Julie.*

He reached out again to get the stick. When the panther clawed at him, Marcus grabbed its paw and pulled it into the water. The alligator approached the thrashing cat, clamping its mouth around the panicked beast. Marcus tore off another branch and put both animals out of their misery.

Marcus climbed out of the other side of the swamp. He limped a few steps before hearing another noise from the trees. Marcus dropped his head and sighed. A bear roared out of the tree line. Visions of his fight long ago against Urvasus rang through his head. He once again reached for a sword that was not there.

## Chapter Thirty-Seven

Julie—Speculus

Julie returned each night to talk to Callista. She learned that the warriors there could do everything they did in life. The only thing different was that they no longer desired to kill each other. The old hatred had vanished.

During the day, she tolerated Azahleah's musings about how he was the only Elder remaining and his plans for the two of them in Speculus.

"I do not believe you understand what we can do together," Azahleah began one morning as the two of them shared a breakfast. "Eryx is using Pallanex as a vessel. She is weak. We can defeat her and rule all of Seras and your world. I would not be stuck here in Speculus. You could have anything your heart desired." It was a grand room with thirty-foot-high windows with red curtains, a fireplace that crackled and popped during their meal, and a full table of bread, fruits, meats, and eggs. Four Death Walkers stood at the ready; two behind Azahleah and two at the door.

"I don't want to be part of your plan. I want to go home. I want to see my family and friends. I want my life back," Julie said.

"You could have a better life with me. Join me, my Heart. I can give you all of that and more."

She pressed her hands on her eyes, hoping beyond hope that this nightmare would end. "You don't understand. I don't want that. I want to be normal. I want all of this to end."

Azahleah stood and walked the length of the long, twenty-foot table toward her. He dragged his fingers across the silky red tablecloth. "I can honestly say, my dear, I have never met anyone quite like you." He stopped a mere two feet from her. "You fascinate me. If I offered this power to anyone else on Seras or your world, they would fall over themselves for this kind of power." He smiled. "But not you. You want the unattainable. You want the, what do the people of your world call it?"

"The fairy tale."

"The fairy tale. Hmm." He contemplated it for a moment. "So, what does this—fairy tale look like?"

"I don't know."

"Of course you do."

"I don't want to tell you," Julie said. She took the napkin off her lap and placed it on the table. "May I be excused?"

"So polite." Azahleah smiled. "My dear, you can do anything you would like."

"So I can leave?"

"Except for that." He hopped up and sat on the table. The dishes clanged, and her glass of juice spilled. "Apologies." He chuckled. "No, never that."

"What do you want from me?" Julie asked, standing.

"I believe I have told you what I want. It is you who has not told me what you want." He wiggled a finger. "Not that."

The two Death Walkers blocked the door.

Julie turned back to Azahleah. "May I go now?"

"As you wish," Azahleah said, waving his hand. The two Death Walkers moved out of her way. "Keep your secrets. I have nothing but time."

Julie stormed out and went to her room.

## Chapter Thirty-Eight

Julie—Speculus

Julie waited once again for what she considered nightfall. Even though Azahleah was an Elder and immortal in practical terms, he enjoyed his nightly slumber.

She made her nightly journey to the depths of Speculus. Julie had grown accustomed to the shadows on the walls, the large statues of the Elders, and the heat of the cauldrons. The images and sounds no longer terrified her. *How long have I been here?* She entered Taryion and found Callista with her Hemoor companions.

"Julie, I want you to meet someone." Callista took her by the hand and guided her past rows of beautiful Hemoor women warriors. Callista stood out as the prettiest of them all in Julie's eyes. She brought Julie to a tall, black woman with long dark hair. "This is my Queen." Callista bowed to the woman. "Queen Zatuyla, this is Julie, the Heart of Tolth."

Queen Zatuyla stood and took Julie's hand. "It is an honor to meet you."

"I've heard about you from Callista and Otta. I heard you were an amazing queen. It is my honor to meet you, Queen Zatuyla."

"I am no longer the queen. There are more Hemoor queens here than I can count, and I count Callista as one of us."

*Callista was a queen?* Julie looked at her friend. "She never told me that."

"That is because I was not," Callista protested.

"You were my Certoris," Zatuyla said. "That would mean you were queen after my death."

"I was not there. I cannot be the queen."

"Nonsense. You were doing the job of a queen. You were

representing me in finding help against the Skorei," Zatuyla said. "Speaking of the Skorei..." She slid over and patted to the area beside her. "Please have a seat and tell me about Marcus."

Julie shrugged. "I don't know. He's a normal guy."

"There is nothing normal about him. He was a monster when I met him. That cannot be what he is now."

"No, I guess not. He isn't a monster. He's kind, caring, smart." Julie paused. "He wants to make up for the things he did. All the wrongs, all the killing, he is sorry for all of it."

"That is what Callista has told me. I am happy for that. I wish it would have happened before he attacked my home, my people, but I am glad."

"You aren't angry?"

"It is hard to explain," Callista said. "We do not have that feeling here. We are at peace here. That is how all of us warriors can be here in one place. There are tribes we have conquered all around us. There are warriors from Allon, like Pertheus and Alanas, here. Skorei are here."

"I would like to see Pertheus and the others from Allon," Julie said. "Would you mind?"

"Not at all. I visit them often. We talk about you quite a lot."

"You do? Why?"

Callista guided her through the valleys of dead warriors. Each area was situated around hills and valleys, with a running stream and lush trees.

"You are the Heart." Callista smiled. She must have noticed Julie looking around the different tribes. They were eating, drinking, and laughing in front of a large building surrounded by small cabins. "We do not need to eat or sleep. The homes and the hall are to help us feel good."

"Does it help?" Julie couldn't resist asking.

"Believe it or not, it does."

They walked into an area, and suddenly, Julie had a sensation that was hard to describe. "Allon."

"It is. How did you know?" Callista asked.

"I just could. I don't know if it was the smells or what, but I recognized this place as soon as we walked in."

Callista gave her an odd smile.

"I know. But it feels like home," Julie continued. She looked around, turning her head to the left and then to the right. "I don't know these people?"

"They were killed before you got there. There were hard times until you arrived. Battles were fought. Good warriors died."

"I am so sorry," Julie broke down. She grabbed hold of Callista. "I didn't mean for any of this to happen." Tears streamed down her face.

"Julie." Callista held her at arm's length. "We would do it all over again if we could. You are this important."

"I agree," a voice spoke behind her.

Julie turned. Pertheus. She rushed to him." I'm so sorry about what happened to you. I never meant for you or any of you to get killed for me."

"You are the Heart. I wish I would have done a better job of protecting you."

"You died for me. I am not worth that."

"You are worth that. And Callista is right. We would not hesitate to do it again for you."

"But I don't want you to die again because of me." She wiped her nose on her sleeve.

"Well, good news for you", Pertheus said. "We can't." He laughed. "But that doesn't mean we wouldn't."

"I've missed you." She hugged him again.

"And we have missed you." He used his head to direct her attention to the horde behind him.

She rubbed her eyes with the palms of her hands then ran to the people of Allon who had been there to fight with her and beside her. She clutched each one as though they were long-lost friends.

After the commotion had subsided, Pertheus asked her, "Why are you here, and where is Marcus?"

"From what he has told me, Azahleah wants me to join him and help him rule Seras." She paused. "And I have no idea where Marcus is."

"There are a few people I think you should meet," Callista said, "during your recent visit to the place named Taryion."

"Who?" Julie smiled.

"Come on." Callista led her to another area of the deceased people of Allon.

Every person she walked by bowed to her. “Will they ever stop that?”

“I do not believe they will,” Callista said. When they got close to a shack, a blonde with long flowing hair came out to greet them.

“Callista,” the woman said. “It is so good to see you.” The two women could not have been more different. Callista was tall and statuesque. The new woman was much shorter and had a smaller build.

“Julie, this is Alanas.”

“Alanas? I have heard a lot about you,” Julie said. She held out her hand.

The woman just looked at it with confusion.

Callista broke in, “This is Julie. She is the Heart of Tolth.”

Alanas’s eyes grew large, and she dropped to the ground. “My Heart, my Heart. I apologize. I had no idea.”

Julie reached down to help her to her feet.

Alanas took her hand and began kissing it.

“Stop, stop, stop. Please.” Julie lifted her.

“If I would have known who you were—"

“Please stop. I am just a girl like you.” Julie hugged her. “I have heard about your bravery and your sacrifice for Marcus. I am sorry this happened to you because of me.”

“No, you are the Heart of Tolth. I am honored to have died so Marcus could find you.” Alanas looked around. “But why are you here?”

“That is what everyone keeps asking me.” Julie directed her attention to Callista. “Azahleah and his Death Walkers kidnapped me.”

“Where is Marcus?”

“I don’t know, but I’m glad he isn’t here,” Julie told her.

“But he should be here, protecting you. That is his job.”

“No,” Julie countered back. “If he was here, that means he is dead. I don’t want him to die.”

# Chapter Thirty-Nine

Marcus—Somewhere in the Abyss

The bear hiked up on its two legs. It stood seven or eight feet tall.

Marcus hunched lower, glancing to his left and right. He knew he could not outrun a bear, and bears climbed extremely well. With no sword, the odds of surviving a bear were slim to none. Marcus made up his mind; he remembered the lesson from his youth when he climbed the tree and was able to fight off the bear by poking it with a stick. Marcus backed slowly, facing the angry bear the entire time. He had to make a move to give him distance between himself and the bear. Here we go.

He jumped back into the water as close to the side of the swamp as possible. The bear dropped to all fours and went after him. Marcus grabbed a tree limb and pulled himself back out as soon as the bear got close. He started up the same tree and was fifteen feet up by the time the bear climbed out. *I was hoping the alligator would have helped a little*, he thought, breaking a branch as he continued to climb. The bear started up the tree and closed in faster than Marcus wanted.

Marcus waited until the bear got within striking distance. When it did, he jammed the stick in its eye. The bear roared in pain. Marcus went a little higher and broke off another branch. The bear freed the stick from its eye and went after Marcus again. Marcus poked the bear in its other eye this time. Blood spurted, and the bear roared, but as it did, Marcus slammed the branch as hard as he could into the bear's mouth.

The bear lost its balance and plummeted to the ground. It rolled into the swamp and didn't move.

Marcus waited a few minutes to catch his breath before climbing down, unsure what else Yarna had in store. The adrenaline helped his wounds heal a little quicker. He walked a bit further into the darkened room, which was designed to resemble a canopied forest. A low growl came from his left. What now!

A Bengal tiger stalked into view, followed by a lion, its mane thick and full.

Marcus cussed under his breath and tensed up. When he did, he felt the demon inside him stir. *I apologize in advance for what I am about to do to you.* He changed into the Skorei demon. *I don't know why Yarna allows me to do this.* He caught the tiger under the front loins and tossed it over his head as he rolled to his back. He pressed his claws deep into the tiger's rib cage, hoping to puncture a lung.

The lion leaped and landed on Marcus before he could get back to his feet. It clasped onto his left arm with its mighty teeth.

Marcus punched it repeatedly under its jaw until it loosened its grip. He grabbed its mane and yanked it down. The lion's face smacked the ground hard. That allowed Marcus to scramble to his feet. He put the lion in a choke hold and held it tight as long as he could. Out of the corner of his eye, he spotted the tiger circling. The lion gasped and clawed at him, skin ripped from his legs and arms until it could not fight any longer and died. The tiger's body breathed hard and shallow. Marcus must have succeeded in puncturing its lungs. It made its move to Marcus. He grabbed it and bit its throat. He clamped down as long as he could. The tiger roared and twisted, trying to escape. Marcus could feel its claws digging deep into his chest and side, but he would not let up. He used his claws to stab repeatedly into the tiger's body. Both were soaked in blood. The tiger's resolve finally gave out with a final gasp.

Marcus tossed the beast off of him and stood with a wobble. Steady, steady.

Yarna entered from the forest, and the trees, swamp, and dead animals disappeared. She gave a slow, monotonous clap. "You continue to impress, demon."

"Just call me Marcus."

"Well, Marcus, you will be happy to know there two more trials, and you are finished."

"Just two? Piece of cake."

"Shal we get started?" Yarna asked.

He dropped through the floor to find himself strapped to a post.

## Chapter Forty

Julie—Speculus

A knock came at the door. "Come in," Julie spoke, rubbing the sleep out of her eyes.

"Good morning, my dear," Azahleah hummed. "I hope you slept well."

Julie hesitated because she didn't want to tell him how little sleep she had gotten the last several nights. "I did, thank you."

"I am thrilled you have grown accustomed to living here. Please clean up and meet me for breakfast." He turned to leave then paused and looked back at her. "I take it you have forgiven me for the other day."

"No, I still don't want to stay, if that's what you mean."

"In time, my dear, in time." He left the room.

Julie rubbed the back of her neck. A massage would feel good right about now. She got dressed and joined Azahleah in the dining hall.

"Thank you for joining me." He pulled out the chair from the end of the table. "Please have a seat."

"Thank you." She sat and placed the napkin on her lap.

Azahleah clapped, and Death Walkers served her trays of meats, loaves of bread, and fruits.

Julie took her time eating, all the while avoiding conversation with Azahleah. But he tried.

"How did you sleep? How do you like it here? Have you thought about my proposal?"

She didn't answer any of them. Eventually, he gave up and began to leave.

"When you are ready, please join me in the throne room," he said. He nodded to two of the Death Walkers and left.

Julie wasted as much time as she could then stood to leave. The two Death Walkers escorted her to the throne room. She looked around the room. All eight of the Death Walkers were in the room. Still no appearance by the dark-haired woman that she met on the first day. The Death Walkers had their swords drawn, and the doors to the two chambers of Speculus opened.

"Ah, welcome, Julie. I hope you had a wonderful meal?"

"It was. Thank you. What's going on?" she asked.

"Your little fun is over," he said.

"My fun?"

He slammed his fist on the arm of his chair. "Yes, I have allowed it for too long. It will come to an end."

Julie approached closer. "What are you talking about?"

"Do you think I do not know? I am aware of everything that goes on in Speculus. Why do you think you could come and go, visiting your old friends in Allon, the Hemoors, and even the Skorei? I allowed it!"

Julie stuttered, "I-I-I—"

Azahleah bent down and took her by the chin. "It will come to an end. I will have my answer and be satisfied."

"What do you want me to say?" Julie wept.

"Say you will be my bride. Say you will stay with me and help me rule Seras."

"I can't do that." Her eyes stung, and snot dripped from her nose.

"I grow tired of waiting." He dropped her face and clapped his hands twice. Two of the Death Walkers brought Callista out.

"Wait, what?"

The Death Walkers forced Callista to her knees. A third held her sword over her head.

"No, no, no," Julie screamed.

Azahleah waved off the execution. "Here is my ultimatum to you, dear Heart. Join me, and I will spare your friends."

"Julie, we will gladly die for you again," Callista said through gritted teeth. "Do not do this."

The Elder began to signal the Death Walker to finish Callista off, but Julie grabbed his hand. "No, please, no. Don't do this. Let her return to her people. I beg you."

"Very well. I will show you I am merciful as well as patient." He flicked his wrist to the Death Walkers. "Let her go back." Then he took Julie by the hand. "I will not wait much longer. You will decide by this time tomorrow, or their deaths will be in your hands."

## Chapter Forty-One

Marcus—Somewhere in the Abyss

"I have tried to help you," Yarna said. Her green robe flapped in the wind. The place they were in was cavernous. "I wanted to give you everything a person could desire. Power, money, sex, and you turned it down for the Heart. I sent four of my best fighters to kill you. I sent eight fierce animals to kill you. Why will you not die?"

"So, are you going to talk me to death now?" Marcus asked. He wiggled around, trying to free himself. He tried to change into the demon to snap the ropes or rip through them, but he couldn't. For the second time, his ability to change had been blocked in some way.

"No, the time for trying to change your mind is over. Now, I am giving you an ultimatum."

"And that is?"

"Simple. An exchange. Your life for hers." Ten bowmen appeared. They set their quivers on the ground and nocked their arrows.

"That's it? Kill me, and Azahleah will let her go?"

"Yes." Yarna nodded.

"Fire away."

"You would sacrifice yourself for her?" Yarna looked surprised at his answer.

"Every time."

The archers lifted their bows and pulled back the strings.

"Are you sure?" Yarna asked.

"Absolutely. Promise me you will let her go."

"I promise, demon."

"Then let's get it over with."

The archers took aim.

"Last chance, demon. Your life for hers. You can go free and live a normal life."

"What are you waiting for?" Marcus said.

"Fine." she held up her hand. "I will not give you another chance."

"You're boring me with the small talk."

"Fire." She dropped her hand.

Marcus closed his eyes, waiting for the impact and death. It didn't come. He opened his eyes and was freed from the ropes; the stake had disappeared, the archers had disappeared, and it was just him and Yarna. He checked his body for arrows. Nothing. "Um, what happened?"

"I have never met someone like you," Yarna said. "You would rather die than to have her here?"

"Yes."

"Why?"

"Have you met her?"

"Just once, when she was brought here."

"Then you don't know her like I do. Being the Heart isn't just what she is. She is so much more than that. She is special outside of anything Tolth may have done to make her that way."

"You love her?"

"Let's not get carried away," Marcus said.

"You love her more than yourself. You were willing to die for her."

"I am willing to die for her. I suspect I will die for her," he told her.

"Then I am truly sorry, demon, that I cannot let you see her a final time."

"I figured it would come down to this." Marcus cracked his neck and rolled his shoulders. "So, what do I have to do now?"

"Nothing." She paused. "It will be over soon." She clutched the dragon emblem on her choker and began to transform, growing larger and larger. Her smooth, white skin, combined with her flowing green gown, transformed into scales. Yarna stretched out her hands as her arms morphed into sleek, mighty wings. Her long black hair cascaded down her back, forming a spiked spine that extended into a mighty obsidian tail. Yarna's beautiful neck elongated as her face twisted into a harsh expression, revealing large teeth. Her ears grew pointed and protruded from the top of her head. Her green eyes shimmered with fiery intent. The choker still fastened around her thick neck and the emblem swung as she moved her head from one side to the other.

Marcus stood, mesmerized by what he had just witnessed. Of course, he had seen Jayna transform, and he grew up watching the Tarracks transform, but that was nothing compared to watching Yarna become a dragon.

"Let me properly introduce myself," Yarna's voice echoed around him in the cavern. "I am Yarna, last of my kind, mother of the Drak'raths."

Marcus could not find his voice. He had fought man and beast, but the idea of fighting a dragon was beyond his comprehension.

"What is wrong, demon?" Yarna asked, her tone taunting him. "I gave you a chance to live as a king. I gave you chances to die as a hero. Now, you will die painfully."

"Why didn't you just let the archers finish me?" Marcus finally asked.

"I wanted to see if you were worthy. And you are. You turned down money, power, fame. You killed my very best. You were willing to die for the Heart. I have never met a more worthy opponent."

"So, these were all your tests, not Azahleah's?"

"Yes. He just wanted me to kill you. He did not care how. I wanted to measure your worth. It is almost a shame to kill you. It has been an honor." The fire in her chest rose.

"Can I at least have a fighting chance?" Marcus screamed. "I've earned that!"

The fire subsided. "Fair enough." A sword clanged to the ground. "Here."

"Can I make a wager with you?"

"You are stalling, demon," Yarna's voice boomed.

"Yes, I am. But it remains. A wager?" He looked back and forth, up and down, at the stalagmites and stalactites around the cavern. The stalagmites made handy natural pillars.

"Speak your wager."

"If I win and let you live, you will serve me?"

"If you win," Yarna laughed. "If you let me live?" She laughed harder.

"Is it a deal?"

Yarna regained her composure. "Yes, demon, if you win and you let me live, I will serve you."

"Thank you," Marcus said with a respectful nod.

"Shall we begin?" Yarna blinked her reptilian eyes that closed and opened from side to side.

"I guess I've put it off long enough," Marcus said. He took off running.

"Good." She whirled around, her tail smashed into the stalagmites, causing them to shatter and splinter.

Marcus dodged the debris and slid behind one of the fallen pieces.

Yarna sent a blast of fire in his direction. The heat seared the stone and mineral around him.

Marcus waited until she caught her breath and ran to another pillar, avoiding Yarna, who was crouching down on her four legs. Her massive body was quicker than he imagined as she roared in his direction, snapping her jaws at him. *Does she want to cook me or eat me?* he wondered.

She sent another fire blast in his direction.

Again, he waited. After it stopped, he ran to a thick stalagmite.

"You are only delaying the inevitable."

"I don't think you want to kill me," Marcus yelled. He spotted an opening in the crevices.

"You are wrong, demon."

Marcus stepped out into her view.

Yarna rose on her hind haunches and flexed her wings in an impressive display of power. Her chest reddened as she prepared for another burst of flame.

"Wait!"

She stopped and dropped back down. "What now?"

"Nothing, I just wanted you to wait." He took off for the crevice.

She screamed and reared back up. "I am going to kill you!"

Marcus made it and ran inside. He hid behind a large stone.

Yarna jammed her elongated neck into the narrow opening. "You will die, demon!" She dug in her claws and pushed her way closer and closer to him.

"I don't believe you want to kill me."

"You are wrong, demon." Her voice was only mere feet from where he sat in hiding.

"If you wanted me dead, I would be," he said. "You're playing with me like a cat to a mouse."

"Maybe, just like a cat, I like to play with my food before I eat it."

He could hear her move closer. The rocks around him crumbled at her massive power. When Yarna got close enough for Marcus to feel the heat radiating from her mouth, he made his move. He jumped out and yelled as loud as he could, catching the dragon by surprise. As she raised, Marcus ran underneath the length of her neck and thrust his sword upward. But, instead of stabbing her scales and not knowing if he actually could or not, he sliced the black collar at the base of her neck. It dropped to the ground, and Marcus scooped it up. He turned, prepared to strike, but Yarna had returned to her human form.

"What have you done, demon?"

"This?" He held out his hand to show her the pendant. "What does this do?"

"Give it to me!"

Marcus closed his hand. "No."

"Give it to me, please."

"Tell me what it does," he ordered.

"I have no choice but to obey," Yarna said. "It controls me. Whoever possesses it controls my power."

"I thought you worked for Azahleah?"

"Only because he had the collar around my neck. I had to do his bidding. Now that you have released the collar but have my medallion, I must obey you."

"Then take me to Speculus and help me free Julie," Marcus commanded.

## Chapter Forty-Two

Julie—Speculus

Julie sat in the lower room of Speculus. Azahleah and his Death Walkers were gathered to witness Julie's decision. He had Callista, Pertheus, and Alanas lined up against the invisible wall. "Why are they here?" she protested.

Azahleah cocked his head and smiled. "They are here to help encourage your decision."

She looked at the Death Walkers; around eighty in total, each had a sword at their side. "If I do not like your decision, I will simply—remove one of them until I do like your decision." He clapped. "Shall we begin?"

"No." Julie stood. "I am the Heart of Tolth. You will not force me to marry you. I was not brought here to be a game for you to play."

"Very well," he said. "Bring one of them to me."

"No!"

Azahleah whipped his head to her. "This is your choice, not mine. Just say yes, and it will be over, my dear."

"Absolutely not."

"Then you leave me with no choice." He motioned to one of the Death Walkers. She grabbed Callista and pushed her to Azahleah.

"No," Julie sobbed.

"You know how to stop this," he told her. "Just say the magic words." His grin stretched across his face.

Julie closed her and sighed. "Fine."

"Julie, no," Callista yelled. "I am not worth that."

"I can't watch you die again," Julie said.

"I will be fine."

Azahleah laughed. "She will not be fine. In fact, I have no idea what happens to them once they die here." He shrugged.

"Okay, okay. Stop." Julie held out her hands. "Let her go, let them all go. I'll do it. I'll do whatever you want."

"That is more like it," he said. "And just to make sure you do not change your mind...kill her."

The Death Walker raised the sword.

"No-o-o-o-o-o," Julie screamed.

As the sword came down, a giant crash rumbled through Speculus. The sword dropped to the ground. Julie rushed to Callista.

"Thank God she didn't kill you."

"I would have died for you all over again," Callista told her.

"Go," Azahleah ordered. "Find out what that was!" The Death Walkers rushed up the staircase, only to be chased back down again. A blast of flame filled the hall, followed by Yarna being ridden by Marcus. "Yarna, I command you to stop!"

The dragon turned to Azahleah. "You are no longer my master." She sent a stream of fire in his direction.

Marcus dismounted. "Yarna, smash down those walls."

Yarna roared, then swung her tail against the side of one wall while attacking the other with as much flame as she could.

Callista picked up the dropped sword and ran it through the Death Walker, who was ready to kill her. She threw the sword to Pertheus, and he used it to cut himself and Alanas free.

The invisible barriers crashed down, and the men, women, and children from both sides poured out of their confinements. Most of the people from Hina screamed and scattered around the room, adding to the chaos. The men and women from the Taryion side took out their frustrations on the Death Walkers.

Marcus reached Julie. "Come with me," he said.

"Thank God you showed up," she said, hugging him.

"We have to go," he said.

"I'm not leaving them here to die," Julie told him.

"Julie, they're already dead."

She wasn't listening. Julie grabbed a sword and jumped into the skirmish.

Callista and Alanas joined her as Marcus caught up.

"Marcus," Callista said.

"Callista! Alanas!"

The Death Walkers were striking down the unarmed warriors at a fevered pace.

Yarna's size was becoming a hindrance to the fight. She tried to avoid stepping on people running around, while trying to help defeat the Death Walkers. She sent flames toward a group gathering to advance on her.

Marcus stabbed one of the Death Walkers as she grabbed at Julie.

Julie attempted to use her powers, but to no avail. Whatever Azahleah had done, it continued.

Alanas battled a Death Walker, but the enchanted woman was more than Alanas could handle. Alanas lost her footing. Marcus ran the Death Walker through before the Death Walker could finish her.

More Death Walkers appeared, and the wave of warriors began to disappear at an alarming rate.

"We need to leave," Marcus yelled.

"I am not leaving them. I promised!" Julie dodged a Death Walker then tackled her.

The Death Walker pushed Julie aside. Julie bounced off of Yarna's leg.

Julie tried to shake off the pain. Her head was splitting; blood drizzled from a gash.

As the Death Walkers converged on the small number of warriors remaining, a mighty yell came from behind them.

The combined forces of the Hemoors and Skorei charged into the room, led by Pertheus and Argos's youngest son, Edwin.

Marcus ran to join his former clansmen. Callista joined the Hemoor tribe.

Julie watched as her two heroes fought alongside each other and their former tribes. She fought back the emotion of seeing Marcus with the men she had only heard of as terrible demons fighting against the Death Walkers.

In a matter of minutes, the battle swung back into their favor. The

Death Walkers began to retreat from sight.

The men and women of the Speculus erupted with a roar of relief and excitement.

Marcus found Arthur, Bones, and the rest of his old Skorei tribe. He embraced each one of them, before holding them by the shoulders so he could gaze at them once more.

Julie caught a lump in her throat watching the exchange between the men. They truly loved him, she thought.

Then, Marcus left them to join Julie and Callista. "Callista, I never thought I would see you again." He wrapped his massive arms around her and lifted her into the air.

"It has been too long," Callista said.

Yarna twisted her head to the group. "Marcus, we should leave now."

"I agree," he said.

"Go," Callista said. "We will finish this."

"Good luck." They hugged a final time. Marcus went to his old friends, wrapping his massive arm around their heads and pressing his forehead to theirs as he said goodbye.

"We had good deaths, and we will have more," a tall, bald black man told him.

"They will return," a small, skinny man with spiked blonde hair said.

"Thomen," Marcus said to a man standing in the back of the group. "Thank you."

"No, thank you," the one named Thomen said.

"Marcus," the dragon snorted.

"Yes, get us out of here," he said.

"Not so fast," Azahleah's voice rang around them.

Death Walkers appeared everywhere and began killing the already dead warriors. One of them struck Julie, hitting her in the leg. Julie screamed in pain.

Marcus jammed his sword into the Death Walker's ribcage.

Rinna, the Death Walker who had attacked Julie all those years ago, appeared before Marcus and Julie.

Marcus grabbed her. "Go," Rinna said. "I want no quarrel with you."

"Thank you."

Two Death Walkers unleashed a flurry of attacks on Rinna, stabbing her repeatedly as Marcus scooped Julie in his arms and ran to Yarna.

Marcus started pushing Julie onto Yarna as the dragon sent blast after blast toward the approaching women. He got a helping hand from Edwin.

"Get up there," Edwin said. "We have this."

Marcus looked at him, "Who did this to you?" He hugged the young man tight. "Tell me."

Through the chaos, Julie could not hear what he said.

"Go," Edwin yelled.

"I will have your revenge," Marcus told him as he climbed on Yarna.

Two Death Walkers appeared and grabbed at Julie's leg. They were the same two that captured Julie in Allon.

Yarna spun and slammed her massive leg on them, crushing both, as she extended herself up through the room, blasting the ceiling with enough heat that she could crash through it without a problem. In a matter of minutes, they were airborne and free from Azahleah and his Death Walkers.

## Chapter Forty-Three

Julie—Seras

Julie refocused her eyes. The natural light caused her to squint. She had no idea where they were in relation to Allon. The wind whipped through her hair as she and Marcus soared across Seras. Marcus's arms wrapped tightly around her body were the only thing keeping her warm and from falling out of the sky. She pressed into his body. "Thank you," she whispered. "I'm sorry it took me so long," Marcus whispered in her ear.

"No, I knew you would come for me."

"Always," he said.

Julie closed her eyes and slept, knowing she would always be safe in his arms.

"Hey," Marcus nudged her awake. "We're here."

Yarna flew above the mountains and began her descent at the edge of the front gate of Allon.

Julie could feel her strength returning. *Was it the nap, being further from Azahleah, or being closer to Marcus?*

The people of Allon rushed out to the sight of the giant dragon coming to a landing. The warriors were armed as Freya, Griffus, and the other leaders rode out, swords at the ready for an attack.

Julie could practically see the relief on their faces when Yarna turned to show them her passengers.

The crowd moved to help Julie as she slid from the dragon's back.

He and Griffus embraced. "I never thought I would see you again," Griffus said.

"How long have I been gone?"

"At least ten days," Griffus told him.

"It didn't feel that long," he said.

"Time moves differently in the abyss," Freya said.

"Hi, Freya," Julie said.

"I am glad you have returned," she said, before turning to Julie. "Come with me. I want to know everything you witnessed."

"Can I just go home?"

"I understand you wanting to leave, but please, I must know what you saw," Freya said.

Julie sighed.

"Go with her. I will see you soon," Marcus said. "There are a few things I have to do."

"Okay." She grabbed him around the neck. "Thank you again. You don't know how scared I was."

# Chapter Forty-Four

Marcus—Seras

Marcus approached Yarna. “Thank you for helping me.”

“It is my duty now, demon.” the dragon snorted. The people of Allon stood and stared at the monster with amazement.

“No, it’s not,” Marcus said. He held out the medallion.

“What do you intend to do with me?”

“May I ask you to change into a human again? It’s hard to talk to a dragon,” he said.

Yarna did as he commanded. She transformed back into a beautiful woman with green eyes, long dark hair, and wearing a green robe.

“Thank you,” Marcus said.

“What are your intentions with me?” Yarna asked.

“This.” He handed her the dragon necklace.

“I do not understand.”

“There’s nothing to understand. You are free. You can choose to do whatever you want,” Marcus told her.

“You do not want me to serve you?” Yarna asked. “Did I do something wrong?”

“No, you served Azahleah well. You served me even better. You helped me save the Heart and brought us safely home.”

“Then why are you doing this?”

““It is for you. You have earned your freedom. Thank you for all you did,” Marcus said. “You are free to do whatever you want; go wherever you want.”

Yarna was speechless for a second. “Am I welcome here?”

“Of course you are. You will be a most welcome addition to Allon,” he told her.

"But I do not have to?"

Marcus tried to stifle a chuckle. "No."

Yarna's eyes filled with tears.

"I didn't mean to insult you," Marcus said.

"You did not insult me. I have never been treated so fairly," Yarna said. "I want to thank you, demo—Marcus."

"No, thank you, Yarna. I could not have done it without you."

Yarna changed back into dragon form. "I will not forget your kindness, Marcus of Allon." Then she opened her wings and soared into the sky. Free.

Marcus watched as Yarna flew away, having no idea where she would go or if he would ever see her again. He then turned his attention to a more pressing matter. He raced to Argos's home.

"Argos, Argos, Gwendolyn!"

Gwendolyn opened the cabin door. "Marcus, you've returned?"

"I have, and I know who—" he stopped mid-sentence. At the family table sat the grieving Argos, Jakob, and Leyta. "You!" Marcus pointed at Edwin's fiancé.

"Marcus," Argos stood. He looked more tired than he was the last time Marcus saw him.

"Get away from them," Marcus ordered. "Get away from them now!"

"What's the meaning of this?" Argos asked.

"Marcus, stop," Gwendolyn said. "Jakob just asked permission to marry Leyta."

"No," Marcus yelled. He looked at Leyta. "Do you want to tell them, or shall I?"

Leyta stood, trembling.

"Tell them," Marcus ordered. "Tell them!" Spit flew from his mouth as he seethed.

Tears streamed down Leyta's face.

Jakob stood to defend Leyta.

"Tell them!"

"Tell us what?" Argos asked.

"What do you want her to tell us?" Jakob asked. His hand was on the hilt of his sword.

Leyta placed her hand on Jakob's. "I'm sorry." She looked at each one of them and repeated it over and over, collapsing back into her chair. "How did you find out?" she cried.

"Edwin told me."

Argos stood. "You talked to Edwin. How?"

"Oh my." Gwendolyn placed her hand over her mouth.

Leyta dropped her head into her hands. Her body rose and fell with whimpers.

"What did Edwin tell you?" Jakob asked slowly, looking at Leyta the entire time.

Leyta lifted her head. "It was me," she sobbed. "It was me. I killed Edwin."

Jakob fell backwards.

Gwendolyn dropped to her knees. "No, please, no."

Argos stood. "How, why?"

Leyta used the table to get to her feet. "I—I am what they call an Akarin."

"No, Akarin are all dead," Argos said.

"I am probably the last of them."

Jakob drew his sword. "You killed my brother. Did you plan to kill me next?"

"No, it just happens. I can't control it," Leyta cried as she broke down in hysterics, her fingers began to grow, and a low murmur came from her throat. Leyta's face distorted, and pincers extended from her jaw. "I'm sorry, I'm sorry," she sobbed. A large tongue shot out at Jakob, hitting him square in the chest.

Jakob hacked off her tongue. Marcus rammed his sword into her chest as Argos removed Leyta's head from her body.

## Chapter Forty-Five

Julie—Seras

"So, it was Leyta the whole time?" Julie asked when she and Marcus entered his cabin.

"Yeah." Marcus wiped his forehead with his hand.

"Is she dead?" Julie asked, knowing the answer but not being able to help the tears rolling down her cheek.

"Yes," Marcus answered quietly. "Freya told me she was an Akarin. She said Azahleah made them. They can pretend to be human but have a taste for blood."

"She told you a lot."

"She did."

"They sound like succubuses; seducing men, sucking their blood until the body explodes." Julie wiped her face with her arm.

"Julie, if you don't mind?" Marcus said. He took off his boots.

"I'm sorry. I just have all this pent-up energy. We've had a helluva couple of weeks."

"You can say that again." Marcus groaned as he sat on the edge of the bed.

"I should go." She sniffed her armpits. "I seriously need a shower."

"A nice, hot shower sounds amazing," he said. "Take a few days off. Heck, take a week or two off. You deserve it."

"You do, too."

"I'll probably sleep for a week. I'll see you later."

"Bye." She rushed over and hugged him one more time. "Thank you again!"

"Of course."

Julie started to disappear behind the wall to return to Earth. She stopped and looked back as Marcus took off his shirt. The scars from his time in the abyss had not healed yet, and blood had dried around his shoulder, his side, his chest, and his back.

"Oh, my God!"

"Hey, you're supposed to be leaving," Marcus said.

Julie grabbed a rag and threw it in the water bowl. "Here, let me help you."

"I can do it."

"Please. It's the least I can do." She pressed the wet cloth over the bloodied areas.

"Thank you."

After she finished, she sat on the bed and pulled her legs up to her chest.

Marcus looked at her then to the corner of the room. "You okay?"

"Yeah, yeah, yeah." The two separate images she had in Speculus blazed through her mind. "Just something I've been thinking about for a while." There was a strange stillness between them. Julie had felt it a couple times over the last few months, but this was different. Being this close to him after everything that had happened left her feeling dizzy and shaky. Her chest rose and fell rapidly, too rapidly. Julie thought for a second that she might pass out.

"Okay." Marcus sat on the edge of the bed. "Talk to me. You know you can tell me anything." That's when she noticed Marcus's right leg, bouncing furiously, betraying the same restless energy she felt inside.

"I'm not sure if I can tell you this." She cocked her head and managed a weak smile.

"I bet you can. We've been through a lot in the past few years. You trusted me before you should have. Look at what just happened to us."

"I know, I know. I'm just being silly," she said.

"Well, stop being silly and tell me what's on your mind."

Julie took a deep breath. "Okay, here it goes. The whole time I was there with Azahleah. He wanted me to marry him. He wanted me and him to rule Seras."

"Yeah, you told me that."

"But the only thing I could think of was you."

"Julie, I don't know what to say." Marcus reached for her hand.

"I know, I'm being crazy. I'm sorry."

"No, I get it."

"You do?" Her eyes widened.

"Yes, I think you and I are feeling the same way," he told her.

"I think I love you." She moved her hand to her mouth. She noticed his knee shaking.

"I'm in love with you, too," Marcus said.

Their words dwindled into silence.

# Part Two

Prophecy Girl

## Chapter Forty-Six

Pallanex—Seras

"Come with me," Pallanex ordered her priests. She had just read a note given to her by the messenger who was in charge of the raven spies. She led them out of the hall and down the steps toward her secret room. They saw the mummified bodies of those who had let her down in the past. Cobwebs and spiders filled the chamber.

"My Queen," the man named Barth spoke in a hushed tone. "Where are we going?" All three men trembled as her large black pets appeared to move in their direction.

"The Heart has returned," she seethed.

"My Queen?" the stocky Barth questioned once more.

A second man said, "But it is our understanding that the Heart comes and goes as she pleases."

"Not from the Speculus," Pallanex screamed. "Azahleah had her, and he failed to inform me." She tossed open the backdoor and went out into her private courtyard. The fallen images of Canis and the others lay crumbled in the dying grass. Propped on the remains of the white statues were picks and shovels. Pallanex pointed to the men. "Start digging."

"Digging, why are we digging?" one asked.

"Because I ordered you to dig!" Then she pointed to Barth, "You, bring me a fat goat."

"Yes, my Queen." He hustled away.

"Dig," Pallanex ordered Salius and Rondal.

The men started their task. By the time Barth returned with a goat tethered by a rope, the other two were stripped to their undergarments and shirtless. Sweat covered their bodies, and they discarded their clothing. Salius's long-stringy hair was caked in dirt. Rondal looked as though his old body couldn't lift another shovel full.

"Bring it to me," Pallanex called out from a shaded area. "No, I will come to you." She moved to the group. "Get out."

The men stopped their digging and climbed out of the hole.

Pallanex took the goat, plunged a knife in its neck, and tossed it in the little pit. She drew the Elder's circle around the holes as the goat's blood began to spill out. Once the goat stopped moving, Pallanex handed a scroll to Rondal. "Read this when I jump into the pit. Do not stop until I am gone."

"Gone?" Rondal wiped the sweat from his bald head.

"Yes, gone. Now, start reading."

Rondal began to read ancient words on the scroll. Fire erupted from the burial pit.

Queen Pallanex lifted the hem of her dress just enough to jump into the flames.

"My Queen," she heard the men yell as the world around her went dark.

She slipped through the portal and reappeared at the large gates of Speculus. *This will be fun.* Pallanex walked through the front lobby. She let her hand graze the tall arches. Such extravagance in such a wasted area. The only sound she heard was the sound of her footsteps on the obsidian-tiled floor. The hall was dark. The cauldrons and candelabras were extinguished. Pallanex moved from the throne room with the tapestries torn, and on the floor to the stairs that led to the white-stoned chamber. Before she descended to the lowest level, she stopped at the Enochian writing in the halls. Pallanex took a heavy candelabra from the wall and smashed the enchantments. She made her way down the steps and paused when she reached the bottom. What has happened here?

Azahleah stood. "Pallanex, why are you here?"

The room was in shambles. The walls were smashed, and the grasslands inside the Speculus were on fire. Some Death Walkers were standing guard, keeping the doors locked; others were lifting the bodies of their dead sisters off the floor. "What have you done?"

"What have I done? What have I done? Look at my beautiful home!"

"Why did you not tell me you had the Heart?" Pallanex shrilled.

"I do not work for you! Our world does not revolve around you," Azahleah yelled.

"You know she is the one who Tolth created to destroy me. What purpose did you have?"

Azahleah walked closer to his sister. "My purpose is my own. I do not have to explain myself to you."

"Then you are the traitor I have always known you to be."

"Pallanex, you are as delusional as ever. The only traitor is you. You betrayed our father, you betrayed your brothers and sister, you betrayed everything and everyone. No wonder you are so miserable. You had everything, and you burned it all. You deserve—"

A massive explosion stopped his words. The shock waves rippled from Pallanex and shook the giant hall. Death Walkers were knocked off their feet, and the weary women prepared for another battle to protect their master.

"Impossible! I have protected this place from our magic."

"You are a fool, Azahleah. I saw the writings. Figure out the rest."

Azahleah vanished in a plume of black smoke then reappeared behind Pallanex and hit her with both fists.

The Death Walkers marched toward Pallanex with swords drawn. She raised her hands and lifted them into the air.

Azahleah shot a bolt of lightning, knocking Pallanex back, and causing her to drop the Death Walkers. He sent another bolt in her direction, but Pallanex vanished before it could hit her.

Pallanex appeared in front of him, grabbing him by the neck and lifting him in the air. "I could have finished this, and none of this would have happened to you!"

"I would never give her to you," Azahleah choked out. He broke free from her grasp and sent a magical blast at her.

"What were you up to, you worm?" Pallanex asked as she formed an invisible barrier around her. "Let me guess, you thought if you could trick her into joining you, you would leave here and take over Seras?"

Azahleah sent lightning and debris from the room toward her. "I could have ruled better than you or Tolth!"

Pallanex's force field held from the attack. "You could not wipe our boots. That is why you were sent here. This is the best you can do."

Azahleah struck out over and over, each time being cast aside by Pallanex. He stopped to catch his breath.

Pallanex transported herself toward him and grabbed his head with both hands. "Why did you make me hurt you? I would have helped you."

"You would not help me. You feel I am below you. You and Tolth both felt that way. I wanted to be worthy," Azahleah hissed.

Pallanex shook his head. "Damn you!" The entirety of Speculus began to explode as life drained from Azahleah's body. Pallanex stood, looked at the destruction, and disappeared in a black cloud.

## Chapter Forty-Seven

Julie—Seras

Julie found Marcus in their practice area, in the clearing near the northern edge of Allon. The sun's golden rays filtered through the tree line. It had been two long weeks since they awkwardly declared their feelings for each other. Marcus was already sweating from a workout. Julie struggled to contain the urge to pounce on him like a spider monkey.

"Are you ready?" he asked, between large gulps of water from his pouch.

Julie stopped, puzzled at the abruptness of his tone. "Yeah." She shook her head. "I guess."

"Good. We have a lot of work to do."

She pulled out her sword and stood ready for Marcus's attack. Nothing like she was hoping for, since they had not seen or talked about their conversation in his cabin.

"Ready?"

"I guess so."

Marcus lunged forward. "Good," he shouted. "Block, block!" His voice carried over the tree line on the edge of the northern forest. He thrust his sword toward Julie then came down with an overhead swing.

Julie barely deflected it; her arms vibrated from the force. She gritted her teeth. *Why won't he talk about it?* It was driving her crazy that he had not said a word about what they shared with each other. Julie sent a wave of power in his direction. The invisible force caught him square in the chest and knocked him off his feet.

Marcus hit the ground hard but rolled through the blast and crouched down, ready to fight again. He opened his palm, and his sword returned to him.

Julie's eyes stung as her blood boiled. She rushed him with a shout. She spun into a double-handed strike, pivoting at the last second.

He blocked it. "You're really getting good at this," Marcus said.

She hit him again with another blast.

He fell back but used the momentum to disappear into the woods.

Julie seethed then chased him into the forest. She looked up, ready for him to jump down from a limb.

But he appeared from around a tree instead.

She swung her sword.

Marcus trapped the width of the blade between his two palms. "I've missed you," he said in a tone just above a whisper.

Julie froze. Her breath caught in her throat. "I've missed you, too," she finally got out. "It was a long two weeks."

Marcus exhaled. "I can't tell you how glad I am that you feel the same way."

"I was worried you'd changed your mind," she admitted, stepping closer, and lowering her blade.

"No," he responded with a slight jerk. "But I can't lie. I still have my reservations."

Julie frowned. "Do you think I'm silly?"

Marcus snickered from the side of his mouth. "Um... a little. But no sillier than I am."

"Why?"

He hesitated. "Mostly because of the age difference. And...let's face it, I used to be your teacher."

"I know." She shrugged, but she didn't waver. "Are you okay with it? Because I am. I've barely thought of anything else in over a year."

Marcus let out a nervous chuckle. "I have too, to be honest. You just caught me off guard."

"Good!" She placed her hand on his chest. She could feel how fast his heart was beating. "Listen, I've been thinking about this a lot. I mean a lot, a lot, and here's what I thought: one, you're not really a teacher, so anything that has to do with that is wiped out; two, even if you were a teacher, it's been over a year since you were my teacher. I looked it up." She bobbed her head. "And three, we are both adults, so age doesn't matter."

He stared at her. "I'm glad you've spent so much time thinking about the details," he eventually said. "And I'm glad we took a little time to step back. I just... still have reservations. I feel...guilty. I don't want to take advantage of you."

"Please don't," she said softly. "You are not forcing me into anything I don't want." Her hands slid up around his shoulders and clasped behind his neck. "I promise." She kissed him. It felt amazing. She had dreamed about this moment for over a year, and it was worth every second. "I am in love with you."

At first, Marcus didn't react, as though she had taken him completely by surprise. Then, he put his hands on her waist and pulled her closer. "I love you, too."

When they finally broke apart, both of them were breathless.

"So... what happens now?" she asked, brushing her fingers to his lips.

"I don't know," he said, still catching his breath. "I think we just make it up as we go." He moved a strand of her hair behind her ear. "We don't have to be in a hurry."

"I like that," she said. "Do you think we should keep it a secret?"

Marcus gave a half-smile. "Maybe for a little while. Until we figure it out ourselves."

Julie nodded. "That sounds good."

They kissed again. This time it was slower, more intense. She stood on her tiptoes as he bent to her. Their breathing became one.

When they finally came up for air, she put her head on his chest. "Now what?"

Marcus whispered. "More of this, please."

"I'm serious," she said, laughing quietly.

"I'm serious."

"Well... then we should probably get back to work," he said, sounding a little disappointed.

"Okay." She gave a devilish grin. "But I wanna do more of this, first." She kissed him once more for good measures.

# Chapter Forty-Eight

Julie—Earth

Julie sat at the kitchen table with a plate of homemade nachos slathered in cheese and topped with jalapenos in front of her. She had just finished taking a shower after a long day of practicing with Marcus. She couldn't wipe the smile off of her face thinking about what had transpired the last few weeks. Never in a million years would she have let herself believe that he felt the same as she did. Just like clockwork, she said to herself when her phone rang. "Hi," she said, finishing a bite of chips.

The images of her mom and dad appeared on the screen.

"Hi, honey," they said in unison.

"How's it going?"

"Indescribable," Michelle answered. "Words wouldn't do it justice."

"Right now, it's lots of sea days, fun in the sun, beautiful beaches, and the drink package," Philip said with a wink.

"Are you eating nachos for dinner?" Michelle scolded her.

Julie moved the plate out of the frame. "It's just a snack before dinner," Julie teased. "So, where are you?"

"Don't try to change the subject—"

"We just left Fort Lauderdale," her dad saved her. "Heading to the Yucatan Peninsula. We're going to take an excursion to Chichen Itza."

"That sounds like fun." Julie took a drink of water. "How's grandma?"

"She's taking a nap," Michelle told her." I think she is loving it, but there is so much to see and do. I'm glad she came with us."

"Me too", Phil added.

"What have you been up to?"

Julie paused. "Not much right now. I will start my new job at the

Coffee Cafe tomorrow morning."

"That's great, honey," Phil said.

"We are so proud of you," Michelle added.

"It's just a part-time job," Julie reminded them.

"I know." Michelle looked at Phil. "We know, but we are."

"Stop," Julie said. "I'm good. I promise. I'm better than good. I miss you guys, but I'm excited to hear all about your adventures. And I promise to keep you updated on everything here."

"We miss you too, honey. Remember, we're always just a call away."

"Love you, Jules," her dad told her.

"Love you, too. Have fun. Bye."

"We will, bye-bye," Michelle finished before hanging up.

Julie got up, put her nachos back in the microwave, and refilled her water glass; then, when the timer went off, she sat and thought, *I wonder what Marcus is up to?*

## Chapter Forty-Nine

Julie—Seras

Julie wiped the sweat off her forehead with the back of her hand. She and Marcus practiced in the heat of the day.

"I've told you not to jump in the air", Marcus said. "This isn't the movies."

"But it looks cool," Julie chuckled.

"Cool or not, it will not work in real fighting," he told her. "Now, come on."

"Okay, okay." Julie took her stance.

Their swords clanged.

"Good," Marcus yelled. "Swing, swing, block."

Julie followed his instructions. She sent a blast toward him from her hands. It knocked Marcus on his butt. "Are you okay?" Julie couldn't help but laugh.

"Yes." Marcus got up and brushed himself off. "That was a good one."

"Can we be finished for the day?"

Marcus looked at the setting sun as it began to shrink behind the mountains and trees. "Sure, I think we've been out here long enough."

Julie wrapped her arms around his neck and kissed him. "It's not that I don't want to stay out here all night with you, but I think people are going to get suspicious. Especially Bobo."

"I agree. We have to be careful a little while longer," he said before kissing her again. This time, they didn't hold back. Eventually, Marcus pulled away. "It's getting dark."

"Okay, okay," Julie said as they returned to the northern gates of Allon. "I didn't know a fierce demon warrior would be afraid of the dark," she laughed before asking, “Can I be honest?”

Marcus cocked his head. “I hope so.”

“You surprise me,” Julie said with a smile.

“How?”

“In a good way,” she continued.

“Okay, how?”

“Well, I never guessed you would be the romantic type. But you are.”

Julie watched his face turn red.

“No, I'm not.” Marcus kept walking into the gates. Cauldrons and torches lit up the courtyard.

“You most certainly are.”

“I disagree with you.” He stopped near the center of town. “Prove it.”

“Whatdya mean prove it?”

“I mean, if you think I'm some kind of romantic, prove it.” Marcus laughed.

Julie stopped and cocked her head. “Right here?” she whispered.

“Yes, right here, right now. I want you to tell me what makes you think I'm a romantic.”

“I-I-I don't know what you want me to say?”

“Let me help you.” Marcus held up one hand while bringing her closer with his other. At that moment, fireworks erupted into the night sky.

Julie's mouth fell open.

Marcus couldn't keep the smile off of his face.

“Are you kidding me?” Julie squealed.

“Does this prove your point?”

“Oh my gosh! I love you!” Julie threw her arms around him and kissed him. She couldn't believe her eyes. Marcus had set up an entire fireworks display for her and, in doing so, publicly announced their feelings for each other. “I can't believe you just did that,” Julie said afterward as they walked from town.

“I wish I could do more.”

“Like what?” Julie protested.

“I don't know. I wish I could be more for you. I can't be your...your boyfriend. I can't visit you whenever I want. Heck, I can't even show my face on Earth."

"I don't care about that stuff. I have wanted this longer than I want to admit."

Marcus smirked. "Come on. You know, if you hadn't had to spend all this time with me here, you could have any guy you wanted."

Julie took him by the shoulders. She felt the strength in his muscles and had to catch her breath. "Listen to me," she said gently. "There was a time when I had a different boyfriend every month. My brother used to make fun of me because of it. I don't want that. I want someone who I can talk to, someone who is funny, someone I don't have to keep secrets from."

"But I'm the reason you need to keep secrets," Marcus protested, holding the door of his cabin for her.

"I want you." She kissed him just as he closed the door.

Marcus sat her on the bed. "Listen." He knelt in front of her. "I know you don't think it's a big deal now, but I've been alive quite a bit longer than you, and I've seen things and done things you can't imagine."

"But I can," Julie argued back. "I know what you are and what you've done."

He touched her face. "I want you to be one hundred percent sure. Because when I say I love you, I mean it. You are everything I have ever wanted. Anyone before you was just a mistake, a big mistake."

"Are you finished?" Julie took him by the hand and led him up from his knee to the bed beside her. "I have seen you at your best, and I have seen you at your worst. I understand more than anyone who you are." She placed her hand on his knee. "I have dated a bunch of boys, and I'm tired of boys. So, when I say I love you. I mean, I love you with every fiber of my body." A tear ran down her cheek. "I didn't even know I was capable of this kinda love. It's scary."

Marcus took a breath. "I hope I don't let you down."

"Never." She kissed him.

# Chapter Fifty

Javan—Seras

Captain Javan and his men returned to their ships. Frustration was etched on the men's faces. After traveling several miles through the river passage and marching an additional ten miles through the northern wilderness, they came up empty once again.

"Sir, the days and nights are endless. When will we be allowed to return?" Javan's trusted navigator, Ranu asked.

"We all want to go home, Ranu," Javan answered.

"No, Ranu does not have a home. Destroyed by your Queen. I do not wish to die in another man's land for nothing."

Javan rubbed his eyes. The stress of leading his men through the treacherous waters and unchartered territories of the north had taken its toll. "I understand," he said. "I will send word to the queen and let her know we have traveled as far as we could with no sign of Marcus or his fortress."

"How will the words pierce her ears, sir?"

He smirked. "How do you think she will take that news?"

The man bowed his head. "Apologies, my Lord."

"I agree with you. I do not see the sense of moving on. We will make camp here, and I will prepare a message."

"Yes, Captain." The man turned to a group of men. "You heard the captain. Go! Get supplies and food from the ships. We will make camp here."

The men hustled to the small boats and shoved them out from the shoreline.

Javan looked around. "You know, it is quite pretty here. It would make a nice place to settle." He smiled at his oldest friend and shipmate, Ranu.

"You mean, hide from Pallanex?"

"We will keep that to ourselves, Ranu."

"Yes, my Lord." He turned his attention to ordering the men to make preparations to set sail.

The men got to work as Javan returned to his cabin on the main ship. He sat at his desk to pen the words that would surely be the death of him.

*My Queen,*

*I regret to inform you that we have again failed. The men grow restless, and I do not know how much longer I can—*

Before he could finish, there was a brief knock at his door.

"Enter."

One of his men came into the cabin. "Captain, I apologize for interrupting you but come look. There is something in the sky."

Javan stood and followed the man out the door. He pointed northeast of their location, beyond the trees and a mountain range, where strange colors burst across the night sky, lighting it up like magic.

"Sir, what is that?" the man asked.

"That, that is a sign from the Elderess," Javan said, slapping the man on the back. "Thank you, thank you!" He rushed back to his cabin. "Send for Ranu," he ordered a man.

"Yes, my Lord."

Javan returned to his desk. He threw away his previous note and rewrote it.

*My Dearest Queen,*

*I have seen the sign from the sky and will continue our venture north. The enemy is in sight.*

*Javan*

He rolled the paper and attached it to the leg of a raven. He carried the bird outside and released it. "Fly, my wonderful friend. Fly." He returned to his men. "Make notice that we will travel at first light."

"Yes, Captain," the man said.

Javan then walked to Ranu, who had made his way from his room on the opposite side of the deck.

"Change of plans, Captain?" Ranu asked.

"Look." Javan pointed to the explosive bursts in the sky. "That is a sign."

Ranu just stared. "It raises questions, my Lord."

"What questions, Ranu?"

"I do not mean to insult," the pilot said.

"No insults. Please speak clearly."

"Why do they show themselves now, and why do we charge headlong into a place with that type of power?"

"The Elderess Eryx has shown our path," Javan said. "And, we have all of the firepower we need and the will of the Elders. We will be victorious in the name of Pallanex." He looked at Ranu. "You and I know all too well her power."

"I pledged my oath to you, Lord Javan. Ranu is your faithful pilot."

"Good, then sleep now. We sail at first light."

## Chapter Fifty-One

Julie—Seras

The morning sun peeked above the northern mountains, casting a golden hue over the green fields where Julie practiced with Redderick Bobo. She would much rather be with Marcus, but Redderick's teaching had proven to be beneficial, plus he and Marcus insisted she spend time learning everything the ancient scribe of the Elders had to teach her.

Julie clenched her fist, looking at the parchment in her hands. The symbols on it shifted in a dizzying blur. Some were written in the Enochian angel language, which she could barely decipher with over a year of practice, and the rest...well, to her, it seemed like a chaotic jumble of lines and circles. "I can't make heads or tails from this," she muttered. "Half of this is in Angel language, and not to be rude, I think the other half was just someone doodling."

Redderick's voice was calm, which irritated Julie even more. "You are distracted. You must concentrate."

Julie rolled her eyes and blew out a deep breath. "Maybe because I have other things on my mind, duh."

"Regardless, my Heart, you need to get better."

"Why?"

"What has you bothered today?"

Julie paused. "Why am I so important?"

"You do not understand how important you are, Julie. You are not just here to pass the time. You are the gatekeeper."

Julie tilted her head. "What does that even mean?"

"It means your role is far greater than you realize. You are the gatekeeper to Seras, your world, and beyond. You hold the key to everything that is and will be."

"I don'—" She stopped herself, shaking her head. "I don't understand. I can barely read this." She held up the parchment. "I can't control this...this *power* you keep talking about. How am I supposed to be some...gatekeeper?"

"I am sorry, my Heart. Because you were born for it. Not everyone can carry the weight of this world, and the fear of what will happen if Seras would fall."

"See! That's what I'm talking about." She swallowed hard. "I don't think I can do it."

"You can," Redderick insisted. "And you will. I have faith in you. But you must focus."

Julie bit her lip. "Fine. I'll try again." She raised her hands, closed her eyes, drew in a deep breath, and tried again. A flicker of heat sparked in her palm.

"Yes, yes, my Heart, you are doing it. Keep going!"

Julie's entire body strained as she tried to push the energy out. Finally, a burst of fire shot from her hands, searing the brush at the edge of the field.

Redderick clapped. "Marvelous," he said. "Try again."

Julie blew out a zerbert from her lips. "Seriously?"

"Yes, my dear. This is important. If you are going to face Pallanex, you will need to harness all of your power."

"Fine." She extended her arms again, focusing all of her concentration on unleashing the energy inside her. This time, a stream of fire surged from her hands, scorching a path along the field.

"You are so close, my Heart!"

"Are you kidding? Look at what I just did."

"Read the letters again. Think about those words."

"I've told you I don't understand half of these scribbles."

"But they are the key to unlocking what lies within you. And we must hurry. Time is running out."

Julie stepped back. "What are you talking about?"

"Pallanex. She grows stronger every day we do not face her. I fear she has become too strong already. We do not have long before she grows impatient and acts against us."

"Why, I don't get it?"

"Julie, as I said, you are the key. The gatekeeper. The Heart of Tolth. You are the one Tolth wanted to protect Seras. Without you, we are all lost. That is why Azahleah wanted you. You do not realize how powerful you are. That is why you must understand what I am trying to teach you. Time is running out."

# Chapter Fifty-Two

Marcus and Julie—Earth

Marcus and Julie sat facing each other on the couch in her parents' house.

"Can I get you something to drink?" Julie asked with a slight tremble in her voice.

"No, I'm good," Marcus answered.

"I loved that you snuck back to Earth and left me flowers in the hut last week. But you shouldn't have," she said.

"I wish I could have dropped them off in your house."

"Why didn't you?" she asked.

"Well, I didn't have any clothes for one." Marcus held up a finger. "That would have scared your neighbors." He held up a second finger. "And I'm wanted by the police." He lifted a third finger. "Three strikes."

Julie grimaced. "Good points."

**"I'm glad you left me some clothes so I could finally come in, Marcus said. "Is this weird?" he asked.**

"A little, but you've been here plenty of times."

"I know, it just seems...**weird." He cleared his throat and changed the subject. "How are your parents getting along on their cruise?"**

**Good,"** she answered. Before Marcus could respond, Julie continued, "Do you have to sit way over there?" she asked, **her face flushing red.**

He opened his mouth and shut it again comically. Not knowing how to answer. "No, I can move closer," he said, half rising and landing next to her; his student, no, his former student, a girl whose fate had brought them together six years earlier, was no longer a girl. Marcus could feel his heart racing, his mouth dry, and all he could think about was touching her, but he hesitated.

Julie rotated toward him and crossed her legs in front of her.

Marcus mimicked her action; now the two warriors were facing each other, knees touching, pulling away, and then lingering to the point they no longer moved apart.

First contact.

"So, what did you want to talk about?" Julie asked. She knew he was fully aware of what they needed to discuss.

"I-I don't know," Marcus stuttered. He gently brushed a strand of hair from her face.

Julie softly laughed at the touch.

"What do you want to talk about?" he teased.

"The weather, college, ya know...the regular stuff," she joked. Her heart beat like a drum. She kept her head down, avoiding eye contact. The thoughts of her schoolgirl crush flooded her mind. A crush now turned into a full-fledged young woman's yearning.

"Can I say something?"

"Of course." Julie gave a slight grin.

"You are," he paused. "Words cannot describe you." He leaned in and kissed the top of her head. His lips grazed her brown, wavy hair.

Julie felt the blood rush to her face. "Why?" she had to ask.

Marcus reached out and lifted her chin and stared into her soft brown eyes. "I don't know," he responded, then kissed her on the forehead.

"I couldn't believe you said that to me," Julie admitted.

"I couldn't believe you said it, either," Marcus responded. "I thought I was alone with these feelings."

"I thought I was alone with these feelings," she replied. He moved to kiss her cheek.

Julie did not back away. She breathed in his essence, his fragrance, his chiseled features, the warmth of his body.

"I never want you to feel alone again," he said, taking a chance and kissing her gently on the lips.

"Are you sure about this?" Julie asked, returning the kiss.

"I am very sure," Marcus repeated, kissing her a bit longer this time and then backing away. "Are you sure?"

"Oh yes, I am very sure." Julie leaned closer and kissed him, this time allowing her mouth to part slightly.

Their tongues touched gently. "Julie, I am in love with you."

"I love you, too," she answered.

Their words dwindled into silence.

Marcus pulled Julie onto his lap.

She moved both legs out to either side of his waist.

He moved his hands across her back, making his way under her shirt.

The sensation of Marcus lightly touching her back gave Julie goosebumps.

"Tell me when to stop," he told her between long passionate kisses.

"I will," she promised. "But I won't want you to."

Marcus moved his mouth lower to Julie's neck; there, he tenderly kissed her neck, shoulder, and earlobes. This drove Julie wild.

Julie's kisses were unlike anything he had ever experienced. Her soft lips and her gentle, active tongue were all foreign to his previous experiences.

"I love you," he whispered in her ear.

"I love you," she moaned.

## Chapter Fifty-Three

Pallanex—Seras

Queen Pallanex approached the entrance of the cave, which belonged to her sister. Steam rose from vents as Vestus's companion, the red-clothed Greagon, confronted her with a spear in his hand. He screamed and poked his weapon toward her.

Pallanex was in no mood to play. She threw back her hand, and the poor creature crashed into the side of the large opening.

"What did you do?" Vestus's voice roared through the cave.

"I have come for you," Pallanex said. "Not some little imp."

"I knew this day would come. You have finally come to finish what you started."

The queen navigated through a series of mazes to the great cavern. The interior walls dripped with sweat.

Molten rock rose to form giant hands to strangle Pallanex. Vestus closed in around her. "I will destroy you."

Pallanex stomped her foot, and the cave went still. "I showed you grace before. I will not show it again."

"Why have you come here?" Vestus questioned. "You left me here to rot until the end of time."

"You know why I am here, sister. I should have guessed it from the start. You gave that fool your gift."

"What did you expect? You are a traitor. You are wicked!"

"Enough!"

"No! You stand before me as some queen. You are nothing but a vile worm. You are willing to give us up and all of this up for what purpose?"

"I knew you would not understand. That is why you are here. I did not want to kill you, sister. I wanted to keep you safe and out of my way. Now, I know you are the reason the demon and the Heart are here to destroy my plans."

"Do you expect me to apologize?"

The ground under her feet shifted. "Oh no, I expect you to be another casualty in their hopeless quest."

"You are the one who does not understand," Vestus said. "They have the blessing of Ostram and Tolth on their side. You will be defeated, and the world will never remember your existence. All for what, the love of another traitor?"

"Do not mistake me for a fool!"

"I do not mistake you for anything other than what you are. You have destroyed everything precious in this world that we built. You betrayed us. You betrayed what we held so true. You betrayed our father."

"Shut up!"

"Kill me if you must. Kill me and put me out of my misery. But if you are to kill me, do not dishonor me by killing me like a coward. Give me my body. Take this curse from me and let us finish what we started so long ago."

"You could not beat me then. You will not beat me now," Pallanex laughed. "So be it. My curse is lifted, and you are restored." Pallanex held out her hands and released Vestus from her molten prison.

Vestus formed out of the shadows of the cave. She ran her hands over and down her raven locks. She stretched and flexed the muscles she had not used in a millennia. She took a moment to reflect and admire her dark skin tone. "Tell me, sister, what finally led you to me?"

Pallanex smiled. "It was our brother, Azahleah."

"Is he?"

"He is." She nodded.

"Then one of us will join him soon."

"Indeed."

"Shall we begin?" Vestus asked.

"I was going to allow you to enjoy being in form once more, but if you insist." The wind began to whirl around them, and lightning crackled.

Light shone around Pallanex as she flicked her wrist and lifted a boulder, tossing it toward Vestus.

Vestus shielded herself from the large rock and broke it in half with her fists. She countered by moving her hand in Pallanex's direction. A rope from inside the cave wrapped around Pallanex's ankles.

Pallanex began to hover. She lifted her hands upward and smashed the cave ceiling. Debris fell all around the two elderesses.

Vestus leaped out of the way and followed her sister into the sky. Lightning formed and struck to the left and right of Pallanex as Vestus guided them toward her.

Pallanex dodged the bolts and lifted a chunk of the ground, sending it hurling at Vestus.

Vestus lowered herself out of the way then scrambled to her feet and raced at her sister. She crashed into Pallanex, knocking her out of the air. Vestus grabbed a post her Greagon companion used to climb and flung it at Pallanex. It hit its mark and splintered around the queen.

Pallanex shook herself off.

Vestus repeated her last attack. Unfortunately, Pallanex was ready.

She raised her hand, and the post smashed into an invisible wall. Pallanex stood. The queen flicked her hands, and bursts of fire exploded at Vestus, sending her flying backwards away from the cave that used to be her prison and into the dead forest.

Fire reigned down around Vestus. It consumed the area in flames.

Pallanex landed twenty feet away. She flung rocks toward Vestus with multiple hand movements.

Vestus blocked the attack with swipes of her hands. Sweat poured from every inch of her flesh.

Pallanex calmly walked closer to her. She put her thumbs and index fingers together, facing Vestus, and, with her palms open, moved them away from each other. A large sword appeared. She struck out at her sister.

Vestus blocked each attack with her golden wristbands. One blow glanced off and sliced her in the cheek. She scrambled away, using her power to pick up large pieces of Seras and toss them in Pallanex's direction.

Pallanex used her sword to cut through the flying sections of the ground.

It distracted Pallanex enough for Vestus to create her own sword out of thin air.

"This is the end for you, sister," Pallanex said. "You are no match for me." She could see the panic and desperation in Vestus's eyes. "You were no match for me when I took pity on you and allowed you to live."

"You allowed me to live stuck in a cave!"

Just then, Vestus's Greagon companion jumped on Pallanex's back. The attack gave Vestus a chance to regroup. The little creature took a large bite out of the back of Pallanex's shoulder.

Pallanex turned and twisted to grab the Greagon. She took it by the head and broke its neck.

"Sa'mon!" Vestus lunged and attacked Pallanex with a flurry of blade strikes in a fit of rage. She knocked the sword out of her sister's hand and then grabbed her by the neck. Her eyes darkened, and clouds raged above the Elderess of the Sky's head. Her hot breath heaved like a wild animal. Blood covered her teeth and lips. "I hate you!"

Pallanex laughed. "Where was this when I needed you?"

"I hate you," she repeated even louder. She held Pallanex out at arm's length in one hand and her sword in her other, ready to plunge Pallanex to her death.

A lightning bolt struck Vestus's blade. The shock temporarily stunned her. Just enough for Pallanex to conjure a blade and jam it into Vestus's chest. Blood soaked her cloak as Pallanex turned the blade, causing her sister to drop her sword. "My poor sister. You never stood a chance," Pallanex told her as Vestus began coughing up blood. She guided Vestus to the ground. "If only you would have joined me. If only you would not have helped the demon and the Heart."

"They will make you pay for all you have done," Vestus spit out.

"No, they will not, and all will be in vain." Pallanex took the blade out of her sister's chest then picked up her sword and cut off Vestus's head.

# Chapter Fifty-Four

William—Seras

William rubbed his tired eyes. It had been too long with nothing to show for it. His second in command appeared in total disgust.

The man looked at him with gritted teeth and a panicked face. William's men were strapped at the ankles, waist, chest, arms, and forehead. "We are soldiers of Pallanex! We trusted you!" He spat at William.

"And you are going to make me proud?" he said. "Trust me. Your sacrifice will be for the glory of Pallanex and me." William smiled.

"This is not the way it should be done," he protested. "I will report this to the Queen."

William grabbed him by the throat in his demon form, lifted him up, then as the man choked and jerked, William jammed his sword into the man's abdomen. While the man withered in pain, he snapped his neck. "I guess you won't be part of that experiment," he chuckled.

The number of men who died taking part in the experiment could fill a gorge. Indeed, it had filled a gorge. William had tried something new with the current crop. He treated the men of Pallanex's army to large, healthy diets. In the past, he fed the experiments only meat and water, hoping to attract their instinctual needs. It did not end well for them. This time, he took a slower approach: meals full of meat, loaves of bread, vegetables, fruits, and drinks of water, milk, and ale. They thrived under the new plan. They could eat and drink to their fill as often as they wanted. They had no idea what he was doing. Other soldiers not part of the project were jealous. *If only they knew,* William would say to himself as the complaints grew. He had to brutally stab one of his officers when they began to wonder why the men under William were being fed and treated so well.

As the men grew accustomed to their routine of eating and training,

William began adding his potion to their food and drink. The men never noticed. William added more and more until it was time for the final dose. He contemplated how to do it but decided that this approach would yield the best result.

"Why, General?"

"In time, you will understand," he told the man. "Now, I want you to drink this, all of it." He lifted the man's head and poured the contents of one of the many bottles he had extracted and created from Thomen's blood.

The man spat, then shook violently.

"Fight the pain. Fight the pain," William shouted.

"No, please, it hurts!"

"Show me!"

The man yelled. The others, who he had strapped on similar cots in the room, started to struggle to free themselves.

William rushed to each of them and followed the process of lifting their heads and pouring the fluid down their throats. Soon, each of them convulsed and screamed. He returned to the first soldier. "Let the beast come out. Fight the pain and let it free."

A ridge formed across the man's nose as it expanded, then sharp teeth began to emerge, causing blood to ooze from his mouth.

"You are almost there. Keep going!"

His skin peeled as his muscles grew. His fingers extended, and his nails turned brown and hard.

William looked to the others who were in the process of turning. "Yes, yes, yes!"

# Chapter Fifty-Five

Marcus—Seras

The clashing sound of swords rang through the open field, echoing in the stillness of the northern edge of Allon. Marcus and Julie sparred in the early morning light. She was able to match him blow for blow.

"Make sure you use both," Marcus said, stopping to give her advice. "When I become a demon, I don't use one strength over the other. I use both. You have to do that, too. Don't just rely on one at a time."

Julie took a breath. "Okay."

The two started again. This time, Julie flicked her wrist and used her free hand to send waves of energy in his direction as she parried against him.

He dodged, jumped, and blocked to keep her at bay, but Marcus could see the subtle hesitation in her eyes, the way she seemed to pull back ever so slightly, as if unsure of something more than just the fight. "Better, better, but you're still holding back."

When they stepped into the tree line, the shade was a welcome relief. Julie dropped her sword to her side.

Marcus paused. "I'm sorry, Julie. I just want to help you."

"That's not it," she started, then stopped. She took a few deep breaths. Her chest rose and fell as she seemed to be gathering her thoughts. "I don't want you to think I'm too young for this," she said, her voice low and reserved.

He took a step closer, unsure of how to proceed. "Too young?" He cleared his throat. Her brown eyes sparkled like honey in the sunlight. "Julie, what do you mean?"

Julie looked away to the trees above as if searching for a way to say what was on her mind. "I mean...I know I'm still figuring myself out. And believe me, I'm not *done* yet. I've learned so much since I came to Seras. I've had to grow up fast. Too fast, sometimes, and I know in many different ways, I'm not *finished* yet. But I'm sure of one thing. You and me."

"Hey," he spoke softly, but was cut off.

"Do you still think I'm too young?" she asked again. "Too young for this...for us?"

"Julie," he started, "no, I don't see you like that. Not in the way you're worried about."

"Listen, I know I used to be your student, and I know I used to joke about you being a hundred years old, but that's..." She paused. "Just me being silly. I really didn't want you to stop. I never want you to stop." She took a breath. "I do worry, though. What if I'm not enough for you?"

The doubt in her eyes broke Marcus. He closed the distance between them, reaching out and gently taking her by the shoulders. "You've already given me everything I could ask for," Marcus said. "You don't have to be *finished* for me to see you. For me to see *us*."

Julie looked up at him. "Are you sure?"

"Of course, I am. I'm not expecting you to be perfect. I'm not expecting anything but you. And that's enough. Always has been."

She hugged him tightly, burying her face into his chest. "You really mean that, don't you?" she asked.

"More than anything," Marcus replied. He took her face in his hands. "And I'm not going anywhere. We'll figure all this out together. I'm not in a hurry." He kissed her.

## Chapter Fifty-Six

Javan—Seras

It took Javan and his crew several days to reach their destination. The ship's navigator put them in a narrow river where he calculated the large lights in the sky appeared. From his spyglass, Javan watched a scout return to the small rowboat on the shoreline.

Once aboard the ship, the man took a large drink from a pouch handed to him by another shipmate.

"What happened to the other two men I sent with you?" Javan asked.

"I left them there to learn more while I reported back to you, my Lord," the man answered.

"Excellent." He had the scout follow him to his cabin along with Ranu. He sat down and sliced off a piece of bread. Then waved the knife around. "Tell me what you learned," Javan commanded.

About three miles in, there was a fortress. Trees concealed it, but it was easy to see from the inclines on what would be the northern side, the scout said.

"Men? Positions? weapons?" Javan asked in rapid fire.

"It was difficult to get a count, but it is well-manned. The large weapons are on the eastern side of the fortress. They have turrets and posts on the east and west wings but nothing on the north that I saw."

"They have been arrogant about the north, Ranu," the pilot from south of Eranada said.

"Their arrogance is our good fortune." Javan smiled. "Have them men unload the ships. We will set up camp here and invade at first light."

"And what if they have scouts who spot us before that?" Ranu asked.

"Yes, yes, set up perimeter guards and posts. Ranu, take command and wake me when it is time."

"Yes, my Lord."

"My Lord?" The scout looked at the bread. His sunken jawline and pale skin gave his face the resemblance of a skull.

Javan looked at the bread and smirked. "Of course." He stabbed the remainder of the loaf with his knife and tossed it to the man, who grabbed it with both hands and began devouring it. "Not in here." He stood and kicked at the scout.

"I am sorry, my Lord!" He ran out of the room.

~ * ~

At first light, Javan got dressed in his blood-red outfit and pulled his long, thick black hair into a tight ponytail. He covered his weather-worn face with paint that matched the color of his jacket, then wiped the rest through his beard. He looked monstrous. It was the face his enemies saw before they fell.

Words could not express his joy in finally finding the fortress his queen, Queen Pallanex, had charged him with finding. The crew was beginning to doubt him. They were running low on food, and there were no other trading posts this far north. Luckily, the cold weather had broken, and the warmth of the sun thawed the land as well as his men's moods. Javan knew he had to take advantage of this time, as waiting too much longer would make the heat just as dangerous as the cold. As he placed his sword in its sheath, he let his thoughts drift slightly to the fight inside the fight. He had heard the stories and rumors of Marcus, the former Skorei leader. Javan looked forward to seeing for himself if the tales were true. Could he beat the great demon?

Javan led his men the three miles through the cover of darkness and thick wooded overgrowth to the hidden fortress of Allon. It was obvious to the captain that his opponents were not worried about invaders coming from the north. *Had they wiped them all out? Were there any people north of this position?* Either way, it made preparation for the invasion easy. While the terrain posed some challenges with its slopes, soft ground, and dense tree lines, there was nothing to suggest they expected visitors this far north of their location.

"It is as we thought, my Lord," his trusted pilot, Ranu said. "They are fat and lazy. There are no reinforcements for the wall."

"How close can we get? Without the use of large ballateers, we need to get within range of the long archers."

"We should be in range once we hit the clearing," Ranu answered. "We should have them pause and get set up at the flanks, so they are not warned of our presence."

"Good. Send two units to the east and two more to the west. The bulk should come from the middle."

"We should avoid the eastern wall. That is where they are most protected. That is where their long-range projectiles are kept."

"That is exactly why we should have men there. If we destroy their strongest area, they will fall much like the people of Vateros."

"Yes, my Lord." Ranu turned to give the orders to the awaiting men. "My Lord, this is where I must leave you."

"Ranu, you are a brilliant strategist. I need you here."

"My Lord, forgive me. Ranu is no fighter. I would only get in your way."

"You damned Eranadans," Javan cursed. "If you were not the best pilot in all of Seras..." He waved his hand in dismissal. "Go, protect the ships."

"Thank you, Lord Javan." He kissed his captain's hand.

Javan waited until his men were in place then commanded his army to rush toward the fortress.

The barrage of projectiles from the long archers caught Allon by surprise. Before they could fire upon the rushing enemy, the overwhelmed sentries fell from arrows. Jarvan ordered the second charge with a wave of his hand and rushed across the field with the rest of his men.

## Chapter Fifty-Seven

Marcus—Seras

As the light of day broke through the curtain of the cabin, the sound of an alarm bell woke Marcus. His first instinct was to reach over and check for Julie. He felt her body move next to him.

"What's happening?"

"I don't know." He quickly got up, threw on his shirt, and opened the door.

The sound of hooves from dozens of horses filled the dusty streets as soldiers made their way to the northern wall.

"They have breached the outer wall," one of the horsemen shouted above the commotion.

Marcus mounted his horse as Julie emerged from the cabin. "Go back inside. Go back to Earth!"

"No," she yelled. "I am going with you!" She hopped on the back of his horse.

Marcus had no choice but to spur his horse toward the attack. A spray of arrows filled the sky. "Cover!" Marcus guided his horse under a roofed building as the ground was littered with arrows. He snapped the reins, and the horse moved closer to the wall. Debris and burning beams left the area clouded with thick, black smoke.

Allon's warriors were rushing up the ramps to the parapets to give aid against their attackers. They countered against grappling hooks and ladders that were flung against the inner fortress wall. Some of the men held firm against the gate as it swayed under the thrusts from the other side. They blocked the giant doors with large beams, boulders, and their bodies.

Marcus moved the spearmen into rows on the ground level as Jakob and Julius directed the men and women along the upper rampart. They threw rocks, spears, and scalding water on the men trying to climb the walls. Otta, Freya, and Darius joined him and Julie.

"Open the gate," Marcus commanded as Griffus and Argos rode up in front of fifty horsemen.

Two soldiers removed the beams holding the gate against the brutal push from the other side, as two other soldiers slashed the ropes with their swords. The giant stones fell as the pulley system caused the secondary gate to fly up.

A horde rushed through the gate. Many of them collapsed at the suddenness of the opening. It made the first wave easy targets.

Allon's archers shot rounds into the attackers as they poured through the gate.

"Now!" Marcus yelled, and the men rushed forward. They used the chaos and cluster of the gate to funnel the onslaught of men toward the waiting swords of Marcus, Julie, and the others.

The two armies clashed. Sword and axe met with a terrible collision. The men continued to pour into the courtyard. The walls crumbled under the barrage. Chunks of wood and brick lay broken on the ground as the continuous barrage widened the gate's opening.

Marcus kept one eye on Julie as he delivered a fatal blow to one of the invaders. He watched Julie use her left hand to send blasts into the wave of men, knocking several to the ground and wielding her sword in her right hand. She engaged in combat and fought with two men.

Marcus recognized the mist that began to cover the ruined courtyard. Freya. He heard the clashing of swords. Julie was somewhere in the fog. Men grunted or gasped as their lives were taken. Blood covered the dirt streets.

Otta spun low, parrying a downward stroke from a man's longsword. She used her free hand to pull a knife from her waist belt and plunged it into his thigh. In the brief moment of pain, Otta used it to finish him with her sword into his chest.

Griffus's battle axe cleaved bone as he struck down two men with a mighty swing. The sound of shattered bodies echoed off the crumbling walls.

"Behind you," a shout rang out. It was Seren. She had warned Argos just as a man jabbed at him with a spear. She sent a well-aimed arrow into the man's neck. He fell to the ground as blood sprayed with every pulse of his heart.

Otta, dressed in black leather, faced off against one of the mercenaries. The man swung wide, Otta repaid the mistake by slashing him across the thigh. He stumbled with a deep cry as she drove him into the ground with a flurry of strikes with her two small blades.

Jakob twisted away from an attacker cloaked in crimson. The man lunged at Jakob with an oversized saber. Jakob barely escaped the blow. He hit the ground and rolled from another strike. He blocked the man's blade, but the impact reverberated against his sword.

Blood stained the fallen stones of the fortress wall, and smoke filled the courtyard. Griffus brandished his double-bladed axe and moved with a limp from one attacker to another, hacking off limbs with each stroke. Behind him, his men helped the giant man back a group of the unknown assailants into a corner. Surrender or die, Griffus commanded. The biggest man of the group surged at Griffus, who separated the man at the waist. As he crumbled to the ground, the others dropped their weapons and held out their hands.

Argos made his way to the top of the wall with Seren and Julius close behind. Blood seeped from his wound. There, from the high position, they were able to deliver arrows to the men trying to make their way into Allon. Seren aimed with precision with each release of her bow. Argos launched a series of spears into the crowd. Blood continued to pour out of him. He fell behind the stone. "Cover me," he told Seren.

She nodded.

He took an arrow from the body of a man and placed it over a fire. Once the tip turned red, he pinched the wound together and blew out a breath of air as he cauterized it with the hot arrowhead.

Julius helped those who had survived the onslaught of the attack topple ladders cut grapples and send huge chunks of rock to those below. He ran to aid two men fighting off the marauders as they continued to try to breach the wall. Julius struck down one man in his path then he grabbed the remains of a wooden beam and swung it hard against a tall, still-intact portion of the wall. He repeated the motion a second and third time until it gave way and collapsed outward onto the enemy below. Their screams died out as the rock fell on top of them.

In the courtyard, Julie, Otta, Freya, Jakob, and Marcus led the warriors of Allon in battling back the intruders.

Julie caused the wind to shift. She turned to Marcus. "Let's finish this!"

Together, they surged forward.

Jakob took three men, and together, they lifted a broken pillar and used it as a battering ram to push the horde back through the open gate.

Julie and Freya combined their powers to send waves of wind and blasts into the men, knocking them off their feet and making them easy fodder for Otta and the others to finish off. Many of the would-be attackers gave up, surrendered, or began to flee.

Those who fled were quickly overwhelmed by arrows and spears.

Marcus rushed ahead, looking for the leader. He saw a man in the center of the field wearing a red uniform, trying to control the escaping men. "There you are." Marcus fought his way to the leader, who spotted Marcus and moved to meet him on the field of battle.

"You must be Marcus," the man said. He slashed an x in the air with his sword. He had a full beard, and what was left of his hair was pulled back into a ponytail. He wore a blood-red chest plate with the markings of three sharks forming a circle.

"I am, and I will be the last face you ever see." Marcus struck at the man.

"I am Lord Javan, Captain of the *Sea Tiger*, loyal servant to Queen Pallanex." The two men traded blows.

"I don't care," Marcus told him. "You are going to die right here, right now."

The captain swung his blade with impossible speed. He parried with wide arcs. It was a fighting style Marcus had never seen before.

"I have heard about the great Marcus," Javan said. He moved around, avoiding direct contact. "I consider it an honor to kill you." Javan thrust twice. The second one sliced at Marcus's side.

As Javan continued to dance away from Marcus's sword, the rest of his men had surrendered or been killed.

Marcus had had enough of the foolishness of the captain. He waited until Javan jabbed, spun out of his way, and brought his sword across the man's arm.

Javan let out a scream as his hand and sword fell to the ground. He grabbed his arm with his remaining hand and brought it to his chest. Though severely injured, Javan wasn't finished. In a blind rage, he retrieved his side blade and lifted it toward Marcus. As he did, Marcus leveled his sword and removed Javan's head.

"Marcus," Julie's voice carried across the field.

He turned to see her running in his direction.

When she reached him, she buried her head into his chest. "Thank God you're okay."

## Chapter Fifty-Eight

Julie—Seras

"You really thought that was me?" Marcus asked.

"Yes, don't make fun of me." She wiped the tears from her eyes. "That was horrible." Julie noticed the blood that came off his clothes onto hers. "You're hurt."

"I'm fine." He pulled up his shirt to reveal the gash. "It will heal."

"I don't know if I'll ever get used to this."

Griffus, Argos, and the others rode to them. Freya and Otta held the reins of two horses.

"We need to find out where they came from," Griffus said.

"They came from the North River. He said he was Javan, Captain of the *Sea Tiger*," Marcus explained. He cleaned his blade on the grass and resheathed it.

"Then that's where we will go," Argos said, his voice firm. The general turned to Otta, Seren, and his two sons, "Take the prisoners to the hall and make them tell you everything they know."

"Yes sir," the four said simultaneously. They spread out and gave commands to the men and women who had moved into the battlefield to overtake their assailants.

Julie and Marcus mounted, and they rode north toward the river. After several minutes, they came to a stop and witnessed nearly fifty ships anchored silently on the water, waiting for the crew to return. "Oh wow," Julie said. "What the heck?"

"There, look," Argos pointed to a lone figure on the deck of one of the ships with a red and black striped banner on its mast.

"I hope he likes company," Marcus said. He bucked his horse forward, and the group followed him to the shore. They prepared one of the rowboats that the crew had left for their return, which would never happen.

Marcus, Argos, Griffus, and Freya took the oars as they rowed toward the massive ship. Julie noticed the figure of a woman on the front bow. The well-endowed body had the head of a tiger and a shark's tail. "That's one ugly mermaid," she said. Her comment drew a wry smile from Marcus.

They boarded the ship with weapons drawn. There, waiting for them near the helm, was a skinny bald man. He was unarmed and sitting in a chair with a pad of paper and charcoal. His fingers were dark from his sketching.

"Don't move a muscle," Argos ordered, nearly fully recovered to his former self.

"Ranu has no intention to move," he answered as he gestured to put his drawing material down. "May I?"

Argos drew back his bow. "Slowly."

"As you command."

"Who are you?" Freya asked.

"I told you, I am Ranu, son of Banran, child of the island of Eranada, pilot of the *Sea Tiger*," he answered. "I am a man of peace."

"Peace?" Freya yelled. "Peace? Why are you here, who sent you, and why did you attack us?" Freya continued her line of questioning. Spit flew from her mouth.

"All good questions. The answer is one and the same: we serve Queen Pallanex," Ranu told them.

"I say we kill him," Argos growled.

"No." Julie moved between Argos and his bow and the strange man. "I think he could help us."

"Help us, how?" Marcus asked.

"Will you come with me?" Julie asked the man.

"You are the one they call the Heart?"

"I am," Julie answered.

"You are the one the Queen wanted destroyed. You and the one called Marcus."

Julie looked at Marcus then back to the man named Ranu. "We are."

"Ranu was told evil lurks in you and runs through your veins, and you deserved to die."

"Well, maybe to her, we are evil, but if you want to judge for yourself, please come with us."

Ranu looked at her in curiosity. "I will agree to go with you."

"Good. Thank you," she said before turning to Marcus and the others. "I'll show you."

They helped the man named Ranu onto the little boat and took him into Allon. Men and women were in the beginning stages of the inevitable task of removing bodies and cleaning the destruction of the battle.

"Do you see the peace following what Pallanex caused?" Freya spat out in anger.

"My apologies," Ranu said as he rode on the horse Julie had given him.

She rode behind Marcus, holding tight against his chest, breathing him in. Even in the heat of battle, she found comfort in his scent.

"It appears you speak bitter truth. The Queen gave false noise to the captain. He, in turn, gave it to Ranu with absent direction."

"And good men and women died because of it," Freya finished.

The party stopped in front of the hall. Eight guards greeted them as they dismounted. Otta, Jakob, Julius, and Seren were inside with the prisoners.

"What have they said?" Griffus asked.

"Not much," Seren answered. "They are slaves. All they said was they were told to attack us, so they attacked us."

Griffus looked at Julie and Marcus for direction.

Julie, in turn, looked at the man named Ranu. "Will you help me?"

"How does Ranu help?"

Julie bent down to one of the men sitting on the floor and looked at Ranu. "Convince them we are not bad and that they should help us defeat Pallanex."

The man snarled. "You tie my hands. Now you want to use them!"

Julie stood.

"Seize your tongue," Ranu responded in a calm but commanding manner. "We have been deceived. It is not the Heart who is evil but Lord Javan and the Queen whose treachery led us astray."

"How can you be sure?" the man seethed.

Ranu looked at Julie. "She showed kindness when none was needed, and unlike those who commanded without asking."

"I will follow Ranu," the man said.

Julie smiled at Ranu. "Thank you." She turned to Argos and Griffus. "Can we get them some food and water?"

"Of course," Griffus answered.

"What are we going to do with them?" Argos asked.

"I don't know exactly, but it's better to treat them well, and maybe they can offer us some kind of assistance."

"As you wish," Argos said.

Julie nodded then started to walk out of the room; she brushed Marcus's hand. "Now, let's get you cleaned up."

## Chapter Fifty-Nine

Julie—Seras

After her visit with the prisoners, Julie and Marcus returned to his cabin. She had an idea but was distracted watching as Marcus struggled to remove his shirt, the brown all but gone from the bloodstains. "It hasn't healed, yet," she said, not a question but a concern.

"It will."

Inside the dimly lit room, Marcus winced. Deep blotches of purple and blue camouflaged his back.

"Does that hurt?"

"Just a little. You know it'll get better."

She stood behind him and touched the bruises with her fingers.

Marcus turned to her. "Julie..."

She could tell by the look in his eyes he was going to say something she didn't want to hear. Julie shook her head and placed a hand on his chest. "No. Stop. Whatever it is, whatever the reason, excuse, logic...we're here now. Together. And everything's the way it's supposed to be, for once. Haven't we waited long enough?"

He paused before saying, "Not here. Let's go back to your place. Get cleaned up and talk alone."

~ * ~

A little while later, Julie came down the stairs with a towel wrapped around her head, damp strands of hair falling across her cheeks. She wore a pink football jersey with a faded number eighty-two across the front and back, the hem of her jersey brushed mid-thigh over a pair of black shorts.

Marcus waited patiently on the couch. It looked like he had washed his face and arms in the kitchen sink while she was upstairs taking a shower and deciding what to wear.

"Where's Shakespeare?" Julie just assumed his cat would be all over him.

"I let him outside."

"Cool." Barefoot, she folded herself beside him on the couch, legs tucked beneath her, leaning into his shoulder.

He put his arm around her. "You smell good."

"Thanks."

"Julie..."

"No." She placed a finger on his mouth. "I told you before. We have waited long enough. This is the way it's supposed to be. We deserve to be happy." Julie pulled away slightly and drew her knees up to her chest, wrapping her arms around them. Her head rested atop her knees, hair fell around her cheeks and neck. "Let me ask you something. On a scale of one to ten," she asked before he could respond, "how bad did you want to kiss me the night you told me you loved me?"

Marcus grinned. His face flushed. "On a scale of one to ten?"

"Yep." She lifted her head with a smile.

"One hundred."

She laughed softly, then looked away. "Why didn't you...?" She stopped herself. "Never mind. Silly question." She curled tighter. "You should kiss me," she said, her voice barely above a whisper.

"I want you to be sure."

She climbed on his lap and straddled him. "Shut up." Julie kissed him. Passion grew as her fingers worked the buttons of his shirt, sliding it from his shoulders. His lips found the curve of her neck. A soft, high-pitched sound escaped her. Julie's body tingled as he traced the subtle curve of her lower back. She melted into him as his mouth found its way to her neck. Julie couldn't take much more. She reached her arms up and looped around his neck, drawing him closer. "Please," she whispered.

His hands made their way to her bra strap. She did not stop him. He released the tiny metal clasps, and her bra fell into their laps.

Julie arched to allow him to explore her more with his mouth.

Marcus helped her remove her top. Her breath shallowed as he nibbled and kissed her chest and belly.

Julie tugged at his shirt and begged him to take it off. She traced the muscular landscape of his chest and back with her fingers. “How are you such a great kisser?” she breathed out.

Marcus smiled. “Stop.” He moved her around so his legs reached the floor and stood, cradling Julie in his arms; again, she did not stop him.

She wrapped her legs around his waist.

“It’s getting harder and harder to stop.”

Julie pulled back just enough to give him a sly smile. “I’ve noticed.” She winked and giggled as he carried her upstairs to her room. “I know. I’m a little devil.” She laughed. “I couldn’t resist.”

They lay next to each other, barely taking time to breathe.

The moon outside her window was full, and the night was not long enough for either of the two lovers.

# Chapter Sixty

Marcus—Earth

Marcus adjusted his position and brushed a strand of hair behind her ear. The low hum of Julie's ceiling fan cooled the room. Watching her lie in bed with her head resting on her folded arms, everything seemed right. He ran his fingers across her naked back. *So, why did he feel this way?*

"Do you ever think about the way it used to be?" she asked.

"What do you mean?"

"I mean, before you had to leave Earth, being here, your apartment, being just a normal guy?"

"I don't know. Hmm, maybe a little." He thought about it a second more. "I miss your mom's cooking."

"Yeah, I miss those days, too. I used to steal looks at you when you came over for dinner. I can't pretend I didn't notice you looking at me as much as I was looking at you."

Marcus chuckled. "That was different. I was trying to figure out why it was you."

"Are you happy that it was me?" Julie rolled on to her back.

"I don't know."

"Hey!"

He could feel his heart racing, his mouth dry, and all he could think about was touching her, but he hesitated.

"What?" Her soft eyes lit up her face.

He opened his mouth and shut it again, not knowing how to respond. "Um, can I ask you something?"

"Of course."

"Are you okay? I mean, really okay with this?" He used his head and eyes to point to them in bed.

She slowly inched her way closer to him, like a caterpillar. The scent of lavender lingered in her hair. “I am. It hurt a little.” She cocked her head with a slight smile.

“I’m so sorry.”

Julie swatted at him playfully. “Don’t be silly, I’m more than okay. Are you okay? Did you not want to?”

He smirked. “I shouldn’t have been your first.”

She sat up. “Why?” Julie stared at him with those beautiful brown eyes.

Marcus joined her in sitting up. “How many reasons do you want?”

“Stop,” Julie begged. “A person’s first should be someone who she loves dearly, and she knows loves her more than life itself. And I know that you, above anyone I have ever known or anyone I will ever know, love me. You would die for me.”

“I would.”

“I know, and that is why you alone are the most worthy of my gift.” She quickly rolled on top of him.

“Thank you.”

“Now,” she cooed with renewed energy, “are you ready for a second round?” She giggled in delight.

## Chapter Sixty-One

Julie—Seras

The men and women of Allon boarded the freshly built docks on the river, north of their fortress.

Julie stood with Marcus, Griffus, Argos, and Freya around a table at the edge of the bank. They looked over a map unfurled and pinned down by four stones. She traced the route the ships were to take to Cauleta.

At first, her plan was viewed as too risky, but it was eventually deemed necessary. "We use their ships," she had said to them, a month after the attack from Javan and his men. "They were sent here to destroy us. So, we take them back to her and end this once and for all."

She convinced Ranu, Javan's once loyal navigator, to teach the soldiers of Allon to sail with the help of the captain's slaves. "Can we trust them?" she had asked.

"Those who were forced to serve, yes," Ranu answered. "The others? No, they remain loyal to the queen."

That was good enough for Julie. Griffith, Argos, and Jakob divided their forces, dedicating a third to mastering the ships. Men and women who had never seen a rudder were taught to read the wind, to patch torn sails, and to steer through the narrow river bends out into the open sea.

Over the months of training, every person in Allon was required to take the trip out to learn how to adjust to the new form of transportation. They vomited over the rails, slept in makeshift hammocks, and fought the unforgiving churn of waves. Little by little, they grew to accept the challenge and embrace the mighty ships and life on the water.

As the sun rose over the mountains of the north, the last of the supplies was loaded. It was time to go.

Julie felt a hand on her arm. It was Marcus.

"This is going to take time," he said. "Maybe you should return to Earth."

"What? Why?"

"You have things to do there. You don't need to travel with us."

"You don't want me with you?"

"I always want you with me," he said. "And this was a great idea. Pallanex will never see it coming. But there's nothing more you can do right now."

Julie wrinkled her face and blew out a breath of hot air. "Fine. But can you at least set up a place for me in case I want to pop in?"

He nodded. "Of course."

"Take me there now," she said, grabbing his hand.

"Okay, but why?"

"It's important that I see where I'm going." She practically dragged him up the ramp and onto the ship's deck.

Marcus laughed trying to keep up. "Come with me." He escorted her to the back of the ship where Captain Javan's cabin was located. "Here you go. I cleaned it up a little and took out any unnecessary stuff. I burned his bed and put in one of my own."

Julie took it all in. "Good." She looked around, memorizing the space. "So, how long should I wait?"

"Wait for what?"

"I'll come visit." She winked.

Marcus's eyes grew large.

"I know." She gave her best evil smile.

Marcus gave a half laugh, half sigh. "You're going to be the death of me."

"Stop," she squealed.

"Your little friend, Ranu, gave us the log. It took them a few months. But they also spent time traveling through every river head from here to there. So, it might be a lot sooner than that." He stopped.

"What?" Julie's breath caught in her throat. "Say what you're going to. Just say it."

He turned serious. "This isn't a pleasure cruise. We are going to war."

“I know.”

“Are you sure you’re ready for this?”

“I am. I’m ready for all this to be over. We’ve put it off long enough,” she answered. “Are you?”

“I am. I just worry about you.”

Julie hugged him. “I don’t know what this means to you, but I know what it means to me. And I will not spend another day pretending like I don’t feel it. That’s why it has to end now.”

# Chapter Sixty-Two

Julie—Earth

The late afternoon sun streamed through the smudged windows of Julie's dorm room. Her roommate, Brooklyn, was down the hall taking a shower while Julie sat on one of the twin beds half reading excerpts from *The Odyssey*, half thinking about her and Marcus. *I didn't see it coming, but wow. Stop smiling,* she said to herself. The thought of him and the brave men and women of Allon sailing toward Cauleta dampened her mood for a second.

Her phone buzzed. She picked it up and answered.

Claire's face appeared. "Hey, stranger!"

"Hey! What are you doing?"

"Just finished with practice and had about an hour before team dinner. How 'bout you?"

"Just reading, trying to catch up on stuff," Julie said with a sing-song tone.

"Wow! Someone's in a good mood. What's up?"

Julie flopped back onto her pillow. "Nothing."

"Bull larky!" Claire narrowed her eyes. "Okay, spill. What's going on with you?"

"Nothing," Julie repeated with a giggle.

"Wait a sec...that guy you mentioned...are you in love?"

Julie fluttered her legs against the bed. "Maybe."

Before Claire could ask another question, the door opened, and Brooklyn walked in wearing nothing but a towel around her waist and another towel around her head.

"Oh!" Brooklyn said, her eyes going directly to the phone.

Julie waved her in. "It's fine! It's Claire. Claire, this is Brooklyn.

Brooklyn, this is Claire."

Brooklyn let out a large sigh of relief.

"Finally! I've heard *way* too much about you not to know your face."

Brooklyn laughed and sat on the edge of Julie's bed. "Same! I was hoping you weren't her mystery man..."

"Ha! I knew it," Claire yelled.

Brooklyn smirked. "Did she tell you anything about him?"

"Only that he exists. Not so much on the details, though."

"Nothing but secrets here, too," Brooklyn said, getting up to put on clothes.

Julie groaned and hid her face behind a pillow. "You two are the worst."

"Yeah, yeah," Brooklyn said as if she was loving every minute. "We're the best."

"Come on, Jules. Who is he? Does he go there?"

"I'm going to go with *no* on that one," Brooklyn said as she pulled on a pair of jeans and a black top. "She's almost never here."

"What?" Claire shrieked with an excited laugh.

Julie peeked out from behind the pillow. "Stop! You're not getting anything else, okay? Let's just say... he surprises me. In a good way and it came out of nowhere."

Brooklyn rolled her eyes. "That's *nothing*. Come on, even a first letter?"

"Nope."

Claire sighed. "Fine. Keep your secrets. Just know, I'm happy for you. And if he hurts you, I'll hunt him down like a dog."

"Same," Brooklyn added.

"Thanks, guys. I promise you both will be the first to know."

Brooklyn stood and grabbed her coat off the back of the chair. "Alright, I'm heading to a party. Wanna come?"

"I'm good. Thanks."

Brooklyn laughed on her way out.

"So...now you can tell me everything," Claire said.

"I can't", Julie said with a whine. "It's too soon."

"Okay," Claire relented. "But I want to be the first to know. Not her."

Julie laughed.

"Changing subjects, let's do something fun next time I'm home."

Julie nodded. "Absolutely. Let's plan something. Road trip, lake house, something. I need a distraction."

Claire smiled. "Deal. I miss you."

"Miss you more."

"Hey," Claire said just before Julie ended the call, "I'm glad you finally found someone, and he makes you happy."

"Thank you." Julie blew her best friend a kiss and hung up. She looked around the room. "I think I'm going to go pay him a little visit," she said aloud with a smile.

## Chapter Sixty-Three

William—Seras

The doors to William's quarters flung open as Queen Pallanex stormed into his chambers. The torches lighting the room flickered, casting shadows that danced on the stone walls. "What do you have for me?" she demanded.

William did nothing but smile. "I think you will be pleased."

"I hope so," Pallanex said. "I fear the worst for my dear Captain Javan. I am sure he is dead."

He chuckled. "I could have told you that fool was no match for Marcus. You should have waited for me. This could have been over by now."

Pallanex raged. "Give me your news."

William waved her to follow him. "Come with me. I want you to see it for yourself." He led the queen down a narrow corridor. The sounds of growling and clanking metal grew louder until they entered the practice arena. The place where William and other boys his age, including Marcus, had trained.

In the center of the dirt-floored arena stood ten prisoners. Guards manned the four entrances of the arena from above the iron gates.

"Are you ready?" William asked his queen with a bow of his head.

"I am."

William raised a hand.

The guards gave the orders to open the gates from somewhere below the stadium. As they did, twenty beasts charged in. Their howls and shrieks rang through the arena. They were half-men, half-animal, like hairless dogs with protruding jaws, sharp teeth, and razor claws. Their muscles rippled in the hot sun. Some raced on all fours like dogs, others walked upright and slightly hunched.

The prisoners didn't stand a chance. Within seconds, screams filled the air. Blood sprayed across the dirt and sand as the men were torn from limb to limb.

After the last man fell, and the beasts fed off of their carcasses, Pallanex stood silent for a moment before saying, "I am impressed."

"I knew you would be." William laughed. He clapped his hands like a proud father. "I told you this would work."

"How many more do you have?" she asked.

"This is half," he said. "I could create more if you gave me more men."

"And you can control them?"

William shouted into the arena. "Return!"

The beasts jerked their heads to their leader.

"Return!"

They stopped their feeding and hurried back through the gate.

"You will receive more slaves," Pallanex said.

"No," William answered. "Slaves are too weak from lack of food and health. I need soldiers. I need warriors."

"I am afraid we may not have that kind of time."

"I know what I am doing. Let me prove it to you, My Queen."

She stepped toward him, shifting her tone. "You will get what you need, but I also have another task for you."

William smiled. "Yes, My Queen."

"I need you to train my soldiers. They must be able to defeat Marcus."

William hesitated. "No mortal man will ever defeat Marcus in single combat. Not one-on-one."

"They cannot know that," Pallanex said. "You must convince them they can."

"I will do what I can."

"Very good." Pallanex placed a hand on his cheek. Her metal ring shaped like a claw drew blood. She smiled as she placed it on her tongue.

"When should I begin?" William asked, not moving to clean the cut, knowing it would heal in a matter of seconds.

“Right away,” she said. “Well, maybe not right away.” She turned away, her black cloak swept by him. “Come.”

“Marcus is mine,” he whispered before following Pallanex back to his chamber.

## Chapter Sixty-Four

Julie—Seras

The commanders of Allon gathered on their horses as the army spread out across the field just a mile from Cauleta's gates. Blue and gray clouds swirled with the feeling of impending rain. The imposing fortress, with its tall towers of rock and iron, stood before them. A cloudy fog encircled one of the back spires.

"That is where you will find Pallanex," Jayna told Marcus and Julie from their positions on horseback.

Griffus rode up to the small group of commanders. "My men are set. Just give the word."

"Thank you, Griffus," Marcus said. "Just like we planned."

"So, this is the famous Cauleta," Argos said.

"It is." Marcus stroked the stubble on his face as though he was recollecting brief moments from his childhood. "Good riddance."

"What?" Argos asked.

"Nothing. I was just remembering the last time I saw this place."

Close by, Freya brought the navigator, Ranu, into the conversation. "Have you talked to your people?"

He nodded. "It is as you wish."

"And what have you decided?" she asked.

"I cannot die in another man's land," Ranu said.

Freya looked to Marcus and the others. "If we are successful, I will give you and your people freedom."

Julie's head snapped toward Marcus.

He held up a hand to keep her from shouting.

"My enemies have won," the pilot answered.

"What does that mean?" Freya responded.

"We will serve you faithfully." Ranu left to instruct his people.

"They were going to get their freedom anyway," Julie protested.

"We need all of the help we can get," Freya answered.

Julie seethed but had a more pressing problem on her mind. She moved her horse closer to Marcus. "Can we talk?"

Marcus looked at her, then to the army gathering in the opposite direction, and back to Julie. "Okay, but it has to be quick."

They moved away from the group.

"This is a bad idea," she said.

"Julie, we've talked about this. It's the only way."

"No, I've changed my mind. I've been here before. I know how this ends, and it doesn't end well for us." She dismounted and walked further away from the army.

Marcus climbed off the back of his brown charger and followed her. "Julie, you know I don't want you here. It's my job to protect you, but Pallanex will not stop until she kills you. I can't let that happen, so I have to kill her first."

"But what if you don't?" Julie began to cry. "What if you die and she kills me?"

"I'm not going to let that happen," Marcus said, trying to comfort her. "Do you know how many have died in order for you to come here?"

"Is that supposed to make me feel better?"

"No! It's supposed to make you feel like you owe them something."

"I can't owe them! I didn't even know half of them!"

"I did! And you are letting their sacrifice die with them in vain."

"Stop, just stop, and listen to me, please," Julie begged. "I never told you what I saw when I was with Azahleah. I have been here before," she repeated it slower for effect.

He took her by the shoulders. "What did you see?"

Julie took a breath. "We all died. We all died. We all died!" She started pounding his chest.

"Julie, I am not going to let anything happen to you. But this has to end. Right here, right now."

"Please, Marcus, I'm begging you not to do this."

"Why did you wait until now?"

"It didn't hit me until I saw the fortress. I thought it was just a nightmare Azahleah made me watch. But I've seen all of this. William kills you."

"Stop. Just stop." He gently rotated her toward the army.

Julie focused on a warrior praying with his eyes closed.

"These people have come here to fight for what they know is right. They know why they are fighting. They believe in you. I believe in you. Many of them will die today. They have to know that you are with them." He turned her back to face him. "Nobody wants to die. Nobody wants to be in battle. But this waiting on the edge has to come to an end." He brought her close to him. "I love you. I believe in you. I will die for you if I have to." He kissed her then went back to his horse and rejoined the commanders. "In the heat of battle you have to know what you're fighting for, and I do."

Julie followed behind.

"Are we ready?" Marcus asked.

Argos nodded.

Jayna, Julius, Jakob, Seren, and Otta nodded in agreement.

"Griffus and Freya are in place?" Marcus asked.

Each nodded again.

Marcus looked at her. "Welcome to Operation No Chance in Hell," he mumbled under his breath.

It made Julie chuckle. "I hate you."

"I know." He smiled then spurred his horse. "Let's go!" They marched slowly toward the front gate.

As they got closer, the Queen's army began stamping their spears on the ground in unison.

Marcus held his sword out in front of him. "Forward!"

As the front line closed the gap, a windstorm cropped up, cloaking the advancing army in dust and distracting their enemy. It was followed by large ballistic fireballs and spears flying overhead. Men screamed as they burned and died. The attack continued as archers from both Tanda and the Evandell and the Hawkmirs led by Lord Atrow and Lord Avery filled the sky with arrows.

Both sides volleyed back and forth.

"Swords and spears," Marcus ordered. "Advance!" He urged the riders as Pallanex's army moved toward them. Alongside Pallanex's men were creatures that looked similar to the last time he saw Thomen. What the hell?

The creatures outran Pallanex's men and rushed into Marcus's army. They were an amalgamation of Skorei demons at their lowest form, almost dog-like in their appearance. Allon's warriors were no match for them.

Marcus was pulled down from his horse as the beasts ripped and bit at it and him, forcing Marcus to turn into his demon self. He thrust his spear into one of the creatures and drove it back with such force it jammed into two more. He swung his sword and took the head off of a fourth one.

"For Allon!" He heard the rallying cry. "For the Heart!"

The young warrior Julie watched get killed in her experience with Azahleah started running into the fray. Julie followed him and threw him to the side before he could get stabbed. She dispatched two with a wave of her hand and thrust her sword into another. The boy gathered himself, thanked Julie, and reentered the fighting.

Jayna the Tarrack flew into the fight, changed into a bear, and ripped men to shreds. She moved quickly from hawk to bear to cougar to avoid being struck.

Julius and Otta rode through the enemy. Their swords left a swath through the horde.

Jakob and his foot soldiers clashed violently with Pallanex's men.

Griffus rode up after his ballateers stopped their assault. He used his ax to remove limbs, heads, and lives with each swing.

One of the demons took the legs out from under him. He stabbed a Skorei demon in the neck with a small blade.

"Marcus," Julie yelled to him as he was fighting off three of Pallanex's soldiers. She pointed toward an archer aiming at Griffus.

Marcus threw his sword at the archer, and the man fell over dead.

Griffus got up and continued to fight with his giant ax. Marcus joined him, and the two fought off several advances against them. The bodies piled up, and blood soaked the ground around the warriors of Allon, the soldiers of Pallanex, and the beasts of William.

Julie tried to recall her nightmare from the Abyss. Just as she remembered, Argos was shooting arrows from a high position. But she was too far away. She ran as fast as she could to the commander, sending men and beasts flying with each flick of her wrists.

"Seren," Argos yelled. He ran to help the Hemoor girl, who was fighting off two soldiers. He put himself between her and three of William's creations. The two fought off the men and the monsters bravely.

He launched himself, taking an arrow for Seren. Argos cut it down with his sword as more men rushed toward him. He killed three more men with his sword and a spear.

Seren killed a beast with her sword, but it stuck in the creature. She pulled out two short blades.

As Argos defended himself against more soldiers, he was stabbed in the stomach.

"No, no, no, no," Julie said as she tried to get to them. She shot energy blasts toward them, knocking five of them away from the pair. It wasn't enough.

Argos stumbled back. Another soldier put a sword in Argos's back.

Seren screamed before slicing the man in his neck and chest.

Argos fell.

Seren helped Argos up, but neither of them was able to fend off the onslaught of advancing soldiers. Severely wounded, the two warriors battled until their last breaths.

Julie sent more blasts at the men. They were sent twenty feet in the air. But she was too late. Argos and Seren lay dead. "No!" Julie screamed at the top of her lungs. It was as if a bomb exploded around her. Everything crumbled around them. Men, women, and demons flew back a hundred yards in every direction.

As they regained their position, the brothers, Julius and Jakob, went to their father's body. Otta joined them to grieve the death of Argos and her Hemoor sister, Seren. Over a dozen of Pallanex's soldiers and William's monsters lay dead around the two warriors.

Darius and Freya went to Julie.

"We need to go now," Freya said. "We might not get another opportunity."

Darius called out to Jayna. "Make us a path to the gate."

Jayna flew headlong toward Cauleta's large iron gate. As the soldiers in Pallanex's army climbed to their feet, they were knocked back down by Jayna in bear form.

As Julie went with Darius and Freya, she saw Marcus fighting his way to her. William met them along with a dozen soldiers. Darius turned into his demon form, as did William.

William ordered his men to attack Darius first.

"You are a coward," Darius yelled, fighting off the men.

"But I am alive," William said as he made his way toward Freya.

Julie stepped in his path. "Not this time."

William gave her a puzzled look.

She grabbed Freya and pulled her away to safety.

Before William could go after them, Darius faced off against him.

Julie took Freya to the gate. "We need to get this open!" The two combined their powers and began blasting the iron gate with white-hot light.

"I thought you were dead," William hissed. He swung his sword playfully at his side. "But, no, you abandoned me for Marcus."

"You lied to me. You were with her the entire time. You helped her destroy my family. You helped her kill my mother and father. You abandoned us," Darius growled.

The two demon-warriors squared off. They parried and blocked, and metal clanged as they circled each other. Darius was able to block four of William's strikes, then thrust his sword toward William's midsection, missing his target only to cut his arm.

William struck a gash on Darius's leg.

Darius clawed William with his free hand, dropping William to a knee. Darius moved in for the kill.

William pulled a small knife from his belt and wounded Darius as he tried to finish him.

Darius's left shoulder hung limp. Blood poured from the cut. He fell to his knees.

William moved in for the kill. He opened his hand for his sword to return to him.

Marcus blocked the death blow. "I can't let you do that."

## Chapter Sixty-Five

Marcus—Seras

Marcus stood between Darius and William. He was covered from head to toe in blood and mud. Hatred filled his eyes as he watched his brother slowly slump to the ground.

William backed away.

He moved toward William and plowed into a soldier who tried to get in his way and cut the man down. He took William's feet out from under him, gashing William's calf.

William was able to avoid three of Marcus's strikes.

Marcus caught an arrow in the back of his shoulder. It caused him to lower his sword.

William spun behind him, hitting the arrow further into Marcus's body. The point protruded out of the front. Then he used his claw to rip across Marcus's back.

Marcus bellowed.

William directed his attention toward Julie as if to taunt her with killing Marcus.

Marcus switched his blade to his left hand. The two former friends traded blows.

William jabbed his sword into Marcus's stomach.

Marcus returned the favor. He sliced William's side and clawed his neck with a painful move with his injured right arm.

Both men were covered in blood. They slipped and fought to keep footing in the soaked ground. Marcus looked over his shoulder. Through the blur of sweat and blood, he glimpsed Julie, Freya, Griffus, Julius, Jakob, Otta, and Jayna who were busy leading the Allon warriors in completely wiping out Pallanex's and William's armies. Argos and Seren were dead.

Hundreds of others lay dead or dying. Darius, his long-lost brother, was he dead, or did Marcus arrive in time? It was a high cost, but a risk that had to be taken. The two Skorei demons continued to trade blows. They cut each other, stabbed each other. Blood covered every part of their bodies as the heat of the sun cooked overhead. Would this be enough to stop Pallanex? Would it be enough to keep Julie safe? He ran his blade across William's side.

His old friend howled then, in a desperate move, William lunged at Marcus with fierce abandon.

Marcus blocked and dodged the best he could to avoid William's sword and claws. The two embraced each other tightly. Their swords penetrated the other's midsection. Marcus headbutted William repeatedly as his vision blurred. I can't let him kill Julie. He ripped a chunk out of William's neck with his teeth.

William roared in pain as blood spurted over the two demon-warriors.

Marcus continued to pound his head into William's until they both collapsed on the ground. He rolled to his back. He was finished. If William were still alive and able to move, he would kill Marcus right there. So, he waited for death.

Instead, he heard Julie's voice. "Marcus, Marcus, wake up, wake up!" He felt her lift his head and wipe his eyes free. He still couldn't see her through the light of the sun. "You can't die," she cried.

"Julie, we have to go. This isn't over," he heard Freya's voice.

"Julie," Marcus whispered. "I've done my job. Go do yours."

"No, no, no, no!"

"Come, Julie. We have to do this."

Julie let go of his head as Freya dragged her away. Marcus closed his eyes as darkness overtook him.

## Chapter Sixty-Six

Julie—Seras

Freya took Julie's hands and aimed them with hers toward the large wooden gate. Their combined power left the doors splintered in pieces. Freya dropped to her knees.

"Are you okay?"

Freya took her hand. "Go."

Julie saw Pallanex high above the melee from behind the walls of Cauleta. Her red gown flowed in the wind. Pallanex wore a golden crown that fit snugly on her head, with spikes of varying heights sticking out like sun rays. Julie seethed. "I want her to suffer!"

Julie crashed through the thick gates, Pale Fire in hand.

Pallanex's reserved army stood at the ready to defend their queen.

She dodged a blade and hit the man with a blast from her hand. Julie cut another man nearly in half, then sent a man reeling back with another power blast. Two soldiers charged at her. She dropped her sword and put both hands out in front of her, burning them to a crisp. Julie opened her palm, and Pale Fire returned. She blocked another attack and ran the man through his chest. Blood spurted across her face and chest. More soldiers advanced. Julie punched, kicked, and swung her sword to dispatch them. In a flurry of moves, she wiped out six at once; their bodies lay broken and bloody. In a final attempt to stop her, the last of the men rushed with spears in one hand and their swords in the other. Before they could make contact, Julie rolled out of their way and sent flames in their direction. They fell, screaming in agony.

Julie looked around at the carnage. She didn't have time to feel anything but anger. She tightened her grip on her sword. "Where are you?" Julie screamed. "Where are you?"

"Now, now, now, why are you in such a hurry to die?" Pallanex's voice echoed off the walls.

"No, I'm in a hurry to kill you, bitch!"

"You are a foolish girl if you believe you can kill me," Pallanex's voice rang all around her. "Besides, after all of these years of waiting to meet each other, should we not take time and get to know each other?"

"I don't know what kind of game you think this is, but those people out there are my friends, and you are going to pay for what you have done," Julie yelled as she made her way to the looming castle staircase, where she suspected Pallanex was hiding in wait.

Julie looked around the large hall, decorated with lush tapestries and gold torches that adorned the pristine walls. "What do you call what just happened? How about killing Canis, trying to kill Marcus, his brother, and his sister? How about turning Vestus into a cave?"

Pallanex's laughter filled the deserted hallway. "She does not have to worry about that now."

Her comment made Julie stop for a second. "How about wanting to turn your demons loose on Earth?"

"You believe you have everything figured out. You know nothing about what I want or what was done to me. You only know what you have been told."

"Great! Then, come on out and tell me your side," Julie said as she followed a set of steps up the heart of the castle.

"I shall do no such thing."

Julie opened the door to Pallanex's throne room. There, Pallanex sat waiting. Julie pointed Pale Fire toward her. "Fine by me. Let's finish this right here and now."

"Not so fast." Pallanex waved her hand, and a side door to Julie's left opened, allowing thousands of black spiders the size of her shoe to pour into the room.

"Oh my God!" Julie retreated to the opposite wall as Pallanex laughed. She started sending energy blasts at the eight-legged creatures, causing them to fly in multiple directions. There were too many to shoot at once. She sliced several of them with her sword. Then, in a panic, Julie waved her open hand back and forth as heat radiated toward the spiders.

They caught on fire, shriveled, and burned.

Pallanex screamed and ran through the open door.

Julie made sure Pallanex's pets were all dead before giving chase. She ran down the steps and passed three mummies where more spiders were beginning to emerge. What the hell? She chased Pallanex to the courtyard. There, Julie saw the broken statues of men she had only heard about or learned about from Redderick Bobo, except for the one that resembled Marcus when he was younger. "Nowhere to run."

Pallanex turned to her. "I was thinking the same thing." She spread her hands out in front of her.

Julie readied herself.

"We shall not do this here," Pallanex said in a voice that sounded as if it came from another place. Stars appeared in the sky as Pallanex and Julie rose into a purple-hued veil. They were in a large stone amphitheater with five thrones and an altar above a dais.

"What is this place?"

"Welcome to the birthplace of Seras. The home of the *Khamsah Aryad Ilalo*, the Five Lions of God. This is the very place my brothers and sisters and I created all that you see in Seras, the good and bad."

"I don't care about any of this," Julie yelled. "I want all of this to end!"

"Very well, I will finish you, and it will all end just as you wish." Pallanex lunged at her. A ripple of light reflected down the length of her blade.

Julie ducked as Pallanex's sword reverberated on the marble altar. She swung Pale Fire, but Pallanex blocked her. Julie sent a blast toward her, but Pallanex countered with a shot of her own. In a flurry, Julie and Pallanex exchanged blows with their swords and whatever magic the two women possessed. They attacked, blocking and deflecting fire, while invisible blasts and lightning flew from their hands. There was a jarring impact on Julie's side. The pain sheared through her body. *Pallanex will pay for that.* She touched the area, and her hand came back covered in blood.

"Marcus and Redderick have taught you well," Pallanex said. "It will not be enough."

Julie surged, whirling around and striking Pallanex's back. The blow knocked the queen down. Her back was sliced from one side to the other.

"I disagree," Julie said, readying herself for another attack.

A light emanated from the cut on Pallanex's back, and the queen began to laugh. The wound peeled back, and the rest of her skin ripped and fell by the wayside. In Pallanex's place stood another woman. She was taller than Pallanex with the same raven hair. "It was too soon," the woman said. "No matter. I will finish this whore of Tolth."

"Who are you calling a whore?"

"Who are you to speak to me? I am Eryx. You are not worthy to look at me."

Julie attacked her with Pale Fire. It did nothing to the elderess.

Eryx backhanded her.

Julie flew across the amphitheater. Her sword fell in the other direction. She got up to shake herself off. She spat out blood.

Eryx used both hands to attack Julie with a heat blast.

Julie strained to hold off the force with both of her hands. Her wound throbbed as blood soaked the side of her garb.

"Die now, rodent. You are nothing compared to me," Eryx said.

Julie pushed with all of her might against the force of Eryx's power. Her feet slid backwards. Fire raged around her. Julie felt the heat. Flames engulfed her clothes, searing her body. She was on the verge of collapsing when she heard an unfamiliar male voice inside her head.

"Who are you?" it asked.

"Julie Ayers."

"Who are you?" it asked again.

"I am Julie Ayers."

"Who are you?" it asked, again, louder.

"I am Julie Ayers," she repeated through gritted teeth. "I am the Heart of Tolth."

"Who are you?" the voice asked a fourth time.

"I am Julie Ayers. I am the Heart of Tolth. I am the Protector of Seras. I am Seras's gift from Tolth. I am Seras's final hope." A fierce wind whipped around her. The power Julie used to block Eryx's attack turned into a force all its own. It began to change colors from white to blue to red.

She began to push Eryx's stream of magic back.

"No, this is not possible," the Elderess said. "You are an unworthy speck of a human."

"I am Julie Ayers. I am the Heart of Tolth. I am the Protector of Seras. I am Seras's gift from Tolth. I am Seras's final hope," Julie chanted repeatedly. Images of Marcus's body lying on the ground popped into her head, as did visions of the dead bodies of Argos, Seren, Pertheus, Callista, and all of the men and women who died because of Eryx, Pallanex, and William. The more she thought of them, the more powerful she became. Then she saw her mom and dad, her brother, Grandma Franklin, Claire, Jimmy, her high school friends, her favorite teachers, and the people of Sunset.

Eryx screamed. Lightning flashed as the Elderess exploded into nothingness.

The voice spoke to Julie as she lay on the ground surrounded by the mark of the Elders. "You did well, my child."

"Who are you?" Julie asked, realizing the absurdity of the question.

A man with long blonde hair and violet eyes materialized. The strange man was wearing a white sarong and a blue cloak with a golden belt. "You know who I am, Julie."

"Tolth?"

He looked at the ashes and charred remains of the dais. "I wish it had not ended this way."

"What?" Julie struggled to her feet. The Elder towered over her. "Did you want her to beat me?" She was afraid she had one more battle that she had not counted on.

"No, no, I wish Eryx would not have turned on us. We were The Five Lions of God, the *Khamsah Aryad Ilalo.* We helped our father defeat the traitors. We helped banish Lucifer to Hell."

"I've heard."

"Only to have Eryx want to free him and join him in ruling Heaven, Hell, Earth, and Seras."

"Or destroy them," Julie added.

"You are wise, my Heart."

Having Tolth say that snapped something in Julie. "Wait!" She held out her hand to block him from moving closer to her. "Betrothed. What does it mean?" She looked around the chaos around her. "Am I supposed to marry you?"

"No, my Heart. I am not here. I am just a memory to be forgotten."

She looked at him. "I can't imagine you being forgotten."

"If my plans work, the people of Seras will forget me. They will remember my father and worship them as we should have had them do from the beginning. That was how it should have been. If we had done that, none of this would have been needed."

"I would have liked that," Julie said.

"As would I." He sat on the only remaining marble bench.

"What happens now?" Julie sat beside him.

"Now, it depends on you. A new day will dawn over Seras. The people will have freedoms like never before. There will be good days and bad days. People will live, people will die, and babies will bring forth hope and joy into this world." He stopped to look at her. "And on Earth. You have fulfilled your purpose on Seras. The evil that Eryx reigned over this world is gone. You can be as you want to be."

"And what about you?"

"I can join my brothers and sisters once more."

"I don't understand?"

"Where Ostram, Vestus, and Azahleah reside, I will reside also."

"You're going to die?" Tears rolled down her face.

"Julie. I am already dead."

She broke down and cried. The amphitheater vanished. Julie fell to the ground. She was back inside Cauleta's courtyard. Julie looked around the temple. The columns were broken. The palace sat as quiet as a grave. It was in total ruin. She stared at the toppled statues. Canis was broken in two. Many of the others she did not know or recognize were in similar states of destruction. She looked at Pallanex's and Eryx's statues. They were shattered and intertwined much like they were in real life. One meshed with the other. Then she saw Marcus's statue. His head was cracked, chipped, and broken away from the body...it snapped her back to reality. "Oh my God, Marcus."

## Chapter Sixty-Seven

Julie—Seras

Julie left the gates of Cauleta. She found Freya lying on the ground where she had left her. "Freya, are you okay?" She helped the Oracle to her feet. "Thank God you're alive."

"No, I feel...I feel different."

Julie looked her up and down, front and back. While dirty and bloody, she didn't have any major wounds. "I have to get to Marcus!"

"Did you see him?" Freya choked out.

"Marcus? No."

"No, did you see Tolth?"

"Um, yeah, yeah, I saw Tolth. He helped me defeat Eryx," Julie said, wanting, no, needing to get to Marcus.

"Then he is no longer with me," Freya cried.

"I'm sorry. I need to get to Marcus." She sprinted across the field to where she left him. To her surprise, he was struggling to his feet. "What are you doing?"

"Trying to help you." His voice was weak and cracked.

"Lie down. It's over," she told him.

"Over? Pallanex?"

"Dead."

"Eryx?"

"Dead."

"You did it." He forced a smile, the sun blinding him as he rolled to his back. "I knew you could do it. How?"

"It's a long story that I'm never going to repeat, and God help me, I hope I never remember."

Marcus stood and opened his hand. His sword returned to its master, and he propped himself on it. "Julie, I don't know what to say.

"How are we alive? I saw us die." Tears filled her eyes.

"No, he showed you what would happen had you not been here," he answered.

"What?"

"That's what Azahleah showed you. What you saw was us without you," Marcus explained. "He didn't want you to see what you are capable of. He was afraid of you."

"I hate him even more now."

Marcus chuckled, then held his ribs, and blew out a breath.

"How long will it take you to recover?" Julie asked, wiping away tears and smearing dirt over her face.

Marcus looked at William. "I'm good."

"How long?"

"I don't know." He swung his sword across William's neck, removing the head from the body.

Julie shrieked, "Why did you have to do that?"

"I didn't want to take any chances." He forced a tired smile. "Come on, we need to find the rest."

"I'm scared."

"I know."

They found Freya back on her feet. Her robes were torn, dust-covered, and covered with blood. She was mumbling to herself.

"Freya?"

"He's left me," she said.

Julie stepped closer. "Who left you?"

Freya spoke slowly. "Tolth has...Tolth has left me."

"Are you sure?" Marcus asked.

"Yes." She looked at Julie. "Did he come to you?"

"I already told you he did." Julie looked at Marcus, worried that Freya had lost her mind. She lowered her head. "He did. He helped me defeat Eryx."

"Then, I have served my purpose," Freya said.

"Stop," Marcus ordered. "We have more important things to worry about. You are alive." He moved his hand back and forth, "Not everyone can say that. Help them!"

"I don't know how," Freya cried, pulling at her hair.

"Find the ones who are alive and take care of them," Marcus yelled. He grabbed his sister by the shoulders. "We need you!"

Freya tried to control herself. She agreed to do what she could between shallow sobs.

The air was thick with smoke as they trudged through the chaos of the battle. The screams of the dying echoed through the valley. But there wasn't any time to dwell.

Griffus had already begun giving orders to the soldiers. He was overseeing the grim task of separating the two armies. Those who followed Pallanex and William were placed on carts and taken to the walls of Cauleta. Warriors from Allon were placed on carts and sent to the ships they had arrived on the day before.

"How many did we lose?" Marcus asked.

Griffus nodded toward the horse-drawn carts where bodies were being laid gently across the planks. "Plenty," he said.

"How many is plenty?" Julie asked.

"Hundreds."

Julie turned away. "Oh God...all this...for nothing."

"It wasn't for nothing," Marcus said quietly. "Pallanex and William had to be stopped."

"I know," she said. "But it just seems like such a waste. So much death. For what?"

"There *was* a reason," Griffus said. "She wouldn't have stopped until she ruled every inch of Seras."

"Earth, too. She would've taken everything," Marcus added.

"I could have done more. I should have done more!" She pounded on Marcus's chest. Even though he was in pain, he let her vent and get it out. The deaths of so many people they knew and loved. He joined her in watching the flames rise over the battlefield. Her face streaked with tears and the blood of their enemies.

One of the carts carrying the fallen warriors caught their eye. It carried the bodies of those who served on the council: Argos, Seren, Tanda, and Lord Avery. Their bodies were broken and bloody.

“I let them down,” she whispered. “I let them down.”

“You did not let them down,” Marcus said, stepping beside her. “They gave their lives for freedom. For peace. You think they didn’t know the cost?”

Otta climb into the cart, crying as she held Seren’s hand. “Now, Otta is the last of her kind, the last of her tribe, the last Hemoor.”

Julie patted Otta’s leg. “I am so sorry.”

“Thank you, my Heart. It means everything that you recognize our small contribution.”

Julie looked at Marcus then back to Otta. “Losing a friend is not small. I loved Seren, and I love you. I will always remember the way you took me in and made me laugh.”

“She loved you, and so do I,” Otta said, gently caressing Seren’s brown hair, wiping away the dirt and blood.

Once the carts were loaded, the remaining members of Allon’s warriors followed the procession back to the camp, where those who couldn’t fight waited for their return. As they got closer, the crowd surged toward them.

Griffus spotted his wife, Laila. He spurred his horse to her, dismounted, and greeted her with a massive hug, picking her up from her feet.

Marcus found Gwendolyn. Her eyes caught his. One look was all it took.

The matriarch of Allon crumpled to the ground. “Who?” she screamed. “Who?”

Her two sons, Julius and Jacob, ran to her side.

“Not Argos. Please, no.” She embraced her two surviving sons, who knelt with her.

“I’m sorry”, Marcus whispered. “I’m so very sorry.”

# Chapter Sixty-Eight

Julie—Seras

The funeral pits were dug. Each of the fallen warriors of Allon was placed in the holes, covered with branches and bark, and set to flame. Those who lived gathered to mourn their losses and comfort each other.

Gwendolyn, wife of the fallen Argos, mother to the fallen Edwin, watched as her husband's body was lowered into the ground and set ablaze. Julius and Jakob held her up from each side. The front of her gown was soaked with tears. Both sons held their breath as they watched the flames and smoke rise.

"He is at peace now," Julius said. "He can watch over Edwin."

"He taught us well, but words cannot express how much we will miss him," Jakob said.

Julie watched from the perimeter with Marcus. Over the last six years, she'd watched too many of the good people of Allon die. It was such a waste. "Why do people have to be so evil?" she asked Marcus. "Why did there have to be a Pallanex, a William, or an Eryx?"

"I wish I knew the answer to that. I think evil is just everywhere. Some people are born with it, some are created..." He pointed to himself. "We have to accept that good people will always have to sacrifice themselves for the worthy cause of peace. We must remember what would have happened if we had lost the freedom we would have lost, how many more lives would have been lost."

"I will make sure no one forgets," Julie said.

The smoke continued to rise, filling the air.

"I will as well," Marcus stated. "I hope with Pallanex and William gone, there will be no need for more war or death."

Redderick Bobo joined them at that moment. "Your mouth to God's ear," he said, then turning to Julie. "Those who died in the Battle of Cauleta will be remembered, not as casualties, but as champions of all of Seras."

Griffus approached through the haze. "What should we do?" His eyes pointed toward Cauleta.

"Burn it to the ground. I want it gone," Marcus said. "Burn it all. Every last stone."

Julie looked at Marcus through the flames. He returned her gaze.

"Are you okay?" he mouthed to her.

She could see the pain in his eyes. He had lost just as much as she had, no, more. "I don't know if I'll ever be okay again."

## Chapter Sixty-Nine

Marcus—Earth

Julie curled up on her parents' couch, her bare feet tucked under her. Marcus brought her a cup of hot tea. "Thank you."

He sat beside her and took a sip from his cup. "Julie?"

"Where's Shakespeare?" she asked. After the battle and the long days of burying the dead, she looked exhausted. Her face was pale, and the sparkle had left her golden brown eyes. She was numb, and Marcus couldn't blame her. He blamed himself and the madness of it all.

"I let him out."

"Thank you."

"Can I get you anything else?" he asked.

"No, I'm good," she told him.

"Are you?"

Tears rolled down her cheeks. "No, I'm lying. I'm not good. Did you see what I just did? What have I become? I...killed...so...many...people. And the only thought I had was that I lost you. I thought you died, and I wanted every single one of them to feel my pain...feel my wrath. Especially Pallanex." Julie dropped her head in her hands. "I don't know what to do. I can't do this anymore. I can't...I can't be a part of this. I never want to go back. I don't want these memories haunting me for the rest of my life." She looked up at him. Her eyes were red and swollen. "Help me, please!"

Marcus patted her on the leg. "What can I do?" He had never felt so helpless in his life.

"I don't know." She leaned into him. His shirt wet with her tears.

He ran his fingers through her wavy, brown hair and kissed her forehead. He thought about the first time he realized she was the Heart. At that time, he had no idea what it meant or what it would do to her. She was a wide-eyed, curious girl full of fire and fun. She wasn't that girl any longer. She was no longer the spirited young girl in his classroom.

Julie looked up at him. "What do we do now?" She wiped her eyes and nose with her sleeve. "I'm sorry."

"Don't be. You have no reason to be sorry. I'm the one who is sorry." He slid from his position and knelt in front of her. "Listen. I don't know what you're feeling right now, but I've been doing this a lot longer. Sometimes I wonder how much of a monster I really am." He lowered his head, not wanting to look at her. "I've done horrible things for the sake of doing it, things I'd rather you not know about. I followed war, killing, and chaos for so long, I didn't know right from wrong."

Julie placed her hand on his cheek and brought his face to hers.

"I've made more mistakes than you can count. But there's one thing I am sure of, and that is you."

"Stop," Julie whispered. He could tell she was trying to regain her composure.

"I just want you to know when I say, 'I love you,' it has nothing to do with you being 'the Heart,' it has nothing to do with some silly prophecy. It has everything to do with you. Your strength, your passion, your—"

She interrupted him. "I'm nothing special. I'm only a girl."

"No." He shook his head. "You are my everything."

Outside, the sky rumbled.

Julie got up, walked to the window, and took three deep breaths. "It's going to rain," she said. "I hate the rain."

"I know." Marcus went to her and slid his arms around her waist. "It will pass."

"Promise?"

He pressed his lips to the back of her head, breathing in the scent of her hair. "I promise."

"When?"

Marcus knew she was no longer talking about the approaching storm. He reached into his pocket and pulled out the vial, the 'Breath.' The Elder Ostram's gift to Seras Marcus had used to help him learn English, the ways of the people of Sunset, and how to become a teacher. He knew once he saw the pain on her face, he could not let her live with what she had done or had seen. “Do me a favor.”

Julie turned to him. “Okay.”

He kissed her once. “Take care of Shakespeare for me. He likes you better than me anyway.”

She snorted and cocked her head to the side. “I will.” She kissed him.

The storm outside moved closer. The sky lit up and drops of rain pounded the window.

“Look at me.” He lifted her chin, so their eyes met.

“Why?” she asked as tears returned to her eyes.

“Because I never want to forget the sparkle in your eyes or the taste of your lips.”

Julie sighed. “Can we not,”

Marcus took her by the hand and led her back to the couch. “Close your eyes.”

“Why?”

“It’s easier this way.”

“What’s easier?”

“Please trust me.”

Julie closed her eyes.

Marcus poured the contents of the vial into her teacup. “Drink this.” He handed her the cup as her eyes were still closed.

“Why?”

“Still asking questions.”

She smiled, opening her eyes. “Always.” She took a drink.

“It will help you relax,” he said. “I love you.”

“I love you, too.” Julie forced a tight-lipped smile.

He took her by the shoulders and moved her to arm’s length, wanting to take her all in one final time.

“Are you okay?” she asked.

“I am. Close your eyes.” They kissed for the last time. “Time to sleep,” he said.

“Sleep—" Julie barely got out before falling limp in his arms.

He lay her on the couch and brushed her cheek. “Goodbye, Julie.”

# Chapter Seventy

Marcus—Seras

Marcus went through the portal. The mysterious fire swirled behind him. He found Freya, Redderick, and Griffus, who were waiting for him to return.

"Where is the Heart?" Redderick Bobo asked.

I left her there. He placed the vial, the lamp, and the three rocks on a table.

"The Breath, the Blood, and the Bones," Redderick murmured. "Why?"

"She's done."

"No!" Redderick rose from his seat. "That is unacceptable! She is the Heart!"

Marcus slammed his hand on the table. "And she is done. She is on Earth, and she will never set foot on Seras again!"

"You dare oppose the will of Tolth and the Elders!"

"I do!"

Redderick Bobo stormed out of the tent.

"Are you okay, brother?" Freya asked.

"I'm alive."

"That's not what I asked," Freya responded. She placed a hand on his shoulder. "Are you okay?"

"I watched helplessly as the love of my life turned into a figment of my imagination."

"Then why did you let her go?" Griffus asked, picking up the stones that make up the Bones of Azahleah.

"I miss her voice, her scent, her smile," Marcus said, he chuckled. "It's only been, what, an hour? Less? I miss her eyes, her lips, and her kiss.

I miss her laugh...the way she whispered, ‘I love you’,” He looked at Griffus. “I let her go because I loved her.”

“What’s next?” Freya asked, breaking his sorrow.

“We have a world to fix. I would rather not do it alone.”

“That’s more like it,” she said. “What should we do first?”

“I have an idea. It’s called The Council of Hope. We will spread out and create new borders with trusted men and women of Allon to lead those regions. If disputes arise, we convene to resolve them through voting and collective advice. There will be alliances within the land.”

“I like the idea,” Griffus said. “What can I do to help?”

“I will count on you to lead one of those regions,” Marcus answered. “This idea will take a lot of work.”

“Consider it done,” the mighty Griffus answered.

He turned to his sister. “How are the wounded?”

“Brother,” Freya whispered.

“Stop.” He took his sword and smashed the first stone.

“Marcus?”

He smashed the second and third stones. “How is Darius?”

“Darius is healing. He suffered greatly, but he is being taken care of by Eryana.”

“That’s good.” Marcus smashed the fourth and fifth of the Bones of Azahleah, the only way to transport back and forth from Earth.

“Do you think that’s wise?” Freya asked.

“She will not remember anything about this Godforsaken place or me.”

“She is a Goddess, the blood of the Elders, the blood of angels pump through her veins,” Freya responded.

“And I made sure she will never remember anything that happened here.”

“Very well,” Freya said. “You will regret it.”

“I already do.” He looked at her through gritted teeth.

Freya left the tent.

Marcus was alone. His spring was gone. Summer had burned through with great fury. Autumn had come and gone with fallen tears. The only thing left was winter. And springtime would never find him again. A tear dropped down his cheek as he destroyed the final stone.

# Epilogue

Julie—Earth

Julie sat behind the wheel of her car, staring up at the familiar slope that wound its way to Cedar Creek High School. It still looked like a castle on a hill. Images of her and Claire riding the bus for the first time flooded her mind. So many memories, a couple of them sad but mostly happy: cheerleading, track meets, and late-night talks with Claire and Jimmy.

She debated waiting for Claire or going in by herself. Julie called her best friend since third grade. Who would have thought sharing a box of crayons would lead to a lifelong friendship?

"Hey," Claire answered. "I'm running late. I'll be there in fifteen."

"No prob," Julie said. "I'll meet you inside." Even though they don't talk to each other as much as they used to, it was nice knowing they could reach out and pick up where they left off in a moment's notice.

"See ya soon."

The call ended, and Julie got out of her car. It was a newer car. The Jellybean lasted through college, but it was on its last leg, and she sadly traded it in. Her 'new-to-her' car, as she liked to say, wasn't nearly as fun as her old purple car but more practical. She named it Tink after the famous fairy from Peter Pan because of its forest green color.

Opening the front door of the school and walking across the marble floor tile with 'Welcome to Cedar Creek' written in the middle seemed surreal.

The hallway was decorated in the school colors of green and yellow. A giant arch of balloons framed the gymnasium entrance, welcoming the alumni to their five-year reunion. The soft music grew louder as she approached the place where she had spent two years under the guidance of the gym teacher known by all as Schultz.

At the check-in table in front of the gym, a familiar voice called out. "Julie! Oh my gosh, I can't remember the last time I saw you!"

Julie snapped out of her dreamlike fog to notice her former cheerleading teammate. "Tiffany!" Julie laughed.

"You look so amazing," Tiffany said. "We need to get caught up."

"We will." Julie smiled and hugged her old friend.

"Great! And don't forget, we're getting a cheer team picture later."

"I won't," Julie promised. That's when she started to regret her outfit of choice. Not that there was anything wrong with jeans and a black top, but Tiffany and the girl beside her were wearing brightly colored pencil dresses. She now felt a little underdressed for the occasion. Happy she fought the urge to wear anything green and gold.

Tiffany gave her a 'Hello My Name Is...' tag to stick to her top. "Not that anyone would not know who you are." She smiled.

Julie wrote her name, but the thought of writing 'Inigo Montoya, you killed my father. Prepare to die!' crossed her mind.

Inside, she paused for a moment to soak it all in. Streamers draped across the bleachers. She noticed the drink table and headed in that direction.

"Jules?" a voice called out behind her.

She turned. "Jimmy!"

He looked like he had walked straight off a football field: broad shoulders, thick chest, arms that could bench press a truck. He was more chiseled, more handsome, and every bit the goofy grinning boy he'd been in high school, just a little older and bigger. Julie launched herself into his arms with a squeal. He hugged her tightly, lifting her off the ground for a moment.

"Look at you," he said, flashing a bright smile. "You haven't changed a bit."

Julie laughed. "You're crazy!" He placed her back on the floor. "What have you been up to?"

"I signed with the Bengals' practice squad for a couple of years. Now I'm heading into coaching. I'm going to be an assistant linebacker coach for Ohio State starting this fall."

"That's amazing!" she said. She handed him a full cup of punch.

"Thank you."

Then she poured herself a drink. "Let's find a seat."

Jimmy followed her. "So, what have you been doing?"

"I just started my second year as a fifth-grade teacher," Julie said as they found a table and took a seat.

"That's great."

"It's fun. I love fifth grade. The kids still like to learn and like teachers." She laughed. "I did some student teaching at the high school. I can't say the same. It's a different ball game."

"I bet."

"Can anyone join, or is this a private party?" A voice cut in behind them.

Jimmy and Julie stood up. "Claire!"

"How are you?" Jimmy asked, giving her an awkward hug.

"I'm good," she answered. "It's good seeing you."

"You, too," he said.

"How's the job?" Julie asked.

"Good."

"Where are you working?" Jimmy asked.

"I got hired as a media coordinator for Three Bucks, an advertising firm in Columbus."

"That's awesome," Jimmy answered.

As the three of them continued to get caught up, they spotted former teachers entering the gym.

"Oh my gosh, Mrs. Larson, Mr. Frye, and Mr. Langston," Claire pointed out.

"Where's Shultz?" Julie asked.

"He passed away two years ago," Jimmy answered.

"Oh no, I didn't know," Julie said. "He was so much fun."

Jimmy stood. "I'm going to grab another drink and maybe something from the snack table. Can I get you guys anything?"

"Sure." Julie held up her punch cup. "I'll take another one of these."

Claire shrugged. "Yeah, I'll take one. Thanks!"

"Yep, no problem." He left the two girls and headed to the makeshift punch bar.

"You doin' okay?" Claire asked.

"Yeah, yeah. I love my job. I work with some great teachers, and my students are so much fun."

"How 'bout you? We seemed to have gone different ways over the last couple of years."

"I know. I'm sorry." Claire leaned closer to hug her. "I got busy with school and track and work." She rolled her eyes.

Julie gave a lopsided smile. "I got busy with school, and...nothing, really."

"Whatever. You have a lot going on," Claire dropped her head and gave her a look like a doubtful librarian.

Jimmy came back with drinks. "Larson, Langston, and Frye said they would make their way over to us in a few." He gave each of them a new cup. "I heard they're serving dinner at eight."

The three of them talked, laughed, and reminisced as they ate a catered meal of salad, chicken, au gratin potatoes, and al dente green beans.

"What happened to the one guy you were dating?" Claire asked between bites of her salad.

Julie crinkled her nose. "When?"

"The guy you started dating during your sophomore or junior year? The guy you wouldn't tell me or Brooklyn about?"

She scoffed. "I have no idea."

"So, no boyfriend?" Claire continued, then clenched her teeth like she had said something wrong.

Julie rolled her eyes. "Nah, still looking for someone who can tolerate me."

Jimmy smirked. "That makes two of us."

"I guess I'm three." Claire gave Jimmy a shy, knowing look.

After dinner and dessert, Julie and Claire took a picture with their cheerleading teammates, as well as their track teammates. Jimmy did the same with his football and track buddies. Julie watched Claire's face light up as she watched Jimmy. *True love.*

As the night dwindled, they spoke with their former teachers. Mrs. Larson had two children. Mr. Frye retired, and Mr. Langston, still wearing Ohio State shirts, was still teaching and coaching. The history teacher was thrilled that Jimmy was coaching for the Buckeyes. Jimmy promised him front row seats for the home games, and they thought Mr. Langston was going to cry.

As they were talking, Claire said, "It's too bad Mr. Campbell turned out to be some conman."

"Don't remind me of that—" Mr. Frye held his tongue from saying more.

"I haven't thought about him in years," Larson said. "He had us all fooled."

"Who?" Julie asked.

"Mr. Campbell," Jimmy told her. "Remember the teacher who broke up that fight our freshman year?"

"And the thing with the swords in gym class?" Claire added.

"I can't believe you don't remember him," Langston said.

"That's what I said," Claire added.

"The one good thing he did was save you from Trotter," Mr. Frye said.

"Amen," Langston said.

"I don't remember any of that," Julie said.

The five stared at her in silence.

"Well, maybe that's a good thing," Mrs. Larson added.

Jimmy clapped. "So, how about those Penguins?"

The group's conversation came to a stop, and they moved on to Coach Langston's track team and the school's football team.

Julie excused herself, said her goodbyes to her former teachers, and hugged Jimmy.

Claire followed her out. "Hey, you doing okay?"

"I'm good. Just tired."

"Alright, I just worry about you. I didn't mean to bring up that thing about your old boyfriend. I know it wasn't good when he ghosted you."

"It's okay. I seriously don't remember him," Julie said.

Claire frowned. "Are you sure—"

"I'm sure," Julie interrupted her.

"You don't remember him, and you don't remember Mr. Campbell. Either you have the perfect case of situational amnesia, or I really need to be worried about you. I mean, we both had major crushes on him." Claire brought her shoulders up almost to her ears and gave an awkward grin.

"I love you," Julie said and hugged her best friend. "We need to catch up."

"Yes, we do. I love you right back."

"Now, if I were you, I would go back in there and pick up where you left off before college."

"Stop." Claire's cheeks turned rosy.

"Love you!" Julie left the school and made the thirty-minute drive to her apartment. She changed into her silky pajamas and poured herself a glass of wine.

Mr. Campbell? She went to her bedroom closet, took down a small box containing old memorabilia, and carried it to the living room, where she folded herself onto the couch. Shakespeare, her pure white cat, jumped into her lap.

"Hey, buddy", she murmured, scratching his ears. She reached for the box and opened it. Inside were blasts from the past: medals from track, ribbons from cheer camp, a friendship bracelet from Claire, nostalgic love notes from boyfriends from middle school and early high school, newspaper clippings from her trial against Mr. Trotter, and her old high school yearbooks. Julie began flipping through the pages slowly until she got to the faculty page. She traced the pictures before stopping. Her heart skipped a beat.

There, next to a name she did not recognize, Marcus Campbell, was a face that sent shockwaves through her body. "Oh my God," she cried.

She remembered the fight in the cafeteria. She remembered going into his basement for the first time. She remembered Callista's death. She remembered Pertheus's death. She remembered Azahleah and his Death Walkers, Tolth, training with Redderick Bobo, fighting Pallanex, William, Griffus, Argos, Gwendolyn, Freya, Seren, Otta, Jayna, and Darius. She remembered Marcus. She remembered their fights, their training, their battles. She remembered the unanimous money that appeared in her bank account. The money she used to pay off her college loans. "Marcus." Then, she remembered them making love, and repeated his name. This time softer as she placed her hand over her mouth. "Marcus."

She felt the deluge of tears overcoming her.

She remembered everything.

Then she remembered the words Redderick Bobo said to her about traveling to any place she had been before, and she knew where she wanted, no, needed to go.

# Letter From the Author

Thank you for reading the fifth and final book of The Heart of Seras. The story of Julie and Marcus was a passion project that spanned twenty years and over 385,000 words. What started out as a college class essay, became so much more for me.

In the fall of 2005, I took a mythology class. For the final, we were given options to present all we had learned during the course. I chose an essay in which I would create my own mythology story in the way of Homer. That story became time consuming and too large to finish before the end of the class. So, I switched gears, wrote a subpar essay about Mt. Olympus and the NFL, and quietly worked on my original idea to turn it into a book. At the time, as mentioned, I was taking classes at The Ohio State University.

My journey as a writer began at a much younger age. I was in fourth grade when the writing bug bit me. I wrote my first story, "Super Joe," in which I saved the president and his wife from a villain. The kids in my class loved it, it made them laugh, and I never stopped making up stories after that. My imagination got me through tough times growing up. Anyway, I began taking writing seriously; I wrote poems, I wrote a cowboy adventure inspired by Clint Eastwood's spaghetti westerns, during my junior and senior years in high school. I wrote two comedic screenplays: *A Twist of Fate*, and *The Boys in the Mailroom*. *A Twist of Fate* was about a husband and wife who accidentally switched places with the help of a magic rock. I remember the roles were written for Tom Hanks and Daryl Hannah (fresh off of their roles in *Splash*) as the happily married couple, and Kelsey Grammar as the villain with Jerry Van Dyke as his bumbling sidekick. *The Boys in the Mailroom* was based on my adventures working in the mailroom of Nationwide Insurance during my early-twenties, which I affectionately call my 'college years,' and inspired by the Police Academy movies. Both stories have since been lost but never forgotten.

In the summer of 2005, at the age of 41, I went to college to become a teacher. After 23 years working in the private sector and coaching middle school and high school wrestling and track and field, I realized I had a love of working with students. The timing was perfect. Both of our sons had graduated from high school and were living on their own, and I was given information about how much retirement I had built up through the years of coaching already. It seemed to work in my favor. After figuring out the details with my very patient and understanding wife, I quit my corporate job, moved us to a nearby trailer park, and enrolled at The Ohio State University branch in Newark, Ohio.

Once again, that same fall is when my story began to take shape. At the time, I spent my mornings attending classes, my afternoons coaching, and my evenings sitting at home doing homework. When I wasn't doing one of those three things, I watched a little TV. *Buffy the Vampire Slayer, Angel, Highlander, Hercules*, and *Xena* were my go-to escapisms. I also took a writing class in which the textbooks were the first three Harry Potter books. While I was an avid reader, having been inspired by my mother to read the classics such as *The Hobbit, The Lord of the Rings, Robin Hood, Treasure Island, Ivanhoe*, to name a few, and a big fan of comic books (during the Golden Age of marvel) I had never had the desire to read those books, as I considered them too young for me. I was wrong. I fell in love with them and couldn't get enough. So, as I began creating this mythology essay, the thoughts of Buffy, Angel, Giles, Duncan MacLeod, Bilbo Baggins, Wolverine, Captain America, Hercules, Xena, Snape, Marcus Decimus Meridius, and Harry Potter swirled in my head; and I thought, *What if a girl like Buffy was transported to a place like Middle Earth?*

And that is exactly how Julie, Marcus, and the world of Seras was born.

Using the city of Sunbury and Big Walnut High School as the backdrop for Earth, I spent the first seven years plotting the entire story, creating the world of Seras, the characters, and writing the first draft. Initially, Marcus was the main character, and the first chapter was him landing in front of the Greagons who debated saving him or eating him. I also had him with a magic sword that could talk, and Pertheus as his main sidekick. Poor Pertheus could also travel to Earth, but he would be changed to a cat in the process. Luckily, both of those ideas got scrapped. It was after I wrote the complete draft first that I decided it should be a young adult story, not an adult story, and the main character should be Julie, not Marcus. The story took a much different direction for the better.

Now, here I am twenty years later saying goodbye to these characters I created out of thin air who have meant so much to me (even the ones I felt necessary to kill off). I hope you have enjoyed reading about them as I have enjoyed writing about them.

I decided to make the ending ambiguous. The reasoning was not an easy one, just as Julie's decision will not be easy. Will she forgo her friends and her family to rejoin Marcus in Seras to live out the rest of her life with him, or does she sacrifice true love and stay on Earth? I will leave that to each of my readers' imagination.

Thank you to my wonderful wife, Bronwen, for her patience, love, understanding, and being that person to bounce ideas off of and read my first drafts. I couldn't have done any of this without her.

And thank you, my amazing loyal readers.

Sincerely, Joe

## Other books by the Author
at Rogue Phoenix Press

### Journey to Seras
The Heart of Seras: Book One

Julie Ayers is a normal fifteen year old living in the quiet town of Sunset, Ohio. Her world is turned upside down by the arrival of the school's new teacher, Marcus Campbell.

Marcus Campbell has a secret. He is a warrior from a medieval dimension searching for the mythical Heart-a hero given to the people of Seras to rid their world of impending evil. Marcus's quest is challenged when he realizes that the Heart is the vibrant teenage girl. Now, against his better judgment, he must try convincing Julie to go to his world and begin preparation to face whatever evil lies ahead.

Journey to Seras is the first book in the five part The Heart of Seras fantasy series. It begins the adventures of the two unlikely heroes as they battle the dark forces of Seras.

### The Elders
The Heart of Seras: Book Two

Julie Ayer's freshman year of high school ended horribly. Now Marcus Campbell must try to convince her to return to Seras to learn the secrets of Seras from the mysterious immortal, Redderick Bobo. Going back to Seras is the last thing on Julie's mind. She wants no part of Seras, or her teacher. What secrets does Redderick Bobo have to tell? Who were the Elders known as The Five Lions of God? Why is Julie Ayers the chosen savior of Seras?

Only returning to the dreaded dimension will answer these questions and more for Julie. Can she bring herself to forgive Marcus, and return to Seras? The future of Seras and Earth depends on it.

Revelation
The Heart of Seras: Book Three

The first half of Julie Ayers' junior year is going horribly wrong. Balancing life between Earth and Seras is taking its toll on her. She doesn't know who she can trust; her best friends are fighting, her basketball coach is harassing her, and things are about to get a lot worse. As the forces of evil in Seras strengthen their resolve against those that oppose them, Queen Pallanex moves to secure aid from distant supporters, and launches an attack on those that Marcus feels necessary to protect. William's plan begins to take shape to destroy Allon and give Pallanex power beyond Seras or Earth. As Julie already struggles to figure out the meaning behind Redderick Bobo calling her the Betrothed, a much deadly secret is suddenly revealed that will shake her to the core.

The Dark Warrior
The Heart of Seras: Book Four

Julie now knows Marcus's secret. Her personal life is a disaster and Marcus is missing. He needs to confront his past with the fear it might change him for the worst. Can Julie forgive Marcus in time to save him from himself?

## About the Author

Joe Evener began playing with the idea of writing in 4th grade. He wrote his first story, a superhero story in class. Next, he began taking writing seriously, creating poetry and a cowboy adventure inspired by Clint Eastwood's spaghetti westerns, during his junior and senior year. In his twenties, he wrote two comedic screenplays: *A Twist of Fate*, and *The Boys in the Mailroom*. Both stories have since been lost.

He now has six published books: his YA fantasy series, *The Heart of Seras* which includes *Journey to Seras, The Elders, Revelation, The Dark Warrior, and The Chosen*. His sixth book is a self-published poetry book, *Love, Pain, and Other Things*.

When not writing, Joe enjoys coaching track and field, teaching history, and traveling with his wife, Bronwen, and their family.

www.ingramcontent.com/pod-product-compliance
Lightning Source LLC
LaVergne TN
LVHW010610100826
845148LV00014B/2911

* 9 7 8 1 6 2 4 2 0 8 9 8 0 *